SLAVERS OF THE AMAZON

Cassandra Ward, personal assistant to the chief executive officer of one of the largest mining conglomerates in South America, stretched her lovely twenty-two year old body languorously on the narrow, rumpled bed.

She was beginning to appreciate life in Brazil!

Hovering above her the slim athletic figure of Allessandro, her boss's handsome young chauffeur, smiled as he thrust his still hard cock into the heated depths of her well-satisfied pussy.

The all-but-exhausted couple's final orgasms had been strong and synchronized after more than two hours of ardent lovemaking in Allessandro's tiny garage flat. Inside the cramped bedroom the air was heavy and fetid with the delicious smell of sex. The temperature must have climbed to almost forty degrees, Cassie thought, squirming her body lazily in the heat as the young Brazilian slowly pumped his narrow hips above her.

Cassie moaned softly, enjoying the sensation of their mingled perspiration as it pooled in her deep navel, the warm overflow trickling down her smooth flanks as she moved gently with him. God! her long, dark hair was soaked to the roots with perspiration, whilst her crotch ran with a thickening musk-laden melange of sweat, love juice and semen. She ran her hands appreciatively over the young Brazilian's firm quivering buttocks, enjoying the smooth feel of his olive coloured flesh rocking between her upraised thighs.

Cassie had been discretely partaking of Allessandro's particular physical charms for several weeks now, regularly slipping away from her stylish downtown apartment to rut with her young Latin lover in his back-street garage room.

The awful sounding cliché made her smile - her young Latin lover, what would her colleagues at BRAZCO say if they knew what she had been up to all these weeks with the boss's heart-throb driver Sex, it was her one weakness. Cassie simply loved the physical act of fornicating. Not for her the complications of a permanent relationship she had gladly left that particular mistake behind her two years ago in England. Neither was she interested in the tedium of a tawdry office affair with the inevitable gossip and stationary cupboard gropings, and married middle managers seeking to help her career'.

As she ran her long fingers through Allessandro's damp black hair, Cassie caught sight of her wristwatch and realized the time was fast approaching for her to take her reluctant leave. Christen and Lucy were expecting her at the Racquet Club in a little over an hour. If she left now she would have just enough time to swing by her apartment and grab a quick shower before meeting them for evening cocktails.

Cassie began to smile at herself. Her leaving was indeed becoming very reluctant now that Allessandro was once again turning his devout attention back to her nipples, sucking hungrily on the broad, dark cones, bringing them back to full tumescence within seconds. She groaned regretfully. Christ! she could lie here screwing this boy all night, she simply had to get him off her oversensitive breasts or else she would quite simply never get out of here.

Smiling broadly, she pried herself with difficulty out from under Allessandro and tapping her wristwatch murmured sulkily, "got to go, baby."

A grinning Allessandro nodded and swung himself up off the bed and began to pull on his skin-tight jeans. Cassie was relieved that he didn't try to persuade her to stay a while longer as he usually did. Getting out of Allessandro's flat was always a damn sight harder than getting in, she thought, a wicked smile twitching at the corners of her full lips.

Disappearing into the small bathroom, Cassie quickly towelled the sweat from her body with a threadbare bath sheet and brushed out her damp hair. She checked her face in the stained little mirror above the chipped sink and approved of what she saw there. She knew she was beautiful. It wasn't vanity, everyone told her so. Men couldn't fail to be attracted by the striking green eyes and pale complexion framed by the thick hair falling well past her shoulders, dark brown, almost black. And her figure, full breasted, narrow waisted and long legged, completed the stunning package.

As she repaired her makeup, Cassie wondered for how much longer she would be satisfied with Allessandro as her only lover. For some time now she had sensed that something was missing in her love life, or more precisely, she corrected herself, in her sex life.

As she bent to retrieve her fallen underwear, she caught sight of a sudden movement out of the corner of her eye. She turned in time to see a stocky, hard faced man enter the small bedroom and move purposefully toward her.

With a yelp of alarm, she dropped her bra and panties as she made to cover her exposed pudendum and heavy breasts with her hands.

"Who the hell are you " she demanded sharply, desperately trying to inject a note of authority and dignity into her voice. She looked wildly around for Allessandro, whom she suddenly sensed behind her, moments before he wrapped his arms about hers, pinning her forearms tightly to her sides!

Then, without the slightest hesitation, the tough looking newcomer stepped in close and brought his iron hard fist up in a short, sharp arc to explode on the exposed point of Cassie's perfectly formed chin and after a sudden violent burst of stars everything faded to deepest black.

When Cassie eventually regained her senses it took several moments to re-orientate herself.

The young woman felt a chill hand clutch at her innards as she suddenly remembered what had happened to her Allessandro holding her, the stocky stranger coming into the bedroom and striking her. She was still in the tiny flat above the company's private parking garage, that much she could tell from the sexual odours still clinging to the bed sheet her face was buried in.

She knew that she must have been out for a while because it was now dark in the bedroom, and her panic suddenly became magnified when she realized that her mouth was heavily taped over and that she was tied down. She was unable to move her limbs more than a few inches in any direction despite her best efforts and could only lie spread-eagled on the bed, where only a short time ago she had been writhing in ecstatic sexual congress with her Brazilian lover boy.

She froze breathless as a strange harsh voice began to speak in rapid Portuguese, and groaned inwardly as she recognized the softer tones of Allessandro replying … laughing!

Christ! what the hell was going on Why was Allessandro not helping her Who the hell was this man and what did Allessandro have to do with him Jesus! The more she listened the more it sounded like they knew each other!

Cassie heard the unmistakable crackling riffle of paper money as the older man began to count carefully out loud.

Cassie had been living and working in Brazil for almost two years, long enough to become fluent in Portuguese, and it was with a distinct sinking feeling in the pit of her stomach that she heard the stranger say, "there you are my friend, one thousand crisp U.S. dollars, and not a cent too much I might add, she is magnificent, everything you said she would be."

And then came the final, dreadful confirmation of all her fears. The unmistakable sound of Allessandro's single word of thanks, - "obrogada."

Cassie's breathing suddenly started to become erratic. Her heart slammed like a jackhammer as her frightened and confused mind struggled to grapple with what she was experiencing. It actually sounded like

Allessandro was selling her to this man!

"Get the car ready and wait for me downstairs," the stranger instructed. With a small sound of assent Allessandro left the room and presently she heard the departing chauffeur's footfalls going quickly down the wooden stairs into the large garage below.

Cassie flinched against the tight grip of her bonds as the bedroom door was suddenly kicked shut. From beneath her tightly shut eyelids, she sensed the man move across the room toward the bed, and then felt the old mattress sink as he sat down heavily beside her.

"I know you're awake," he said, amusement evident in his voice. "Let me introduce myself. My name is Gunter Bormann and I'm going to be taking you on a little journey up river to meet some friends of mine, during which time I just know we're going to become really well acquainted."

Cassie jerked in outrage as the man's hand settled on her rump, caressing the soft damp flesh gently.

"Look at me," said the man who called himself Gunter Bormann.

When she failed to move his voice suddenly lashed out, "I said look at me, bitch!" and he brought a hard hand down upon her naked buttock cheek with a sharp crack that echoed around the room and made her rear up, only to be dragged back down by the ropes tied so tightly around her wrists and ankles. She let out a sob of agony, tears suddenly springing from beneath her screwed up eyelids. The pain of the unexpected blow felt like he had put a blowtorch to her flesh.

"I only give an instruction once," Bormann rasped ominously.

Hopelessly and with a feeling of complete dread, Cassie slowly turned her head and strained her neck to look up at the first man ever in her life to have laid a hand on her in anger, and bit down on her full bottom lip to prevent herself from snivelling in front of the cruel bastard. That much at the very least was a satisfaction she would deny him.

Looking at him carefully for the first time, she saw a hard, competent looking man. His coarse brindled hair was worn closely cropped above a broad flat face within which sat two narrow slate coloured eyes. The blunt nose had been broken at some time in the past, giving him the look of a boxer. His bull neck blended smoothly into a massive set of shoulders and upper arms and there was not an ounce of fat on his otherwise stocky frame.

Cassie's heart sank as she realised that she had no realistic hope of immediate rescue. The parking garage was located in an isolated factory area secured behind a high chain link fence. And it was Friday evening! No one had any business in the garage this late save Allessandro, and he was clearly part of whatever was going on.

She despaired when she realized that the privacy and secrecy of this location, the very same privacy and secrecy that had up until now protected her anonymity and excited her, now meant that she was totally alone and at this maniac's mercy.

"Feeling all alone and scared are we " Bormann asked rhetorically, guessing from her expression at the direction of her galloping thoughts. "There's no need to be, Uncle Gunter will look after you." He sniggered, running his cruel eyes up and down the length of her nakedness.

"We'll be off soon," he told her, "but first …"

The man bent low, bringing his nose close to the peerless white flesh of her back, inhaling deeply the smell of musk redolent upon her smooth skin.

Cassie cringed in embarrassment. She had been screwing in the heat for hours and the previously sweet aroma of sex had cooled somewhat so that now she imagined she simply stank like an animal. But Bormann seemed to revel in her odour, running his nose a scant inch above the length of her outstretched body, inhaling every trace of sexual essence.

Cassie became acutely conscious of her nakedness, as the thug now began to run his hands all over her shaking body, his coarse palms following the path his nose had taken only moments before. She gritted her teeth as he began to knead the heavy breasts splayed wide at her sides, stimulating the broad nipples, which despite herself and to her utter dismay began to harden at his expert touch.

Bormann grunted appreciatively. "Alex told me you were hot," he muttered. "Hot, leggy and stacked, well worth a thousand bucks," he concluded, adding mysteriously, "you'll do well at the Fazenda."

Cassie uttered a sharp yelp and reared up in alarm, as Bormann slid his fingers between her forcibly spread thighs and into her still slick sex. She tried desperately to avoid his penetrating fingers by shuffling her hips about, but her movements simply succeeded in allowing him to gain better access to her vulva, which he now began to massage with sure, knowing fingers.

At the same time, Bormann bent to one of her splayed breasts and began to lap at her already turgescent nipple with long, wet strokes of his rough tongue.

Cassie fought desperately to ignore the feelings that Bormann's unwelcome ministrations were starting to generate deep within her, but it was barely an hour since she'd made ardent love and the sexual heat was still smouldering within her.

Moaning into the heavy tape covering her mouth, she screwed her eyes tightly shut and attempted to concentrate on something, anything, which might prevent her arousal.

But Bormann's insistent fingers continued to swirl around her slowly erecting stamen and soft labial petals, teasing the delicate tissues, rolling and pinching them, causing the tense muscles in her smooth belly to flutter wildly, making her choke in shame as her vaginal juices began to flow once again and trickle slowly out on to his hand.

Despite herself, Cassie's hips slowly began to move. Infinitesimally at first, back and forth against her tormentor's relentless fingers, as behind her gag she gritted her teeth in helpless humiliation.

What the hell was she doing responding to this Surely she couldn't get any sort of sexual enjoyment from this situation. Christ! She may have fantasized about being tied up and spanked once or twice, even a gentle rape scene from time-to-time, what girl hadn't but this was the real thing!

Abandoning her now pulsating nipple, Bormann ran his tongue down the length of her spine, pausing briefly to lap at the sweat pooled in the hollow of her back. Again Cassie groaned and shook her head. But it was no use, her wide hips refused to stay still, confirming the realization dawning in her mind that on a purely physical level if nothing else, she was actually beginning to enjoy this abuse. Once again, perspiration was breaking out all over her body, coursing in tiny ribbons over her sides and down into the moist clefts between her luxurious breasts and buttocks.

Bormann continued to fondle her now wildly fluttering sex, collecting her dripping love juice in his big palm and massaging it back into the swollen lips of her vulva and over her engorged stamen.

Again and again Cassie sought to understand her sudden sexual hunger, but could only tell herself, somewhat lamely, that having just been fucked for two hours by Allessandro, she had simply been caught with her defences down.

Unable to breathe freely through her taped mouth, she was forced to pant harshly through her nose, and the difficulty in getting enough air in the incredible heat and humidity caused her to begin to slip into a mild state of asphyxia.

The lack of oxygen greatly amplified her level of arousal, making her strain her magnificent body upward against her bonds, her diaphragm and belly pumping in and out rapidly. The tendons stood out like whipcord against the pale, tightly arched column of her long neck. She groaned long and loud into her gag as she was slowly forced to give up the fight against the patiently rapacious Bormann. There was no point in pretending any further the evidence of her need was painted in the sweat running off her trembling body and in the boiling juices leeching from her hopelessly creaming sex.

To Bormann's immense satisfaction, the now steadily grunting young woman finally signalled her absolute and unconditional surrender by stretching her thighs wide apart for him and rolling her fabulous pale buttocks in perfect time to the erotic cadence of his work-hardened finger tips.

Bormann maintained her in a heightened state of arousal for several long minutes, revelling in the quivering of her body and the harsh, desperate sound of her breathing until, judging her ready and choosing his moment with exquisite timing, he thrust the entire length of his blunt thumb deep into the her sweat drenched anus.

The sudden shock caused Cassie to rear her buttocks up to the absolute limit of her bindings. The ropes encircling her wrists and ankles cut deep into her flesh as the unaccustomed penetration shocked her loins and sent lightening bolts of raw pain through her rectum and sensitive perineum to blaze into her already erupting vulva.

She held her agonized pose for a full five seconds, her anal sphincter tightly clasping itself around Bormann's cruel thumb, before the orgasm smashed through her loins, causing her to thrust her shaking hips madly back and forth against her tormentor's expert hand.

At the height of her climax, Bormann leant forward and ripped away the heavy tape sealing her mouth, allowing her to suck in a huge gulp of air before bellowing out her climax in a series of long shuddering cries, as wave after wave of excruciating pleasure ran through her soaking belly and loins.

Again and again Bormann swirled his fingers around her delicate stamen, prolonging her sweet agony for what seemed like an eternity, until, eventually, he was sure he had wrung her dry. Reluctantly, Bormann released the girl to collapse back into the mattress and drift semi-conscious, as the remnants of her incredible orgasm vibrated through her roiling pudendum like the aftershocks of an earthquake.

Cassie came slowly to her senses, the residual effects of her massive orgasm still making her head swim and her body quiver uncontrollably as she struggled to regain her composure.

Without apparent effort Bormann with one hand dragged the old iron bed around into the centre of the tiny room, so that now she faced him as he sat in front of her, cowboy style, on the room's only chair.

"You enjoyed that didn't you " Bormann smiled tightly, at the same time grasping a handful of her hair and pulling her face up to his. "Well that's good, because you'll be getting a lot more of that sort of thing from here on in, but right now, it's my turn."

Bormann stood up to her face and unzipped his fly before hauling out the largest and hardest cock Cassie thought she had ever seen. It was just like its owner, stocky and muscular, with a pattern of purple veins raised around the surface of the stout shaft and a glans quite literally the size of a small nectarine.

Bormann was evidently in an advanced state of arousal, as the quivering head was already slicked with seminal fluid, which immediately began to drip freely from his slit. She looked at the massive organ and slowly began to shake her head as full understanding of what he was demanding dawned on her.

Instantly, Bormann's hand lashed out and crashed against the side of her face, knocking her sideways. Then he stepped around behind her and she heard the menacing zzzzzzip of his belt being pulled quickly through his trouser loops.

Suddenly terrified, Cassie reared up and opened her mouth to scream, but Bormann simply clamped his hand across the bottom half of her face and hauled her entire body up into an agonizing arch, so tight she thought that her backbone would surely snap.

Held like that, her wrists secured to the bed frame and her arms stretched to breaking point, she found it impossible to move even a fraction of an inch, such was Bormann's strength.

"Now slut," he rasped, "lesson number one, never say no' to me." And with that chilling admonition he began to beat a fierce tattoo across her shoulders with the supple belt.

The sharp cracking of the leather echoed flatly around the small room, as his arm rose and fell over her sweating back and buttocks in a seemingly unending fiery shower of strokes and she shrieked mutely into Bormann's thickly calloused palm. Oh God! when was this torment ever going to stop, she screamed incoherently to herself. Her skin felt like it was literally being flayed from her bones, as agonising nerve fire burned down over the length of her back and across the backs of her thighs.

After two-dozen lashes Bormann stopped, still holding the quivering girl's body in tension whilst he examined the mass of tiger stripes rapidly blossoming across her skin.

His excitement now at fever pitch, Bormann released her to sag back into the mattress, her rib cage heaving with pain and fear as she fought to contain her panic. Tears coursed unchecked down her flushed cheeks and her jaws ached from being clamped tight against the searing pain.

Once again Bormann offered his thick penis toward her mouth. She saw with horror that his erection was even fiercer than it had been before. She could hardly think straight for the pain and shock washing over her, but more than anything else in the World she knew she did not want to be leathered again. Not ever! God no! she simply couldn't go through that hellish agony ever again.

What had she gotten herself into Cassie asked herself desperately, as Bormann cruelly wiped his slimy glans across her cheek, smearing his salty fluids over her beautiful skin. And for the first time, the pretty brunette realised that she had to do whatever it took to get out of this crazy situation alive.

After all, it wasn't as if she'd never sucked a man before, she told herself desperately. Hopefully, she could bring the sick bastard off quickly and then maybe, just maybe, once he'd had what he wanted, she might get the chance to make a break for it.

Bormann grunted sharply, an insistent sound, and once again pushed his cock up against her full lips, and then she was opening her mouth as wide as she could to take in his solid length, extending and flattening her tongue down over her chin to make room for the incredible girth.

For a moment she thought that she would not be able to accommodate his thickness, but by a supreme effort of will she was able to relax her aching jaw muscles and allow Bormann to slip all of the way in, expelling a long groan of approval as he did so. He took hold of her heart-shaped face in his large palms and pulled her long neck straight before beginning to pump himself vigorously in and out, grunting with each plunge, heedless of any difficulty she might have in accommodating his size.

Cassie fought to prevent herself from choking and accept the fearsome cock into the top of her gullet. Calling desperately upon all of her willpower, she managed somehow to regulate her breathing on the outward strokes to avoid suffocation, snorting short breaths in and out as the lunging column of gristle briefly cleared the entrance to her windpipe.

Cassie had always prided herself on being an accomplished fellatrix, but never in all her most salacious dreams had she imagined that she would one day be called upon to deep throat such a monster.

Once Bormann settled into his rhythm, she made herself concentrate on speeding his orgasm by sucking and mouthing the rapidly moving cock as best she could, tossing her head forward as he plunged inward so that her long dark hair cascaded around his belly and groin to increase his level of stimulation.

Bormann groaned in appreciation, speeding his hips and leaning backward. His cock began to thud into her face like an iron piston as his orgasm rapidly approached. Suddenly, with a growl, his lips drew back from his teeth in a grimace of lust, as his scalding spunk flooded into her throat. He held her face tightly between his splayed palms, his cock deep within her mouth whilst he continued to ejaculate over and over.

Despite herself, Cassie felt a brief incredible frisson of pleasure as she struggled to swallow the unnaturally large quantity of cream, gulping

13

it all down, clamping her lips tightly around his girth, instinctively knowing what he would do to her if she lost so much as a drop of the glutinous spend.

After a long few moments Bormann withdrew from her mouth. He regarded her speculatively as he tucked his sated member into his pants.

"If you'd spat it out I'd have leathered you again," he said simply, "but you knew that didn't you "

"Yes," said Cassie slowly, reluctantly licking the remains of his ejaculate from her bruised lips.

"We're going to get along just fine." He smiled thinly. "You learn real quick."

Untying Cassie's bindings, Bormann hauled her up from the mattress and then slapped her roughly about the head with both hands, whilst she stumbled stupidly about trying to persuade her cramped legs to hold her shaking body upright.

Bormann picked up her underwear before saying, "open wide," and then stuffing her panties into her mouth. He secured them by the simple expedient of tying her bra across her mouth and knotting the elasticated straps tightly behind her head. Then came the metallic snapping of handcuffs as he fastened her wrists behind her back.

Bormann stood back for a moment to admire his handiwork.

"Time to go," he said, and taking hold of her by a hank of her hair he pulled her stumbling from the room and down the stairs into the garage, where a disinterested looking Allessandro was on hand to open up the boot of the newest and most expensive Mercedes Benz limousine in the BRASCO fleet.

Cassie attempted to beseech her erstwhile lover with an anguished look, but his eyes passed lifelessly over hers as he turned away to drop into the driver's plush seat.

Without giving her any time to think, Bormann easily flipped Cassie off her feet, pitching her into the capacious boot and then slamming the lid with a theatrical flourish that brought a brief flicker of a smile to his hard-bitten face.

Lying helpless in the total isolation chamber of the car's boot, Cassie had no idea which way they travelled after leaving the garage. The vehicle seemed to twist and turn endlessly through the night-time streets, until finally the sounds of the city traffic faded and the big car began to eat up the highway miles.

And presently, through pure exhaustion, the terrified girl slept.

As the limousine turned off the smooth highway and on to a rough track, Cassie awoke from a troubled sleep with a start.

For several long moments she struggled in the pitch darkness to comprehend the strangeness of her surroundings, praying that she was emerging from a nightmare to find herself safe and sound in her own bed.

Eventually, the car came to a halt. Inside the dark boot Cassie lay dazed and shivering in trepidation as she heard the car door slam and the sound of muffled voices approaching. Suddenly, the boot lid sprang open to reveal Bormann's broad face peering in at her. Beside him, a thin wiry man in his late twenties gazed curiously at her nudity with a pair of dark, close set eyes.

At a grunted signal from Bormann, the pair reached in and easily picked Cassie out of the boot, only to drop her unceremoniously into the dust behind the car. Disoriented as she was, naked and with her hands manacled behind her back, she could not make it up on to her feet and was forced to shuffle painfully forward on her knees through the dirt.

Behind her, Allessandro reversed the powerful car back up the track and was soon driving away and out of her life forever.

Ahead of her in the moonlight, Cassie could see what appeared to be a tramp river steamer moored at the bottom of a wooden jetty. Bormann spoke impatiently to his thin accomplice, "for Christ's sake Marco, help the stupid bitch up and get her aboard sharpish, we're not out for a midnight fucking stroll you dozy twat!"

The man called Marco dutifully reached down and took hold of a fistful of Cassie's dark mane and hoisted her roughly to her feet. Taking no notice of her obvious distress, Marco frog-marched the desperate brunette on tip-toe on to the jetty and down to the boat and herded her toward the forward hatchway. She tottered down the stairway with the lanky mate following close behind, guiding her with prods and swipes of the painful switch every step of the way.

In the dim light Cassie could see that the hold had been converted into several small cells, all of which were presently unoccupied, and to her rapidly dawning horror she realised that she was to be incarcerated in one of the dark, stifling compartments.

As she stood wild-eyed, Bormann came stamping down the passageway behind them and roughly shouldered his way past Marco, who wisely concealed his displeasure at being pushed around by the shorter but far more powerful man.

"I'll string her up," snapped Bormann unpleasantly, clicking on the cubicle's single naked bulb as he spoke. "You get yourself topsides and keep a sharp look out for any nosey parkers sniffing about after all the fucking racket you made getting the bitch aboard."

Marco turned sullenly away, but not before his dark eyes had glittered eagerly over every inch of Cassie's voluptuous form. The younger man

,as promising himself that his turn with the young English slut would come very, very soon.

Bormann took hold of Cassie by her dark hair once more and thrust her belly-up to a stout wooden frame, that stood like a small ranch rail in the centre of the wooden cell.

With efficiency born of long practice, he quickly shackled the girl's ankles to iron rings set into the floor, eighteen inches behind each vertical post and three feet apart. Then he removed her handcuffs and attached chains to her wrists, which he connected to more rings in the ceiling positioned three feet in front of her outstretched wrists and six feet apart. With all the chains pulled bar-tight the effect was to stretch her upper body forward and upward whilst restraining her hips across the horizontal rail. The chain tension meant that Cassie had to stand on the balls of her feet to relieve the pressure on her arms.

The simple pose made it look like the girl was quite literally trying to fly off the floor. It also had the added advantage that it brought out all of the beauty of her straining musculature and accentuated the taut swells of her buttocks and heavy breasts.

Whilst he watched her, Cassie's fear-filled eyes crawled reluctantly around the cell taking in the few features. There was a single un-shaded bulb hanging from the low ceiling. A low wooden bench ran along the back wall barely wide enough to lie on, or so it seemed.

On the wall facing her, a stomach knotting selection of whips, crops and other things she had never seen before hung from various hooks. Below her, a hole six inches in diameter had been let into the floor directly below her genitals and seemed to lead directly into the boat's stinking scuppers.

"That's where you piss, slut," laughed Bormann, noting the direction of her horrified gaze, "but only when I give permission and woe betide you if you miss the hole and mess the place up."

Deliberately, he sought to add insult to injury, "the other you do off the back of the boat, again strictly by appointment." He laughed uproariously as she rolled her huge green eyes and shook her head wildly.

"Oh yes, my pretty," murmured Bormann, coming very close to her face, "you belong to me now. I own you body and soul and you do exactly what I say, when I say, how I say. Nobody is going to come between us unless I decide. So you can forget all about your fancy city friends. No one knows where you are or where you're going, and nobody is coming to rescue you."

Bormann paused, suddenly fascinated by the carotid pulse thudding visibly in Cassie's throat. He knew the girl was terrified of him and that pleased him greatly. It was one of the reasons why he always made a point

16

of tying the sluts up for the first time himself.

There really was nothing more enjoyable that seeing the terror in their eyes when they saw the cells for the first time. Sometimes the silly bitches went completely ape-shit and he had to beat them almost unconscious before they would shut up.

But this girl was different, she was scared, yes, of that he had no doubt. But there was a strength and intelligence about her something in the way she looked at him. Well, that was fine by him. She would not be the first arrogant bitch he had broken on the long trip up river and he doubted very much if she would be the last.

He untied the bra straps from around her head and pulled the wadded panties out of her mouth. His big cock began to swell as he pumped his hand idly up and down the heavy shaft. His narrow grey eyes roamed greedily over Cassie's body, drinking in every detail of her feminine beauty. Licking his lips, he moved behind her and for the second time tonight pushed his fingers deep into her exposed vulva.

"Please, no!" Cassie gasped, trying vainly to close her spread thighs against him. "Oh God! no! look, please let me go," she pleaded miserably. "Please, my boss will pay a lot of money for me, he's in love with me, I'm his mistress, he's crazy about me," she lied desperately, saying anything she could think of to divert the pervert's attention from her body.

"You're lying," replied Bormann in a bored voice. "Alex told me all about you where you live, what you do, who your friends are," he sniggered lewdly, "especially how much you like to fuck."

Cassie groaned through clenched teeth, as Bormann continued to stimulate the pouting lips of her vulva.

Her flesh was still sensitive and moist from her earlier sexual activity and despite her protests she quickly became excited as he manipulated the taught bud of her stamen, liquefying the hunger in her belly and causing the juices to once again run unchecked into her sex. She gasped as Bormann's huge hands clutched at the satin smooth mounds of her buttocks, forcing the perfect white globes apart, further exposing her swollen, juicing labia.

He paused for a moment, staring admiringly into her soft looking crotch before thrusting his monstrous cock straight into her, making her express an anguished grunt as the sensitive membranes of her vagina were stretched to the limits.

Once again, the insidious sensations crawling deep inside her belly. quickly began to demolish her resistance as he worked himself in and out of her sex and for the second time tonight she began to roll her lush buttocks for him, eventually revelling openly in the feel of his massive thrusts.

In a daze, Cassie wondered at the source of her sudden lust. Ordinarily, she knew she would never have looked twice at this hard, ugly lump of a man. But twice tonight he had easily managed to overcome her resistance and make her buck and scream for it like a common dockside whore.

Could this sort of sex be what she had unconsciously been craving of late she asked herself, as she hung suspended in her chains. The muscles of her arms and shoulders slowly began to cramp and burn with the strain of her unfamiliar posture. Helpless to resist Bormann's thrusting, she began to clench and unclench her vaginal muscles, alternatively gripping and releasing his solid shaft as he sawed back and forth within her, threatening to milk the very semen from his balls.

Sensing her hunger, Bormann grasped on to her hips and slammed into her as hard as his massive frame allowed, shattering her sex with his physical power, battering at her buttocks until she screamed her climax out over and over again.

And then Bormann was coming too, roaring at the top of his lungs, pumping the first pulses of his heavy load into her desperately sucking sex chasm before withdrawing to contemptuously spurt his final fluids over her sweating haunches.

Cassie spent the next few hours trying both to understand what had happened to her and to ease the phenomenal aches and pains that had begun to develop in all of her muscles. However, try as she might to adjust her posture, the chains holding her were drawn so tight as to prevent all but the tiniest movements.

How long could she put up with this sort of treatment, she asked herself desperately What time was it anyway She guessed it must be around midnight. Somewhere on the now silent boat she thought she could hear snoring. How long had it been since Bormann had kidnapped her Four or five hours at most she calculated. God Almighty! What if this shit went on for days

What did he want, ransom Her parents were dead and she had no close relatives. Cassie doubted very much that her employer was likely to stump up much cash for a lowly secretary. Anyway, he had shown absolutely no interest when she had suggested her boss might pay well for her. No, ransom didn't seem to be his motive.

And what had he said back at that little fuck Allessandro's place - he was taking her on a trip to meet some friends of his and something about her doing well at the Hacienda. No, that wasn't quite right. He had said something similar sounding, what was it The Fazenda,' that's what he'd said. But that made no sense to her either. A Fazenda was the Brazilian

18

name for a coffee plantation, or some such agricultural concern. Why the hell would he be taking her to a coffee farm of all places

Cassie shook her head in confusion. All she did know for certain was that whatever it was that was going on it was really serious. The dread words white slavery' kept flitting across the forefront of her mind, but she refused to accept that. That kind of thing didn't go on these days, she told herself.

But she had been in Brazil long enough to know that the Amazon was not Europe. Most of it was uncharted and pretty much totally wild. Cassie had heard stories of bandits and pirates operating even quite close to the city limits, and of people wandering around in the jungle for years without finding their way out. She fought to control her increasing panic as the tears welled up again in her eyes. She wondered what Christen and Lucy would have done when she failed to show up at the Club last night.

Would they have gone to her apartment and rung the doorbell, or would they have simply assumed that she had gone off for the weekend with some new boyfriend and forgot to call them to cancel

No, Bormann had been very clever taking her on a Friday night. No one would even begin looking for her until Monday morning at the earliest and by the time someone had telephoned her home and then taken the trouble to call round and see that she was missing. It could be late Monday, maybe Tuesday, or even Wednesday, before the alarm was raised, by which time she would be heaven knew where.

Cassie cursed herself bitterly for keeping her affair with Allessandro so damned secret. There was nothing whatsoever to connect the managing director's dazzling English secretary with his handsome Brazilian chauffer.

Perhaps staring into the pitch black for hours had heightened her sense of hearing, because she heard Marco's stealthy approach through the darkness even before he entered the hold from the companionway.

She knew it was Marco because Bormann didn't seem to be the creeping sort, whereas Marco most assuredly was. Besides, Bormann was obviously the boss and had no need to sneak about on his own boat. He would have switched on all the fucking lights and made as much Goddamned noise as he wanted. She could still hear snoring from somewhere and guessed that would be Bormann asleep in his bunk.

Cassie considered screaming to alert Bormann to the fact that his sidekick was up to no good, but he was just as likely to beat the shit out of her for ruining his beauty sleep.

Marco paused at the entrance to the cell. She couldn't see him in the pitch darkness, but she could smell his sweat. She waited, heart pounding so loudly she imagined Bormann couldn't fail to be woken by the sound of it.

She heard the rasp of the swarthy mate's bare, horny feet on the deck as he moved in so close that the pungent smell of him in the tiny sweltering space was overpowering.

Despite knowing he was so very close, Cassie jumped when he suddenly whispered in her ear.

"Make no sound. I mean you no harm." There was a pregnant pause and then, "I brought you some water, just a little drink, or Bormann will know."

Cassie felt the thick rim of a tin cup bump against her lips and she warily opened her mouth to taste before gratefully letting the cool, sweet liquid run into her throat. Just a single, precious mouthful then the cup was withdrawn.

"More," she whispered, licking her lips, "please Marco, it's so hot down here, I'm parched."

"No, no more," the Mate hissed, "Bormann will know if you piss too much tomorrow."

A few moments later the girl sucked in her breath as the Mate's hand moved slowly across her heavy sweat soaked breasts, testing their weight, gently at first, and then squeezing and kneading the flesh and pulling at the prominent nipples cruelly.

"Please Marco don't," she gasped.

"Quiet," hissed the Mate hoarsely, "if Bormann hears he will punish you severely, with the whip, or maybe worse." Marco let the threat hang before resuming his enjoyment of her breasts. He seemed fascinated by her nipples, repeatedly stretching and rolling them, stopping only when she began to gasp out loud.

"Besides," he continued in her ear, "you will need a friend, to bring you water and a little food, to protect you maybe, eh "

Cassie's mind was racing. Marco would be afraid of Bormann, probably as much as she was. If she began to make a fuss the chances were the creep would leave. She debated with herself what to do for long moments, knowing she should resist him, but somehow she could not bring herself to do so. Maybe, she told herself, she could use this fuckwit to help her escape. Maybe find some way to get the two evil bastards at each other's throats - anything might happen, possibly giving her a chance to escape. As things stood at present she knew that she was desperately short of options.

Marco waited, panting in the cloying heat whilst she deliberated. All the while his fingers gently fondled her nipples, which to her absolute incredulity were once more hardening up and sending waves of sexual heat into her over sensitive breast flesh.

Cassie knew she couldn't send him away incredibly she was becoming intoxicated by his pungent body odour. In the darkness she slowly craned her neck toward him, inhaling him, savouring his masculinity. Swallowing nervously, her head swimming, she whispered, "okay Marco, but only touching, you can touch my breasts, but that's all, okay "

Marco said nothing. She felt him move to her front in the darkness and then his mouth was guzzling lewdly at her breasts, gobbling at her nipples until they ached. He mate suckled hungrily, with no finesse, avidly pulling the hot flesh deep into his mouth before drawing the long teats out with his tightly pursed lips until she hissed. And then swirling his rough tongue all over the wide bowls, licking at her like a dog, lapping up the sweat from her cleavage and the hidden creases beneath the breasts themselves - first one then the other.

"That's enough Marco," Cassie gasped after five minutes spent desperately trying to stop her sensitive buds from hardening. It was no use her nipples were already standing up like rifle bullets, the surrounding breast flesh painfully hot and swollen. If Marco had switched on the light he would have seen the crimson sex flush spreading all over her neck and chest. But he didn't need the light he could already feel her arousal with his lips.

The girl's breath hissed sharply inward as Marco bit down hard on a stiff teat, cruelly grinding teeth into the delicate tissue. The sweating brunette's head strained backward, her mouth forming a huge quivering Ohhh' in the darkness, as she fought to suppress her scream. Only when Marko released the tortured flesh did she groan aloud in agony.

Immediately, he switched to the other teat, sucking it to its full length and thickness for several long delicious minutes before eventually applying the same brutal treatment.

Again Cassie strained against her chains groaning, this time in a much longer expression, this time one of dark satisfaction grunting in shameful gratitude as a fierce sexual heat ignited throughout the whole of her torso. She marvelled at herself as the waves of pain turned to pleasure and swept down into her sex, making her juices roil and flood out on to the heated surface of her pulsating vulva.

Emboldened by her reactions, Marco's palm slid down over Cassie's smooth belly and into the damp hair of her streaming crotch.

Once again, Cassie felt nothing but shame at her body's wanton reactions. She told herself lamely that because of her restraints there was nothing she could do to prevent the mate's fingers exploring her exposed sex. Panting, she closed her eyes and for the third time in just a few short hours asked herself what the hell it was that caused her to flood with juice whenever a filthy raping bastard tied her up and forced himself upon her.

As Bormann had done earlier, Marco was now cunningly masturbating her and her traitorous clitoris was erecting and sending irresistible waves of sexual surf crashing into her loins, threatening to drown her in the depths of her sudden need.

Cassie knew with absolute certainty that Marco was going to fuck her and she also knew that the incredible heat his fingers were building in her sex would not be satisfied until he did. Closing her eyes, she swallowed hard and whispered into the dark, "Marco, I need your cock inside me," and then, throwing her last vestige of shame aside, "quickly, fuck my cunt, I need it now!"

Grinning into the darkness, Marco hurriedly dropped his pants and moved quickly to her waiting rear. Her already stretched body arched further as the now naked man grasped her fevered hips and thrust himself into her clutching heat.

Such was her level of arousal that she began to come immediately, biting down on her bottom lip to silence her groans as the orgasm rolled slowly over her. Marco was not as large as Bormann, but he was equally as hard. She knew that if Bormann hadn't been aboard the mate would have slammed into her wildly, ruthlessly raping her. Instead, he had to settle for a slow, deep motion that kept the rattle of her chains to a mere tinkling.

After many long minutes of carefully controlled thrusting the shivering mate began to pump faster, gasping as his pleasure increased and rapidly built toward his orgasm.

Within her sex the rippling vaginal muscles closed around his straining cock, causing his already engorged flesh to harden and swell still further.

Humping frantically together, the couples' harsh breathing filled the confines of the tiny cell, sounding like a miniature hurricane in Cassie's ears as Marco finally achieved orgasm.

In desperate sweet agony he thrust up on to the balls of his feet, discharging a thick stream of hot spunk into her hopelessly spasming sex. He gasped out loud as he surrounded her with his arms, digging his long fingers into her breast flesh, holding himself in a tightly arched rictus of pleasure, lifting her feet from the decking and stretching the sinews in her legs to breaking point as the last of his cream spurted into her sex.

A sex that throughout the prolonged fucking had rolled continuously from one crushing orgasm to another.

Once again left hanging alone in the darkness, Cassie tried to analyse what was happening to her.

Now that the sexual heat had fully dissipated she felt nothing but loathing for herself and Bormann and Marco, and swore to herself that she would never be a willing sex partner with either of them ever again.

But as she stood sweating in the stifling blackness with her thrashed backside glowing, her bitten nipples throbbing, and the glutinous mix of semen slowly draining out of her smouldering crotch, she could not help but endlessly replay in her mind every single detail of the fabulous sex she had been subjected to over the past six hours, until slow, heavy tears of confusion and shame ran unchecked down her cheeks.

Having fallen into an exhausted sleep in the brief hours before dawn, the exhausted Cassie was soon awoken by the vibrating thunder of the boat's main diesel engine.

It was almost pitch dark in the tiny cell and she had no idea of the time, but guessed from the sounds of activity on deck that it must be early morning. Above, she could hear Bormann shouting orders to Marco and presently the surging motion of the hull and increased rate of the engine told her that they were underway.

Sometime later, Bormann came down to the cells for what he liked to call his morning inspection. Cassie stiffened fretfully when she heard him stamping down the companionway, clicking on lights as he approached. She felt strangely guilty after fornicating with Marco in the early hours, although for the life of her she couldn't imagine why. After all, he had in effect abused and raped her, as had Bormann only an hour or two beforehand.

Nonetheless, Cassie had a sneaking suspicion Bormann wouldn't see it that way. The accusatory smell of sex hung heavy and fetid in the unventilated cell and her vulva was choked with the stink of post coital curd.

Cassie could only hope that the now frankly rank odour emanating from the rest of her sweating body would confuse the issue.

Bormann appeared in the doorway wearing his customary tight-lipped smile.

"Good morning slut," he called, walking right up to the girl and openly inhaling her body odour. Carefully he ran his hands over her taught form, poking his hard fingers into her knotted muscles, smiling as she winced and gasped at his touch.

Finally, he paused to closely examine her bruised nipples, flicking his thumbs over the sore buds and noting her wince at their tenderness. Frowning now, Bormann unfastened her wrist shackles and allowed her to drop to the floor.

Instantly, Cassie doubled up in agony as her calf, thigh and arm muscles spasmed into multiple cramps, making her writhe in agony as the blood supply slowly pumped itself into areas where it had not been for many hours. He growled impatiently at her antics and stooped down. Taking hold of an arm and a leg he easily hoisted her limp form over his brawny shoulder and carried her up through the boat and out on to the stern where he dropped her on to the deck.

Next he took a thirty-metre warp out of the lazarette, lashed one end to a transom cleat and the other around her ankles before tossing her overboard into the boats churning wake before striding up to the wheelhouse, where he grabbed the unsuspecting mate by the hair and smashed his head repeatedly down on to the chart table until the teak splintered. Then he rammed the man's screaming face through a side window and left him hanging senseless in the smashed frame and kicked him viciously in the groin from behind.

Marco sank retching and bleeding slowly to the floor, as Bormann returned to the stern, where he slowly pulled in the warp hand-over-hand and deposited the drowning girl once more back on deck.

Grimacing at the unconscious state of her, Bormann unhitched the warp from the transom cleat and passed the end through a block on the mast so that he could haul her up into the air by the ankles. Here she stayed, swaying ponderously back and forth three feet above the deck, water cascading from every orifice of her limp anatomy.

Bormann then took a fishing rod from a rack behind the wheelhouse and pulled off the four-foot end section. This he used to savagely whip the upturned soles of Cassie's feet until, with a great abdominal heave, she vomited up a couple of pints of river water, immediately followed by a prolonged bout of coughing and spluttering.

Satisfied that she was finally breathing properly, Bormann returned to the wheelhouse where he made sure that Marco was once again tending the course.

Standing beside the freely bleeding mate, Bormann said in his most friendly and engaging tone, "I think that about deals with the midnight shag-fests, don't you Mr Damato "

Marco, who was gingerly plucking bits of broken glass out of his bloodied cheeks, nodded his head in miserable agreement.

"You know what I would have done to you if you'd buggered her, don't you "

Again Marco nodded, shifting his bare feet nervously.

"His Excellency always likes to reserve that particular pleasure to himself," said Bormann, turning to look back at the girl dangling limply from the block under the hot equatorial sun.

After she had hung for a couple of hours, Bormann returned Cassie to her cell, again chaining her to the ranch rail.

But this time he lowered the crossbar, making her kneel on the floor with her back to its centre and with her arms spread horizontally out to the corners of the frame. He spread her thighs wide and fastened them in that splayed position, under the tension of ropes to the bottom of the uprights. Her heels he manacled together. Finally, Bormann wound her long dark mane into a thick twist and used it to drag her buttocks up off her heels and secured it to the ceiling with another rope.

He laughed grimly as he watched the girl vainly trying to keep her body weight from pulling her hair out of her scalp. But after only a few minutes her thighs and calves began to cramp and her weight was inexorably transferred back to her tortured hair roots.

Cassie silently cursed Bormann through gritted teeth as the fire in both her legs and scalp burned through her. Her entire body had developed into a mass of aches and pains as the abuse of the last twelve hours began to coalesce into one great aching morass psychologically she knew she was not doing too well either. Only yesterday she had been enjoying a wonderful cosmopolitan lifestyle, with a good job, nice friends, a sports car and all the freedoms and benefits enjoyed by a young, successful woman abroad.

But Bormann's deeply unwelcome intervention had changed all that. Spiriting her away from her previous life, only to imprison her in this hellish sweatbox of a cell and then subjecting her to the grossest personal and sexual humiliations.

Nonetheless, Cassie could not deny the devastating sexual pleasures she had suddenly begun to experience. She blushed as she recalled the power of the orgasms both Bormann and Marco had given her. Shattering sensations that had her screaming out loud for more. The experience of kidnap, rape and bondage was suddenly beginning to affect her at a deeply visceral level that she had never even known existed.

Cassie had always enjoyed sex and had never stinted herself in either choice or quantity of bed partners. She had assumed that the orgasms her lovers had given her had been perfect, but now she realised that they had been pale imitations of the bittersweet agonies she had recently experienced.

With dawning incredulity, Cassie wondered if she could ever be satisfied in the normal way again.

Ignorant of her thoughts, Bormann squatted down on his heels and took hold of her by nape of the neck, pulling her face toward his. His hard, grey eyes looked into her wide green ones for a long time.

"Now," he said quietly, "maybe you'll learn to do as you're told. No fucking unless I say so, understand "

Cassie nodded her head quickly, desperate not to give him an excuse to punish her again.

"You drink, eat, piss, shit and fuck only when I say," he continued, "whores like you decide nothing, nothing at all, otherwise ..." Bormann let the last word hang between them menacingly.

Cassie again wisely nodded her understanding and Bormann nodded too, smiling his tight-lipped smile, apparently happy that they had reached an amicable understanding. The slaver looked into the perfect, beautiful face for what seemed like an age. Then he bent forward to smother her full mouth with his, forcing his fat tongue past her lips and teeth.

At the same time, his fingers found her nipples and began to stimulate the dark cones, once again tweaking and extending them until they became tumid and she began to moan softly against his lips.

Then he turned his attention to her widely splayed sex, cupping her labia with his palm, slipping his middle two fingers between the delicate petals and massaging the whole mound with his calloused hand, making her gasp open mouthed as he manipulated her sex.

The fire he was kindling spread rapidly and predictably to smoulder deep within her, starting her sexual fluids roiling anew and sending them sluicing into her sex.

Despite her loathing of him, Cassie began to return his powerful kiss hungrily, her mouth falling open to allow their wet tongues to plunge and writhe together.

Incredibly, it did not seem to matter to her that this man had almost killed her only a couple of hours ago. Nothing seemed to have any meaning except the increasing heat smouldering in her belly. So much so that when he stood and pulled open his pants she welcomed his massive cock into her wanton mouth without hesitation, sucking on the broad head and running her greedy tongue around the heavily veined shaft.

The smell of his sweating sex made her head swim. Bormann had not washed since fucking her yesterday and the musk rising from his balls was rich and redolent of their previous fornication.

All Cassie could think of as he started to pump himself forcefully into her gullet was relieving his cock of its molten seed. She concentrated on his bulging glans as it came to the front of her mouth at the start of every stroke, curling her long tongue around it, slurping at the fluid dripping from the slit as Bormann held it there for her to lave.

The young English girl was grunting loudly now, her mouth slavering around the big shaft, the saliva dribbling out of her mouth and running down her chin as she struggled to keep her lips sealed around his huge, pumping girth.

When Bormann's climax arrived, he pulled himself out of her madly sucking mouth, making her gasp in protest as he began to whip his hand furiously up and down the length of his hard shaft.

Bormann grunted harshly as he ejaculated the spray of hot spunk into her wide open mouth and face, laughing as the thick snail like trails crawled slowly down her cheeks and dripped from her chin, and finally plunging his softening shaft back into her mouth so that she could suck off the remaining jism, which she did with obvious relish.

Bormann left Cassie alone in the dark for the rest of the day, during which time the excruciating pain in her scalp and tightly stretched limbs once again began to meld into an all over throbbing agony.

It was a pain that seemed to find its natural centre in her well stoked pudendum where it lay like a coiled serpent, writhing with unpredictable fitfulness causing her belly to churn and her succulent vulva to hang slackly, the labia peeled open in impatient anticipation.

Earlier, Cassie fancied that she had heard the sound of Bormann and Marco going ashore after the boat had docked for the night. But now, all she could hear in the eerie silence was the steady splat, splat, splat, of her sweat as it dripped slowly from her body and pooled on the wooden decking beneath.

The slavers returned several hours later with another captive whom they immediately secured in the cell next door.

To her horror, Cassie was then forced to listen to the sound of the new arrival screaming hysterically, as she was treated to dozens of strokes of the lash and thereafter prolonged and vigorous sex.

The sound of both men's guttural grunting and the girl's protesting groans filled the small hold for over an hour, as both Bormann and Marco repeatedly raped the helpless female perhaps punishing her for some misdemeanour imagined, or real, committed on the way back to the boat.

To Cassie's eternal shame, the sound of the unknown woman submitting to sex and eventually achieving a powerful, if tortured orgasm, no matter how unwillingly, inevitably made her belly begin to flutter and swell with need, her juices once again boiling into her swollen, distended vulva.

And far worse still, the knowledge that Bormann and Marco had exhausted themselves in the other woman's body left her with an incomprehensible feeling of emptiness that once again forced her to confront the incredible depths of the depravity she was beginning to plumb. Cassie wept as the realization struck with dreadful certainty that whatever happened to her in the future, she could never again be satisfied with what passed for normal lovemaking.

After he had finished inducting with the new girl, Bormann came into

Cassie's cell. He was completely naked and the perspiration from his labours next door ran unchecked down his heavily muscled chest in a mass of tiny rivulets. The large cock still glistened with the wretched girl's moisture, as it hung limply between his hairy thighs.

Without speaking, the slaver unfastened Cassie from the rail and pulled her groaning to her feet, holding her closely to him for a brief spell while she unbent her tortured leg muscles.

The girl shuddered at the unexpected touch of their naked bodies. She felt his cock nestle in the damp crease between her buttocks as she hung against him for a few moments with his arms around her, his hands gently cupping the fulsome rounds of her breasts.

Abruptly, Bormann pushed her away from him, perhaps suddenly conscious that he had shown her some tiny measure of undue kindness. Quickly sinking back under his protective shroud of cruelty, he snatched a well-oiled quirt from its hook and sprayed a volley of stinging blows across her naked back as she cowered exhausted and whimpering on the floor.

Then he pulled her roughly to her feet and cinched her wrists and elbows tightly together behind her back, causing her breasts to jut out hugely. Then he clipped a chain to her wrists and pulled her arms up toward the ceiling until she was bent double and forced to balance precariously on her toes.

Next, Bormann gave her water to drink from a bucket, holding her head back while she gulped down cup after cup as he ladled it down her throat. He continued to force her to drink until her belly became uncomfortably distended and she could drink no more without retching it back up.

Bormann nodded at her meaningfully, "make sure you hold on to all of that lot until morning," he growled at her, grinning as she began to moan at the pressure already beginning to throb in her lower belly.

At dawn the following day, Bormann came below for his customary inspection tour, stopping off first at the newcomer's cell.

Cassie winced as she heard the wretched girl whimpering in quiet protest, only to be silenced by a resounding series of slaps as the slaver enforced his rigid code of obedience before carrying on with his perverted inspection.

Then it was her turn. Balanced upon her toes, with her upper arms cinched tightly behind her back, her breasts outthrust, Cassie was forced to endure her purgatory in lip biting silence as Bormann scrutinised every part of her anatomy, inevitably taking particular time over her delicate vulva and anus.

Deliberately, he rested his hand on her deeply curved abdomen and exerted pressure to her excruciatingly swollen bladder. Knowing better than to protest out loud the girl begged him silently with her tear-filled eyes as she teetered on the brink of soiling herself.

Bormann's smile was wolf-like as he said, "time to piss, bitch."

Cassie groaned inwardly, but knew that there was absolutely no way for her to avoid the extra humiliation he was so obviously intent on heaping upon her. In any case, she told herself, she had spent the last few hours in absolute agony as her bladder had become increasingly swollen to the point where her need to urinate had almost outweighed her fear of doing so without Bormann's permission.

Closing her lovely green eyes, Cassie bowed her head and slowly relaxed her aching bladder muscles, sighing out her relief as the golden urine streamed out of her pussy and poured down into the drain between her splayed legs.

Once she was spent, the helpless girl hung by her arms, sobbing as agony slowly receded. She fought desperately to steady and support herself, teetering precariously on legs weak and shaking from the strain of standing all night.

"Now that Madame has completed her toilet, it's time for her breakfast," Bormann announced. He took down a braided leather crop from the wall and began to swish it purposefully through the air behind her. Wild-eyed with alarm, Cassie jerked about, forcing her tired limbs to work, terrified that he was going to punish her further.

Bormann reached up behind her, released her wrists from the ceiling hook and pulled her body upright by her matted hair. And then, to her consternation, he began to shake out the densely matted strands, carefully arranging it about her shoulders and combing it away from her eyes with his blunt fingers.

"There you are, good as new," he declared, pausing to stand back in mock admiration. "The best thousand bucks a man ever spent! Now move your fat arse!" He brought the crop round in a blur to take her across both lush buttocks.

Cassie howled in agony as the explosive leather landed on her soft flesh. She leapt forward awkwardly, her tightly cinched arms unbalancing her, her jutting breasts flogging painfully from side to side as she darted out of the cell, cannoned into the wall opposite and recovering, staggered drunkenly toward the stairway. Bormann pursued her closely, stinging at her with the crop, his avid eyes intent upon the hypnotic motion of her jiggling bottom as she pounded gasping up the stairs and burst out on to the deck to slump, chest heaving, against the wheelhouse timbers.

Cassie looked about her and saw that the boat was lying at anchor under the shelter of the riverbank. All around, the impenetrable greenery of the rainforest stretched as far as she could see with no sign of human habitation anywhere. Her heart sank as she realised how truly isolated she was after only two days travel into the vastness of the Amazonian river system.

Even if she could escape, she had no idea which way to run. From deep within the forest came the weird hooting sounds of unseen animals calling and the young city-girl knew that even if she could escape, she would never have the courage to enter the strange and fearfully unfamiliar terrain alone.

Bormann seated himself beside Marco at a picnic table set up on the stern and the pair began to eat. The two unlikely brigands wolfed down food chosen from bowls filled with a variety of local foods, each swigging liberally from a bottle of cool wine.

Looking up from the feast, Bormann indicated with a wave of his spoon that Cassie should approach the table. Wearily she came forward and stopped where he pointed, her mouth watering and stomach rumbling at the sight of the food set out before her. She guessed that he'd brought her on deck just to torture her again and that the evil bastard probably had no intention of giving her any food, but in this small matter she was to be proved wrong.

"Kneel," ordered Bormann, speaking around a mouth full of roast chicken.

Cassie sank gratefully to her knees, relaxing her leaden limbs for the first time in nearly two days. But the slaver had other ideas. He slashed his spoon from side-to-side and barked, "not like that you stupid slut, get your frigging thighs apart, don't hide your best asset."

Marco giggled like a schoolboy, unable to take his greedy eyes from the secretary's voluptuous body as he rubbed his palm over the crotch of his threadbare pants.

Obediently, the wretched girl dragged her knees as wide as her tortured muscles would allow.

"Lean back!"

Cassie leant backward until her spine was deeply bowed, blushing hotly as she sensed the two men staring fixedly at her dark, richly haired vulva.

Tearing his eyes away from her sex at long last, Bormann said, "right, feeding time." He cut off a piece of chicken with his lock knife. "You only get one meal a day so don't miss," he warned, tossing the meat toward her.

Cassie fumed inside, wanting to scream at both of the two cruel torturing bastards, but she feared the violence of Bormann's response and guessed that if she didn't play his game she would only end up starving.

Craning her neck, she snapped at the food as it flew through the air toward her and amazed herself when she caught it. She quickly swallowed it down as Marco cheered and threw another morsel, which bounced off her nose causing the mate to howl with laughter and bang his fists on the table.

Next, it was Bormann tossing a stream of sweet berries into her wide-open mouth, and so it went on with Cassie snapping her jaws back and forth through the air at the scraps the twisted pair deigned to throw her way until they became bored and Bormann announced it was bath time.

At Bormann's command Marco released Cassie's bonds so that she could massage the pain and cramps out of her aching limbs.

When she could stand unaided, Bormann called her over to the starboard side of the boat and pointed out into the middle of the river. Following his outstretched finger she saw a group of enormous crocodiles sunning themselves on a mud bank about one hundred yards distant.

"They look like they're sleeping don't they," the slaver said conversationally, "but don't you believe it. Just one of those big bastards can pull a full-grown water buffalo under and hold it there till it drowns. Then, he'll rip the corpse to pieces and swallow down bits as big as a suitcase." Bormann nodded sagely. "They're always watching, waiting for something or someone to fall off the boat and then they'll be over here in a crack."

Cassie looked into his eyes, suddenly feeling very uneasy, trying to fathom why he was telling her all this.

The slaver turned to look into Cassie's inquiring eyes, his smile suddenly turning corpse-like, "the ladder's on the other side of the boat," he said, "see you there." With growing horror, Cassie realised what he intended. She opened her mouth to plead, but he cuffed her across the face, spinning her round with the force of the blow, then he sent her flying over the low coaming.

As the sound of her wind-milling body hitting the water, the crocs on the bank instantly launched their hellish armoured bodies into the river, madly thrashing their powerful tails, driving themselves through the churning water toward the boat like a spread of homing torpedoes.

Cassie regained the surface and floundered about waving her arms insanely beside the boat, screaming at the top of her lungs and pleading with Bormann to pull her back aboard. Her carefully manicured nails splintered as she attempted to claw her way up the sheer freeboard, but the deck was many feet above the water line and there were no hand holds anywhere along the smooth hull.

Leaning over the high bulwark the slaver pointed over her head and shouted urgently, "quick the crocs are coming, they'll be here in a few seconds."

Cassie screamed again wailing, "please, please, I'll do anything, help me pleaseeeeeeeee!"

Bormann shouted at her again, "the ladder is on the other side of the boat, stupid!"

Cassie whirled about, sobbing in the water as she looked first to the bow, then back to the stern, but with his customary attention to detail the villainous Bormann had pitched her over mid way so that it was an equal distance to swim either way.

The petrified brunette was totally panic stricken, she knew that there was no way she could swim the long way around in time. Above her head she heard Marco shouting urgently, "under the boat! swim under the boat!" his voice breaking with excitement as he gestured with his palms pressed together for her to dive deep.

Cassie made a supreme effort to compose herself. She realised that she had to dive under the boat to get to the ladder on the other side there was simply no other way. Telling herself that it was no different to swimming a length of the Racquet Club pool underwater as she had done many times, she filled her lungs with a final, huge gulp of air and jack-knifed her superb body and plunged down into the depths.

Desperately trying to put all thoughts of water snakes and piranha fish out of her mind, she pulled herself down through the greeny-brown water, breast stroking rapidly with all of her might, expecting at any moment to feel the dreadful jaws close around her flailing legs – shaking her to bloody death, disembowelling her and ripping her apart.

In the murk, she felt the mat of foul weed and fresh water barnacles lining the boat's bottom rake agonisingly across her back as she made it under the keel, and then she was pulling for the light at the surface on the other side, her lungs bursting with the strain of holding her breath and her heart threatening to erupt out of her chest in pure terror.

Cassie burst through the surface to find both men standing expectantly beside the entry port from which dangled a rope ladder. Without a second's hesitation she hurled herself forward the last couple of yards, reaching out to grasp the ropes and drag herself with what seemed like agonising slowness hand over hand out of the water her exhausted limbs knotted and shaking.

Behind her, she suddenly heard the demonic grunts and snorts of the crocs as they broke the surface thrashing only yards away and with her last strength she dove through the entry port to lay gasping and sobbing on the deck.

Bormann stood over her beaming, clapping his hands slowly together, applauding her.

"That had to be the best show ever," he guffawed.

"She really thought they were going to get her," the Mate spluttered out. The pair continued to laugh uproariously, shaking their heads and wiping the tears from their eyes.

Cassie slowly rolled onto her back, her chest heaving as she fought to regain her breath and control the emotions that were threatening to overwhelm her. She lay exhausted, arms akimbo, her breasts and thighs hanging slackly apart, uncaring as the sadistic duo stood over her, feasting their eyes on her soaking nakedness.

Eventually, she was able to recover herself somewhat and climb to her feet, once again shielding her breasts and luxuriant pubis from their gaze with her pale arms.

Still laughing, Bormann took hold of her shoulder and dragged her strongly resisting body back to the rail to look out at the crocs now swimming lazily around the boat a few short yards away.

Cassie's mouth fell open as she saw the heavy netting rising out of the water the strong mesh surrounding the boat and keeping the disgruntled reptiles at bay.

She looked stupefied into Bormann's grinning face.

"We rigged the nets under the surface before I brought you on deck," he explained. "When you went under the boat we just pulled the whole lot up to the surface on the big winch to keep the crocs out and waited for you to come up. Jesus! You should have seen your stupid fuckin' face, I honestly thought you were going to shit yourself coming up that ladder."

Slowly, Cassie's pent up emotions welled up inside her chest, as all of the humiliation, abuse and pain she had suffered over the past few days came bursting out of her. Her control finally snapped and she suddenly lunged at him, screaming hysterically. "You fucking bastard! I hate you, I fucking well hate you!" she shrieked. Fingers raised like talons she sprang at him, raking his tough cheeks with her broken nails, slapping hysterically at his iron bulk and kicking out at his shins with her bare feet.

Bormann nonchalantly backed away from her flailing limbs his harsh face was impassive as behind her Marco deftly poked the shank of a deck brush between her feet, bringing her crashing heavily to the deck. In a flash, Bormann was on top of her, planting his knee into the small of her back, forcing her arms up behind her back and lashing her wrists together. Finally, he lifted her up with a fist full of her hair and frog-marched her howling over to the fo'c's'le hatch and pitched her back down below.

On deck, Marco busied himself gathering in the croc nets. Presently, he fired up the engine, raised the anchor headed the boat on up river.

Instead of returning her to her own cell, Bormann took Cassie into the chamber now occupied by the girl he'd brought on board last night.

When he flicked on the light Cassie gasped as she instantly forgot her own troubles, her heart going out to the slim blonde girl whom she saw had been splayed backwards over a narrow table like framework, her cruelly extended wrists and ankles chained to ringbolts set into the deck.

The girl's head lolled limply, the soft, golden shoulder length hair trailing across the coarse decking. The blonde's firm body shone with a fine patina of perspiration and her belly pumped rhythmically as she panted in the stifling heat.

Across her pink nippled breasts and down over her flat stomach the results of last night's whipping could clearly be seen as a reticulated pattern of stripes stark on her otherwise perfectly tanned skin. Between her wide spread thighs her brutalised labia gaped wetly with the thickened remains of the slavers' discharge.

Callously, Bormann pushed Cassie to her knees between the supine female's gaping thighs.

"Meet Sandrine, your new flatmate," he said, taking a crop down from the wall rack. "I want you to be real good pals with her and show her that you like her."

Bormann bent the thin braided crop double between his big hands, examining the tasselled end for signs of undue wear before bringing it whistling down to land with an enormous thwack' across Cassie's unprotected shoulders, making the dark haired girl scream and cower helplessly between Sandrine's thighs.

"Now lick her cunt," he commanded, "and you'd better make the French slut come good and hard, or I'll strip the flesh off your back bones, so help me God!"

Mindful of the awful threat, Cassie shuffled forward on her knees, hesitantly offering her full lipped mouth up to Sandrine's gluten filled crotch, the rich tangy smell of last night's sexual flux coming sharply into her nostrils.

Sandrine whimpered in protest as Cassie's tongue slipped into her wide-open vulva. Cassie wanted desperately not to hurt the other girl, but she knew that Bormann would be watching closely for the least sign of mercy on her part. She closed her ears to Sandrine's gasping protests and pushed her tongue deep into the blonde girl's sex, forcing its way past the puffy inner lips and into the narrow channel beyond, drawing out the thickened remains of last night's juices and spreading them back over the bruised labia, trying as best she could to soothe the other girl's injured flesh.

Sandrine moaned reluctantly as the brunette's moist tongue laved at her exposed sex parts, her breathing becoming erratic as the other girl's sensuous ministrations began to force the slow engorgement of her reluctant clitoris.

At first, Cassie found the experience of having both Bormann's and Marco's stale spunk in her mouth repulsive, but as Sandrine's fresh juices trickled into her sucking mouth she began to warm to her task. Never having lain with a female before, she was surprised to find the act of cunnilingus both pleasurable and, as Sandrine began to respond, exciting. Soon she was concentrating hard on the blonde girl's tumescent clitoris, swirling her tongue in the foaming love juice that was now flowing freely from the girl's golden haired sex. As her own excitement rose, Cassie's belly became heavy with need and she shuddered as she sensed the first stirrings of her own liquids within her slowly dilating vagina.

Noting the brunette's burgeoning arousal, Bormann knelt behind her and worked the tip of a thick rubber baton into her sex, roughly pumping the smooth penis-like shape back and forth to further stimulate her vaginal fluids.

In response, Cassie grunted in guilty appreciation, redoubling her assault on the French girl's ripening vulva, her transformation into willing sex slave moving one further inexorable step closer. Leaving the heavy dildo in place, Bormann moved quickly around to the now moaning Sandrine, his hard grey eyes approving the way she had begun to pump her slender hips up to meet Cassie's sucking mouth.

The slaver tweaked Sandrine's nipples between finger and thumb and massaged the pert breast flesh, bending over her to suck the hard pink buds into his hot mouth, and Cassie felt the imminence of Sandrine's orgasm as the now writhing and moaning blonde's clitoris swelled between her adroitly pursed lips.

Desperate now for the satisfaction of her own pleasure, Cassie concentrated upon using her vaginal muscles to milk the heavy dildo lodged in her cunt. Dragging it up against her stamen with her powerful vaginal muscles, endeavouring to induce her own release, which she was now desperate to attain.

Closing her eyes, she was shocked when the image of Bormann, naked and hugely rampant, came into her mind. The dildo in her sex assumed a suddenly devastating simulacrum of the slaver's massive cock, as she began to ascend the short slope toward her own orgasm.

All at once, Sandrine began her climax, rearing up, her gasping mouth falling open allowing Bormann to insert his monstrous veined cock. The French girl gagged for a moment on his girth, as, unheeding of her plight, he pulled her head back to extend her long neck before proceeding to rape her gullet with a series of swift, deep plunges.

Stimulated beyond measure by the huge cock invading her throat, Sandrine's climax continued to move up through her loins, exploding away from Cassie's sucking mouth like a bomb burst to spread into her sensitive breasts and aching nipples. After a couple of dozen thrusts, Bormann withdrew from Sandrine's mouth and quickly moved around to Cassie's up-thrust buttocks, where he positioned himself before ripping out the dildo and ramming his rock hard cock into her.

Shocked out of her fantasy by the arrival of the real' Bormann, Cassie's orgasm immediately began to plough into her belly. The brunette reared up, frantically pumping her hips in time to his powerful thrusts.

Bormann slipped his hands under her armpits heaving her forward and dropping her directly on top of the still climaxing Sandrine, their sweating breasts and bellies slapping together wetly as they writhed together in orgiastic fervour.

Bormann gave Cassie a couple of dozen furious thrusts before pulling out to slam himself into Sandrine's still spasming sex, rekindling her fading climax and sending her careering into further paroxysms of exquisite agony. For the next few minutes he boomeranged back and forth between the two girls' gaping sexes, thrusting into first one and then the other until he orgasmed with a great roar of satisfaction, finally pulling his huge cock out of the exhausted Sandrine, he whipped his clenched fist up and down the curved shaft pumping jet after jet of scalding semen over the two climaxing females.

Having emptied his balls, Bormann still found himself berserk with lust. Growling like a maddened beast, the stocky slaver snatched up the discarded crop and brought it down on the unsuspecting brunette. Cruelly he scorched the wicked braid across Cassie's back and buttocks in a withering blitz that made her howl and writhe atop the helpless Sandrine.

Up and down went his muscular arm, the stinging braid eking out the last remnants of Cassie's intense orgasm, as her quivering buttocks soaked up the punishment.

Still half berserk with his power over the two twitching, whining women, Bormann pushed Cassie aside, exposing the manacled French girl's arched body so that he could slash at her unprotected breasts and belly, revelling in the tortured grunts and squeals the leather elicited from her agonised mouth. He continued to lash indiscriminately at the two screaming women until his madness finally subsided and he stood exhausted over the two naked, sobbing females, his massive shoulders hunched and his barrel chest heaving with the evidence of his effort.

Once the boat had snugged down for the night, Bormann descended to the cells and after making a brief check on Sandrine he turned his baleful attention to Cassie.

Following the tryst with Sandrine, Bormann had returned Cassie to her own cell and suspended her from the ceiling by her wrists, hauling her up so that her feet were off the deck and clamping a three foot spreader between her ankles so that she hung legs akimbo.

After dangling for several hours in the sweltering darkness Cassie's body was once again dripping with perspiration as the muscles in her arms and shoulders gradually knotted up to form an overall mass of pain so excruciating that she began to drift in and out of consciousness.

Bormann ran his hands over the cramped, soft angles and planes of Cassie's body, squeezing and kneading the flesh of her tortured muscles with his thumbs for long minutes until she shrieked out in pain. Smiling to himself, Bormann took a wicked looking flail down from a hook on the wall and swished the horrendous looking implement back and forth in front of the terrified brunette.

"So far you've had it easy," he said menacingly. "Now its time to harden you to the ways of your new profession. Your new master won't want you screeching and yelling your lungs out every time he decides to clip you, will he "

Cassie's terror stricken eyes followed Bormann's wrist as he tossed the rattling flail experimentally to and fro, making a show of gauging the weight for her benefit. The dreadful looking implement had six thick leather tails, each tail sheathed along its four-foot length in a series of short hollow bamboo tubes that rattled like a Sidewinder's tail with every movement.

Cassie filled her lungs as Bormann walked behind her, nonchalantly throwing off his shirt and pants as he did so, to stand naked, his cock quickly rising to full erection as he contemplated the pale, sinuous sweep of her back.

The girl knew by now that there was nothing she could say or do that would alter the course what was about to happen to her. She tried to tell herself that she had simply had the misfortune to be taken up by a latter day slaver from Hell - A true madman, intent only upon his own mysterious criminal purposes. Someone who, for the time being at least, had her completely at his mercy. There was absolutely nothing she could do about any of it except grit her teeth and try to get through this living nightmare one single minute at a time.

"We'll start off hard and get harder," laughed Bormann cruelly, his powerful arm bringing the flail round in a sweeping arc to explode across Cassie's bunched shoulder muscles with a clatter that resounded inside the small cell. The air exploded out of her lungs in a harsh burst that left her gagging and almost paralysed with shock.

Bormann paused to watch a sextet of fiery eructation's bloom on he surface of Cassie's otherwise peerless skin. "I have heard it said that if you can relax your muscles it doesn't hurt so much," he advised her solicitously, "but, having said that, I've never come across a bitch who could stay that relaxed while I was whipping her."

The flail came round again as Cassie finally managed to gather enough air into her lungs to begin to shriek and fight against her bonds.

Bormann laughed as the tall brunette attempted to pull herself up the short chains in a vain attempt to get away from the insidious flail. But no matter how many insignificant inches she managed to climb, her exhausted muscles always conspired to drop her back down until she eventually hung limp as the flail fell again and again in a steady rhythm across the full sweep of her luxurious back.

Bormann worked until his arm ached and the girl's back was a mass of ruby coloured flesh from her shoulders to the backs of her knees, then he paused to take a drink from the water bucket in the corner, standing in front of her as he slaked his thirst. The heat in the tiny cell was almost intolerable, and both of their bodies were covered in a thick sheen of sweat.

The slaver waved the empty cup in front of Cassie's face, but she failed to rise to the bait. Privately, he was impressed with her fortitude - or was it simple stubbornness, he asked himself

Usually, the women begged for water almost constantly, due to the cloying heat down here in the hold, but she had not asked him for water since he had pissed on her that first day, placing him in the unaccustomed position of having to offer her water lest she become dangerously dehydrated.

Cassie stared at Bormann through narrowed eyes. She had bitten her tongue during the flogging and a thin trail of blood trickled from her lips.

The slaver refilled the cup and again offered it up to her face, slopping the liquid into her parched mouth carelessly so that the majority of it ran down through her cleavage and over the richly curving belly to drip from her dark pelt into the drain between her legs.

"Come on girl," Bormann rasped impatiently, "drink the fucking stuff, don't spit it out."

Cassie gagged as she tried to gulp down the cool liquid. The agony saturating her back, buttocks and thighs was incredible and made the previous beatings she had recently taken pale into insignificance by comparison. But even as she floated in her own private pool of pain, Cassie's attention was drawn sharply to the sudden contact of Bormann's upstanding cock sliding across her belly, as he stood close to ladle another cup of water into her mouth.

The slaver was also instantly aware of the contact and jutted his hips forward, rubbing the sensitive underside of the glans over the taught curve of her belly, painting a clear trail of jism across her sensitive flesh. He grinned into her face as he took himself in hand and guided the heavy column through the valley between her thighs. Slowly, he rocked his hips back and forth so that the veined length slid across the sealed lips of her vulva, the ventral surface of the shaft peeling open her ripening flesh like the skin of a peach. He continued to indulge himself in this way for several minutes, eventually wringing a soft mew of regret from her as he finally withdrew his tool from her moist gash.

The agonising sensations left by the flogging began to bore deep into her belly and as Bormann dropped the cup back into the bucket and picked up the flail, Cassie began to experience the first inexplicable stirrings of sexual heat.

Bormann tossed the wicked falls back and forth as he watched her. It seemed to his practiced eye that the girl was not quite so frightened as she had been at the start. He also noted the aureoles surrounding her umber nipples becoming puckered and the first faint signs of a sexual flush had begun to spread from her cleavage to the base of her long throat.

Watching him watching her, Cassie saw, much to her chagrin, the realisation that she was becoming aroused slowly dawn in the slaver's eyes. She bit down on her bottom lip as Bormann grinned lasciviously at her.

"Fuck me," he said, "looks like you could get used to this." He seized a crop from the wall rack and reversing it crammed the thick haft into Cassie's rapidly moistening sex. He ignored her yelps of discomfort as he worked the thickness in and out, reaming her delicate channel with the rough, plaited hide until she sobbed. Then he released his grip on the crop, leaving it buried halfway up its length in her vagina, and stood back grinning even more broadly than before.

"There you go, bitch, that should keep you occupied until we've finished with the whipping."

This time he began with the fronts of her thighs, walking the bamboo clad falls up over the quivering biceps in a steady progression that left the heretofore-unblemished meat covered in a dense latticework of cinnabar stripes. He worked methodically, his huge arm swinging with metronomic precision as he guided the flail across each of Cassie's spread thighs and up on to the rolling plain of her heaving belly. Carefully and precisely he scorched her flesh and drove the wind out of her as he pounded her diaphragm before laying into her splayed breasts.

To Cassie, it felt as if Bormann was intent upon flaying the very breast flesh itself from her ribs, the pain was incredible, sending her into a realm of agony she could not have imagined even in her most macabre moments.

As the scourge blazed across her nipples the densely packed bamboo sheathed falls seemed to bite and snap at the prominent teats, nipping and crushing the delicate cones until she screamed so harshly she retched. She was so traumatised that it took her a while to realise that Bormann had finally stopped and that the pain washing over her was purely residual. Nonetheless, it felt real enough, as her head lolled down between her arms, her scattered mane covering her seething breasts as she panted raggedly in the fetid atmosphere.

Through the fog of pain clouding her mind, Cassie reeled as she felt the unmistakable stirrings of raw lust boiling in her sex, as Bormann once again began to twist the crop he had left embedded in her cunt. During the course of the flogging she had unconsciously leeched a huge quantity of juice into her vaginal tract so that the tool in Bormann's fist now slid easily in and out. The glutinous lubricant slurped audibly as the slaver slugged away at her rapidly over heating sex, pumping the excess juice out on to her inner thighs from where it made its slow way down to her widespread knees.

Stimulated by her response and quaking with barely suppressed excitement, Bormann finally flung the crop away, ignoring Cassie's groan of disappointment as he did so. Impatiently he wrapped his fist in her hair and pulled her lolling head back, arching her body so that the well-flogged bust was available to him.

He bent to her nipples, which were solid with need, the dark umber flesh turgid and smouldering as he plunged his mouth over first one then the other, sucking on the delicious stalks, worrying and flogging them back and forth with his rasping tongue.

The freely perspiring brunette hissed through her teeth as Bormann piled on the agony leaning back to rain a flurry of blows across Cassie's solid gourds with his hard palms, slapping the heavy breast-meat back and forth until the massively protruding nipples seemed turned to stone.

Then the slaver clamped one massive hand over each globe, digging his iron hard fingers into the rubescent flesh before stepping over the spreader separating her ankles and dragging her onto his straining cock. He slid easily into her waiting cunt. The throbbing vaginal muscles instantly enfolded his iron hard shaft and hauled his meat right up to the waiting cervix. Now Bormann shot out his jaw the tendons rigid in his neck as he savoured the initial plunging stroke, at the same time letting out a long groan of satisfaction tinged with not a little surprise as he sank fully home. Then he began to heave her torso back and forth by the tits, pounding her as hard as he could as he sought desperately for climax.

Cassie found herself caught up in a maelstrom of pain-pleasure, pain-pleasure, as Bormann's massive cock skewered her trembling innards. The dreadful agony of the whipping had long since blended into the background to be overlain by the magical sensations now being conjured up in her roiling belly. Even the treatment being meted out to her brutalised breasts by his cruel fingers served only to heighten the pleasure, as the pain seemed to channel itself directly into the boiling cauldron that was her sex.

With a mighty groan, Bormann shot his seed into the waiting chasm, ruthlessly he dragged her on to him, their sweated bellies slapping wetly together, his fingers like red hot pokers in her flesh as he discharged pulse after pulse into her gulping sex.

Cassie threw her head back and howled, the huge scalding bolus of Bormann's semen slugging against her bruised cervix was all she needed to precipitate her own orgasm and that smashed through her with a violence that shocked even the normally unshockable Bormann.

The brawny slaver held her tight to his chest, as she shuddered and vibrated, enjoying the intensity of her climax as one titanic explosion after another thundered through her body for what seemed like an age.

When she had finally subsided Bormann blew out his cheeks with a long breath.

"Your price just went up five thousand bucks," he said to no one in particular, as he peeled the limp girl off his chest and unhooked her from the ceiling, allowing her shattered form to settle limply to the floor. He was still shaking his head in disbelief as he collected up his clothing and made his way on deck.

Cassie stood taut and tall. Her aching body was pressed flat against the cell wall her wrists and ankles were spread wide and shackled to heavy iron rings set into the darkly stained teak.

She had occupied this same position throughout the previous day and night and was, by now, in desperate need of relief and the sleep that had refused to come in her enforced vertical state.

Unusually, the boat had motored all through the night and even down here in the darkened hold she had been able to sense the myriad twists and turns Bormann had made as he conned the craft through the maze of convoluted river channels.

Having been on the boat for well over a week, Cassie had become something of an expert at divining what was going on up top by sensing the boat's various motions and listening to the shouts of the two slavers, as well as the sound of the ancient engine and the clanking deck gear. Right now it sounded as if Bormann was preparing to dock the boat, as the engine rate began to slow and she heard the shifty eyed mate lugging the big anchor about at the bow.

Whatever it was that had occupied Bormann for the past twenty-four hours, Cassie was grateful for the break, however brief, it had afforded in the usual routine.

Up to now, Bormann had established a regular pattern of strenuous floggings applied every other day, alternating between herself and Sandrine in the cell next door. In between the slaver seemed to relish contriving various psychological tortures usually revolving around the provision of food and water. And of course there was the frequent sex Bormann made a point of fucking both girls at least once a day, without resorting to the whip if they were lucky.

That was of course providing it was not their scheduled day for what he laughingly termed their hardening therapy', in which case each girl received both flagellation and sex in large measure.

Inevitably, Cassie had spent many hours of late trying in vain to come to terms with her own incredible reactions to the sadistic treatment Bormann was meting out to her on a daily basis. Each time the dreadful slaver had laid the whip on to her flesh she had found herself eventually responding with the most powerful orgasms she had ever experienced.

On her days off', Cassie was treated to a crude voyeuristic cacophony from the next door cell, as Sandrine was put through the same painful evolutions, invariably ending up with the petite blonde screaming out her own reluctant appreciation as the rapacious Bormann wrung the required number of climaxes out of her.

Now, through the thick old hull timbers Cassie heard the distinctly hollow splosh of the anchor dropping into the water, chased by the rattling of the chain through the hawsehole. Shortly afterward the thrumming of the engine died. They had arrived at their destination.

After ten minutes or so the companionway lights flickered into life, and presently Marco appeared at the entrance to the cell, his quick, dark eyes crawling over her dimly illuminated nakedness as he came close to unfasten her shackles.

The furtive mate had not dared to bother her since the first night she had come aboard, but now that he had been sent down to fetch the two girls, he was able to take advantage of the situation. He pressed Cassie's exhausted body back against the rough planking with his own bulk, forcing his crotch into her naked belly so that she could feel the unmistakable hardness growing in his pants. His hands clutched at her breasts, his work-hardened palms sliding easily over her permanently sweated flesh, kneading the heavy orbs until the sexualised nipples perked up.

Marco groaned fervently, but softly, a feverish shudder running through his entire body as he rubbed himself urgently against her. Cassie held her breath against his rankness, turning her face away from his, ignoring the cajoling importunities as he attempted to close his hungry lips over her mouth.

To her immense relief, the wheedling mate was forced to cease his surreptitious molestations at the sound of Bormann stomping noisily down the narrow companionway. Quickly releasing her, Marco stooped to unlock her shackles and pulled her roughly toward the cell doorway as Bormann appeared. As he entered the confined space the slab-bodied slaver eyed the mate mistrustfully, his glance taking in the girl's freshly crinkled nipples and the surrounding reddened globes.

Bormann raised a warning eyebrow in Marco's direction and jerked his head impatiently toward the deck head. "Get a move on Marco, you randy little shit," he growled menacingly, "I want both these two bitches secured in the stockade before that Irish arsehole O'Driscoll puts in."

Marco bobbed his head obsequiously, "aye, aye skipper, right away." He yanked Cassie forward by the wrist.

Once they had passed by, Bormann entered Sandrine's cell and unfastened the French girl from an exactly similar position of bondage. The slaver dragged the blonde stumbling drunkenly out of the cell, cuffing her roughly across the head to silence her squeals of protest as her legs, which were seized with cramp, threatened to pitch her to the deck.

Sandrine groaned as she staggered to the steps, forcing her deadened limbs to work, trying not to glance behind her at Bormann, whom at any moment she expected to plant a crippling boot in her defenceless rump.

Once on deck, both girls were herded, blinking painfully against the bright morning sunlight, toward the transom where the boat had been tied up stern first to a narrow, rustic jetty that seemed to grow directly out of the dense vegetation that came right down to the river's edge. The slavers quickly shackled the girls' wrists behind their backs before fitting them with well used bar gags, pulling the head straps tight so that the thick leather-covered bits flattened their tongues and forced their jaws wide apart.

Bormann encouraged the women to leap over the low transom with a flurry of blows across their shoulder blades, using a twelve inch knotted ropes end cut for the purpose. The solid wet hemp elicited anguished squeals from the pair as they hopped quickly over the teak coaming, tumbling together in a tangle of limbs on the jetty five feet below.

Once they had regained their feet, Marco stooped to fasten a pair of short chains between both girls' ankles, effectively hobbling them.

As with most things the slavers did, the primary effect, that of preventing them from running away, was complimented by a secondary effect, that of making them shuffle forward in a sort of dancing trot, which in turn caused their breasts and buttocks to bounce and jiggle about. The girls' uneven motion was something, which Bormann enjoyed more than somewhat as he sauntered along behind his two charges, casually swinging the rope end to and fro.

The unlikely quartet moved off into the over-arching jungle, following a narrow trail that appeared well trodden into the greenery by the feet of many previous visitors. After only a few short minutes the path broke abruptly out into a clearing dotted about here and there with a handful of ramshackle single storey wooden buildings built up on short, thick stilts, their spreading roofs covered with thick rafts of greenery.

Nearest, stood a large solid looking storehouse with a door of stout planks, beyond was a bunkhouse with a small cookhouse off to the side a lazy curl of wood smoke issuing from the tall, black iron chimney. The centre of the clearing was dominated by a more comfortable looking bungalow complete with a wide ranch style veranda.

A large tree trunk some twenty feet long and four or five feet in diameter had been laid out in front of the veranda and stretched over the curving circumference Cassie saw the supine figure of a girl, her arms and legs drawn outward by ropes pegged into the ground on opposite sides of the trunk.

Running down over the smooth bark of the trunk between her splayed thighs, a thick trail of slime issued from her gaping crotch bearing silent witness to the huge quantity of spunk she had recently been forced to take by person or persons unknown.

At the far side of the clearing stood a stockade. The eight-foot walls were rudely constructed from sharpened tree trunks dug into the compacted earth. Through the open gates the unmistakable reticulated outlines of numerous slave pens were visible, and it was toward these that Bormann marched the reluctant Cassie and Sandrine.

The two slavers waived with nonchalant familiarity toward the several grinning faces that appeared at the windows of the bunkhouse as they passed. Beside the entrance to the stockade an open fronted lean-to had been constructed against the fence and within, a rancid looking guard in a tattered straw cowboy hat lounged rather incongruously in a rocking chair, a short vicious looking pump action shotgun laid across his lap. He grinned at the approaching party, his eyes closely appraising the women as he called out a greeting to the two slavers, "buenos dias mi amigos."

Bormann raised a casual salute in return, "buenos dias, Paulo," he replied, swiping the two women smartly across the buttocks with the rope, as they both came up short, reluctant to enter the hellish looking place beyond the gate.

"Get moving!" shouted the slaver, grasping both girls by the hair at their crowns and propelling them forward toward the rows of wicker cages. Steering them toward a couple of empty units, Bormann thrust the girls to their knees in front of two small open hatches, forcing them to scramble inside with a mixture of kicks and swipes of the rope.

Once they were inside, Bormann secured the hatches with padlocks he had brought along for the purpose. After thoroughly checking the all round solidity of the rustic pens by heaving on the tough wickerwork, Bormann addressed the two crouching females. "Now listen up, sluts," he said gruffly, "I'm going off to split a bottle with the owner of this here fine establishment and you two are going to get some rest, because later on you're gonna need all of your energy - so no lying here frigging yourselves witless if you get bored."

Bormann winked at Marco who was, in turn, leering fixedly down at Cassie, his febrile imagination obviously going into overdrive wondering what the fabulous brunette would look like frigging herself witless in his bunk back on the boat. He grinned down at the two girls, savouring the expressions of confusion, fear and uncertainty flitting across their pretty faces, as each of them looked disconsolately around at the other pens, the majority of which were occupied by a number of similarly bound and naked females.

Once the two slavers had departed, Cassie settled her aching body down onto the fetid pile of damp leaves and grasses that comprised her bedding. The cage itself was little more than five feet long by three feet wide and barely afforded enough space for her to lie down, whilst the three-foot roof height would prevent her from standing.

The cages were arranged in an oblong pattern made up of four rows of ten, with room left for the guard to walk down between each row. Each cage rested on a pair of heavy logs running the length of the row, which kept them from sinking into the dark moist earth.

Overhead, a large patchwork of grass covered netting and tarpaulin had been suspended above the cages to give some protection from the weather, although from the tattered look of the ancient material Cassie resigned herself to getting wet when the obligatory afternoon rainstorm arrived.

Taking Bormann's advice at face value, Cassie tried to settle her exhausted body down and relax, but as soon as she laid her face down on her folded arms an overpowering stench rose up from below instantly making her gorge rise. Cassie jumped up in alarm, trying desperately not to vomit against the gag blocking her mouth and pulling in sharp breaths through her nose as she fought to quell the almost overpowering urge to puke.

Gingerly, she scrabbled aside some of the bedding, flinching at the plethora of tiny creatures that scurried away from her fingers as she cleared a space to peer through the thick wickerwork floor. Around the gag her full lips curled back in revulsion as she realised that the dark, mass of stinking material beneath the cages was in fact the accumulated excrement of many past tenants and presumably the future repository for her own personal waste.

Holding back the sobs that were already racking through the young French girl in the adjacent cage, Cassie sank slowly back down. Hopelessly, she closed her green eyes and tried her damnedest to visualise something pleasurable from her past, reluctant to let this latest turn of events crush what was left of her rapidly vanishing courage.

After departing the stockade, Bormann and Marco split up. The mate going off to the bunkhouse in the hope of finding himself one of the domestic sluts the management supplied to the men, to keep them from prowling around the slave pens, whilst Bormann went to pay a call upon the Big Man' himself.

Climbing the steps to the bungalow's rickety veranda, Bormann could not help but overhear the harsh, guttural sounds of a male grunting his way to orgasm within. The urgent, rasping male noises were overlain with the softer plaintive gasping of a female almost at the same point.

When he entered, Abdullah was just finishing off in the rectum of his current housemaid, who was at that very moment stretched over the kitchen table. The girl's nose was buried amongst the remains of Abdullah's breakfast, as he lunged furiously back and forth.

The huge Afghani turned Bormann a baleful sidewise glance as he began to ejaculate. His deeply set soot black eyes bulged as he shot his spunk into the gasping girl.

Despite his obvious preoccupation, the thickly bearded giant managed to growl through gritted teeth, "Bormann, didn't your whore of a mother ever teach you to knock before entering, you infidel pig "

Bormann stepped back out on to the veranda, ostentatiously banging his fist several resounding times on the wide open door. A huge grin split his face as he re-entered and slammed the door behind him. Abdullah withdrew his immense cock from the girl's hugely stretched anus. A thick strand of semen followed after his glans, maintaining a tenuous, glistening connection with her pouting sphincter. The giant slumped down into the nearest easy chair and pulled the trembling girl after him by the hair and slipped his partly subsiding member into her mouth for her to clean.

"By the Prophet's beard, I needed that," Abdullah grinned weakly, wiping the sweat from his belly with the girl's bleached blonde tresses, before impatiently pushing her away and hauling up his pants, his shovel sized hands tucking his vest down over the massive, thickly haired belly.

"Make us some coffee, you American slut," he ordered, "and none of that instant shit, put the percolator on for my good friend Gunter here."

Bormann ran an appreciative eye over the slim, high-breasted blonde as she hurried into the kitchen and started to rattle the pots about.

"She's new around here."

Abdullah nodded smiling, "she came in last month," he said in thickly accented English. "She is an American, from San Diego, California – an anthropology student." The Afghan raised his thick black eyebrows as he spoke to signify how impressed he was with the girl's pedigree.

Bormann turned his mouth down to show that he was indeed impressed.

"She came down here with a college professor type to study local Indian rituals, or some such crap," Abdullah explained. "Anyway, a couple of the local Indians did not much like being studied and so one night they slit the nosey professor's throat. She was very fortunate that they had the good sense to sell her to me instead of just cutting her and leaving her to the beasts, as they did with her boss."

"Very fortunate indeed," agreed Bormann, admiring the luxurious sweep of the girl's heart shaped buttocks as she bent over the kitchen sink.

Following the direction of Bormann's gaze, the Afghan said, "I keep her around mainly for the arse-work. She really hates it, but I think she will soon grow to love it if I give it to her every day. What do you think "

"I think you'll probably puncture her spleen if you keep ramming that monster up her like you were when I came in just now," laughed Bormann shaking his closely cropped head incredulously.

"You are only jealous because I have the biggest cock on the river," asserted Abdullah, grinning broadly. "Besides, when I fuck her up the cunt she really comes hard, she says I hit her G' spot."

Bormann tried not to laugh, as he glanced at the girl who he could see was blushing furiously as she set out the cups.

"I have heard that Californian girls like a lot of cock," he agreed affably, "what's she like in the gullet department "

"Ah, not so good, I am still training her, she says my cock is too wide for her throat, but I think it just needs a little more stretching and then she will be fine."

"No pain, no gain, that's what they say," Bormann agreed affably.

The girl handed Abdullah and Bormann their coffee.

"Would you like to see her masturbate " Abdullah asked.

"Is she especially good I have seen it done before you know."

"I think you will be pleasantly surprised."

"Why not then " said Bormann sipping at his coffee.

Abdullah snapped his fingers at the girl. "Up on the table, America, show my good friend Gunter how a real California slut flogs her twat."

The girl turned the Afghan a pleading glance, but he was already speaking to Bormann. "This you will really enjoy, I guarantee it."

"How will I know she isn't faking it " Bormann asked suspiciously.

"This will not be a problem, she is very special in this department, when she comes, you will know it."

The hirsute Afghan hooked his leg over the chair arm and scratched absently-mindedly at his crotch before declaring: "besides, you have my personal guarantee, as the most honest slave trader in the whole of the Amazon basin."

Bormann responded with a non-committal grunt that could have meant anything.

The two men sat back in their chairs as the girl clambered up on to the table as instructed, resignation evident in the slump of her narrow shoulders as she assumed a sitting position directly in front of the two men, her long, smooth thighs outspread. Beneath the flair of the girl's buttocks a small pool of semen immediately began to collect as the massive load the Afghan had recently left in her rectum slowly drained from the still pouting anus.

Beneath the intent gaze of the two men the Californian slipped her index and middle finger tips into her sex, parting the outer labia and began to stimulate the delicate tissues, seeking out her clitoris with the smooth pad of her forefinger.

The girl had been having sex with Abdullah several times a day for almost a month now and so her body was almost always in a heightened state of sexual excitement, due quite simply to the immense amount of pounding the monstrously endowed and virile Afghan subjected her to.

Even the arse-work' the beast had jokingly referred to was becoming enjoyable as her previously virgin anus finally began to relax and accept the Afghan's prodigious tool without the mind blowing pain she had initially been forced to endure.

As she let her mind wander off, the girl quickly slipped into her role of performing masturbatrix, her thoughts drifting back to earlier that very morning when Abdullah had awoken with his usual dawn hard on. As she was required to do every morning, she had taken the huge cock into her mouth, laving the mighty, distended head, hollowing her cheeks and flogging the sensitive flesh with her tongue as he had instructed her, until he ejaculated the first of his three or four prodigious morning loads.

This first one she drank down eagerly, as she had learned to become extremely partial to the taste of his thick semen. After consuming everything, she continued to suck at him, running her tongue up and down the

48

length of his shaft, tracing the throbbing veins with the tip and sucking on the huge dependent testicles one at a time until he signalled that it was time for her to mount him.

Her pleasure really began when she impaled herself upon the huge column of gristle, shaking her hips in circular fashion like a hoola dancer to help her vagina accommodate the huge girth. Riding him with her tiny fists clenched around the iron rail of the bed head until finally, he turned her over and covered her with his immense body. Slamming into her with all of his considerable strength so that it was all that she could do to hang on to his bear-like shoulders, her calves wrapped behind his knees as he plundered her by now freely running sex. The massive thrusting sent her into a long series of colliding orgasms so violent that she shrieked out her gratitude in an unending chorus until he sent his second load of the morning splattering against the entrance to her womb.

Later, after he had eaten the massive breakfast she had cooked for him, the voracious pig had caught hold of her as she had come to clear the table and thrown her face down amongst the remains of his food. Knowing what he intended and always anxious to please him lest she be sent back to the pens, she had pushed her helpless buttocks upward, grasping at the table edge with her long fingers as he had smeared the nervous, pink bud of her anus with a nub of butter and thrust himself home.

Only this morning she had for the first time truly began to relish the feel of the Afghan's great cock plunging into her bowels, as he ruthlessly sodomised her. The huge cock dragging her up the long, uneven slope toward orgasm with him, but then the stranger had burst in and the tenuous link she had established to her climax had been cruelly severed even as Abdullah had seeded her his third stupendous load of the morning.

And now she was once again on the verge of orgasm, her thighs spreading wide to display her sex to the two captivated voyeurs. Her fingers parting the glistening labia as her she flogged at the thrusting clitoris, agitating the turgid nub of pleasure with her thumb as she plunged her three longest fingers deep into her cunt, curling her fingertips up behind the root of her clitoris to press at the thick pad of succulent flesh nestling there.

Through half closed blue eyes she watched the two men leaning forward in their chairs, their coffee long forgotten and grown cold, staring at her animated sex as she performed for them. Abdullah with his deep set eyes burning into her crotch and the stranger, Bormann, sweat breaking out on his broad face, as his hard grey eyes followed the flickering movements of her thumb over the proud stamen.

And then she was coming. The orgasm smashed through her loins in a series of shocks that made her belly visibly heave and her buttocks

49

clench together so tightly that she ejected the final remains of Abdullah's seed from the her tightly puckered rectum in a tiny spurt.

Deep within her vagina she closed her fingers against the clitoral root, wringing the last and most violent sensations from her core, making her drum her heels on the table top, her mouth falling open as she grunted out the dying orgasmic embers.

Leaning forward between her thighs as she climaxed, Bormann was startled when his face was deluged by a fine spray of juice from the girl's cunt, as she pressed down hard on the succulent pad of flesh behind her clitoris, expelling the reservoir of juice contained there as a high pressure mist. He leapt up with a roar, "Jesus H. Christ, I've just gotta shag this horny little fucker!" he spluttered and ripping open his pants he slapped her hands away and rammed his straining cock straight into the girl's still spasming cunt, thrusting into the soaking gash, screwing her mercilessly, as her legs shook uncontrollably about his hips like those of some crazed marionette.

Abdullah was quickly at the other side of the table, the tall Afghan sandwiching the girl's small face in his spade-like hands he stretched her head back over the table edge, straightening the pale column of her throat before lunging into her gullet. He groaned as he felt her throat muscles relax and accept his full length, the girl closing her lips around his shaft as he pumped in and out.

For a long minute the two men pummelled at the shuddering female stretched out between them. Bormann revelled in the tight clutch of her vaginal muscles and Abdullah finally triumphant as she greedily accepted the whole length of him down her gullet.

The Californian snorted loudly and rhythmically through flared nostrils as the Afghan plunged time and time again, sucking deeply on his bulging glans as he withdrew into the front of her mouth only to relax again as he went back deep into the tightness of her gullet.

Both men roared in incoherent unison as they climaxed within moments of each other, flooding the bucking girl with simultaneous gouts of hot, heavy spunk, both of her well plumbed orifices gulping down the precious seed until the grateful donors sagged back into their chairs drained, leaving the twitching, ravished female to drift away in a state of exhausted, concupiscent euphoria.

Abdullah was the first to speak, "well, do you think she was faking it "

Bormann shrugged his shoulders, "its hard to tell," he mused laconically, "some women are really good actresses."

"This is very true."

"Especially Americans … just take a look at Hollywood."

Abdullah looked over at the girl slowly beginning to stir on the table.

"Maybe when she wakes up we should give her an Oscar," he suggested.

"I think she's had more than enough Oscar for one morning, don't you " Bormann sniggered.

"Maybe you are right my friend," agreed the Afghan, shouting at her to fetch some more coffee.

The evil pair laughed uproariously as the startled creature scrambled hastily to her feet and headed shakily toward the small kitchen sink.

Their associate O'Driscoll entered the stockade at the head of a desultory coffle of six girls during the afternoon rainstorm.

The hatchet-faced Irishman looked like a malignant leprechaun as he stood watchfully by in the torrential downpour, as his precious cargo of girl-flesh, each wearing only a heavy iron torc about her neck, was unchained and herded into the waiting pens by his two eager Negro servants who then locked each door with a heavy shackle before handing the keys to the waiting flesh-trader.

As Bormann had done earlier, O'Driscoll examined each cage with the careful attention of the professional slaver, pulling on the incredibly tough wither to test its strength before pronouncing himself satisfied.

From her own cage only yards away, Cassie watched the diminutive Irishman depart with his two cohorts, leaving the newly arrived girls to sit hunched and miserable in the cramped, stinking cages.

From above, the heavy rain poured in on them through the many holes in the ancient, weathered tarpaulin stretched haphazardly overhead.

Before leaving to join Abdullah and O'Driscoll in a night of cards and booze, Bormann secured the twin entrances to Cassie's otherwise defenceless nether regions with a length of well rusted chain, which he wrapped around her waist and snugged between her legs, pulling the links excruciatingly tight, so that they bit deeply into her buttock cleft and sex, spreading her outer labia wide and effectively sealing both her entrances against any possibility of penetration before snapping a heavy padlock shut at the small of her back

Then he laid her across the huge trunk like a stranded starfish. Her legs and arms painfully extended by ropes tied to her wrists and ankles and thence to stakes hammered into the ground on either side of the huge log.

Sometime during the night a band of foraging ants found their way up one of the ropes and began to nibble at various parts of her anatomy, causing her to twitch and moan at the constant irritation, which after an hour or so began to drive her half mad with frustration.

In front of her, the lights of the bunkhouse burned long into the early hours, as the sound of drunken revelry and debauchery echoed around the clearing. Just before dawn things began to quieten down as the drunken revellers gradually ran out of steam and semen and presently everything fell silent.

It was shortly thereafter that Cassie heard the sound of heavy boots coming down the bungalow steps behind her. Almost instantly she felt rough fingers pulling, determinedly but futilely, at the chain dividing her lush arse cheeks. She gasped in agony as the padlock in the small of her back was wrenched from side-to-side in a motion that was more angry than hopeful, but which nonetheless caused the corroded metal links to saw cruelly back and forth against her delicate inner tissues.

The footsteps moved closer and presently she looked up to see Abdullah's bearded face framed in the early light. The Afghan smiled down at her without a trace of discernable humour, "it was wise of Gunter to chain up your arsehole," he said regretfully, "he knows how much I like to shatter sweet white flesh such as yours for the first time."

Cassie's heart missed a beat as Abdullah rove down the zip of his fatigues and hauled out his massively erect prick. Her eyes bulged as she took in the enormous proportions of length and girth, and the big man stood proudly, his pelvis outthrust as her eyes moved disbelievingly over the vein ridged baton of muscle. He gathered up her thick, dark mane above her ears in two bunches and dragged her face toward his crotch.

"But no matter," he said with apparent equanimity, "I like the feel of a woman's warm gullet almost as well."

With an obedience born of helplessness, Cassie opened her mouth as wide as she could manage as the huge plum coloured glans approached her lips. The thought of resistance never entered her head as the indefatigable slave-master sought to ravage her as if by divine right. At the last moment she remembered to extend and flatten her tongue so as to create the maximum possible room for the cock, as she had quickly learned to do for Bormann.

Abdullah gave her only the briefest seconds to become accustomed to his size in her mouth before dragging her on to himself and thrusting forth his pelvis in a motion that speared her throat fully halfway down to her belly in one swift motion.

Lying trussed alongside her, one of O'Driscoll's girls watched in mute, abject horror as the giant stone-hard penis disappeared down the English girl's throat in the first of an unending series of lunges. Cassie's vivid green eyes bulged outward like organ stops as the cock plunged inward, her throat visibly expanding to twice its normal diameter as the elastic tissues were forced to accommodate the stupendous girth over and over again.

For Cassie, her entire world now consisted only in terms of her struggle to service the monstrous weapon surging in and out of her gullet. She closed her mind to all external thoughts other than the regulation of her breathing a constant struggle to achieve a brief snort of precious breath on the out-strokes and the relaxation of her throat muscles as the blunt torpedo shaped head reamed its way inward.

Cassie knew that the only danger was that she might begin to panic and lose her rhythm, at which point she would gag and choke and lose any chance of satisfying the Afghan pig as quickly and as painlessly as possible. Abdullah groaned as her outspread tongue lapped against his scrotum each time he bottomed himself against her face. He marvelled at the way she maintained a tight grip with her lips around his saliva slicked shaft as the rigid flesh slid in and out. And the concentration etched on her fabulous face was nothing short of entrancing, as was her hot breath snorting through her widely distended nostrils onto his penis as he withdrew into the front of her mouth.

Their syncopation was perfect and the ordinarily selfish Abdullah found himself concentrating on maintaining his own timing so that he would not upset her rhythm, such was the perfection of the act.

Once again, Cassie was shocked to find herself beginning to respond to her darkly brutal predicament. The motion of the cock as it surged down her throat, combined with the fetid smell of sexual musk issuing from the Afghan's heated crotch, made her head swim, and she moaned as she tasted the first precious morsel of pre-cum issue from the straining cock onto her tongue and she redoubled her efforts to speed the inevitable ejaculation.

She found herself wondering if the size of the cock would be matched by the quantity of semen and was soon desperately straining forward to meet Abdullah's mighty thrusts, their harsh grunting now also in total syncopation. Her need began to spread to other parts of her body and soon the chain links sawing between her sex lips were slick with love juice as the rocking of her hips worked the coarse metal against her clitoris.

Sensing her growing arousal, Abdullah released her hair and was gratified to see that she continued to hold her face up and pull herself toward his crotch using the ropes securing her wrists for leverage. He let his hands fall to grasp at the splayed breasts lying crushed against the rough bark of the trunk. Cassie moaned as he gathered the heated, sensitive flesh in his hands and kneaded the turgid nipples between his blunt fingers.

Abdullah now ceased his plunging to allow her to lave at the succulent, sensitive glans, her cheeks hollowing as she sucked languorously upon the bulging flesh. Cassie moaned, savouring him, as yet more pre-cum leaked out onto her sensitive taste buds. She put all thoughts of self-disgust to the back of her mind, as she sensed rather than saw the horrified expression of the girl lying watching beside her. She knew that she must look totally wanton and debauched as she willingly swallowed down Ab-dullah's immense cock, but the smell and taste of the mighty organ, cou-pled with the delicious sensations as he raped her gullet had taken their toll on her nowadays all too limited chastity.

Cassie was quite simply gagging for it' and when Abdullah reached down over her swooping back and grasped the heavy shackle securing the chain dividing her sex parts it was inevitable that she would raise her buttocks in an unmistakable signal for him to work the coarse steel back and forth across the sopping flesh of her cunt. The copious lubricant is-suing from her sex easing the friction of the links as they bit into her pout-ing vulva, crushing the delicate stamen again and again until her entire body shivered in mounting ecstasy.

Unable to contain himself further Abdullah bellowed like a bull as he recommenced his feverish thrusting, leaning backward as he strained to achieve orgasm, desperate now for the final moments with this incredi-ble creature. His orgasm was presaged for Cassie by a final, distinct thick-ening of his incredibly hard shaft, which jammed her jaws open, and then he was pumping his scalding fluids down into her belly. Slug after slug after slug of hot, thick spunk surged down her throat as the Afghan giant grunted out his climax.

Cassie hung teetering on the brink of her own orgasm for several ag-onising moments as she felt the heavy discharge pouring into her belly and then, thankfully, Abdullah withdrew into the front of her mouth, at the same time hauling up savagely on the chain separating her buttocks be-fore sending the last gouts of his considerable ejaculate into her desper-ately sucking mouth.

The long awaited taste of the precious semen and the brutal use of her sex finally flung Cassie over the precipice. Her orgasm exploded with a force that made her body flex and shudder atop the tree trunk, as she con-tinued to drink down the final spurts from the cock still held fast within her mouth.

The pair stayed locked together as their orgasms continued to rumble and clatter through their groins, each twitching and groaning as the deli-cious sensations continued to reverberate back and forth between them.

At last, Abdullah was forced to withdraw his sated penis from Cassie's insistent mouth as the post orgasmic sensations caused by her rapacious sucking became too painful even for him to bear.

Instead, the giant shucked his pants down to his knees and allowed her to lap at the heavily dependent testicles, drawing first one huge ball then the other into her mouth, as she sucked deliriously on the large stones, groaning softly as he continued to tweak the chain delving between her sweated buttocks.

"I'll give you twenty thousand bucks for the English girl," said Abdullah as Bormann finished roping up Cassie, the visibly devastated Sandrine, and three other unfortunates he had bought from Abdullah earlier that morning.

"No dice," replied Bormann shortly.

"Twenty five thousand " Abdullah was showing more than a little desperation.

"What the fuck's the matter with you," laughed Bormann. "Jesus Christ, she's only one fucking bitch and you've got your pick of hundreds coming through here all year round."

Abdullah grimaced and shook his head. "I don't know. She's got something special about her. I'd like to keep her around for a while, that's all."

"Well, she's a class bit of cunt I'll grant you that," agreed Bormann, slapping Cassie's buttock almost gently. "I can't say I've ever seen me a better looking bitch and she certainly likes a bit of jig-a-jig that's for sure. But no, she's destined for a better man than you, or me my friend, and a lot richer one too.

Abdullah spat contemptuously into the ground. "His Excellency, Don God-All-Bloody-Mighty'!"

"That's the one."

"If he doesn't want her…" Abdullah left the sentence unfinished.

Bormann simply snorted. "Oh he'll want her alright, I know his taste. And boy, is she ever to his taste."

Their good-byes said, the coffle set off along the track back toward the river and it was with a feeling of immense relief that Cassie clambered back aboard the boat.

Bormann also seemed relieved to be back aboard and rather surprisingly he left the five girls standing around on deck whilst he and Marco hurriedly cast off the mooring warps and motored quickly out into mid stream.

Once they were safely away, Bormann paused to look hard and long at Cassie, until she began to fidget nervously under his scrutiny. "I thought for a moment there Old Abdullah was gonna do something real stupid over you," he mused. "I've known that hard edged bastard for over ten years and never seen him get doe-eyed over a bit of fanny before, but you certainly got to him alright. Care to tell me what your secret is " he inquired cordially.

Cassie shrugged. "He's a swine," she ventured, somewhat more boldly than she felt.

Bormann nodded in agreement, gesturing for Cassie to lead the way down below.

"And you're a pearl if ever there was one."

"I'm in the mood for a little feminine company tonight." Bormann smiled, his hands wandering slowly over Cassie's body. "Now, I'd prefer you to the French whore, she's a bit on the bony side for my taste, but it really doesn't matter to me that much. What might matter to you, though, is that the lucky lady gets to brush her teeth, wash her hair with real shampoo, eat her own cooking and lie in a comfy bed for the night."

"What's the catch " the girl breathed warily.

"No catch," he laughed quietly, "except that you'd have to treat me real nice, cook me your best meal, clean my cabin, fuck my brains out, the usual sort of thing. Oh! And the bitch that stays in the cells gets to enjoy Marco's company all night. Right now the poor guy's walking around up top with a major hard on just praying it's gonna be you."

Cassie knew that she had little if any choice. Much as she sympathised with Sandrine and the other girls, she had to take the opportunity of getting out of her restraints and away from this stifling cell even if it was only for a few short hours.

She had to admit to herself that even fucking with Bormann was a price well worth paying for a few hours of comfort. The tall brunette groaned inwardly as she realised what she now considered to be comfort' in her new life. But she knew that if she was to be forced into having sex, she'd rather it was on a full stomach in a soft bed with the headman than starving in the cells with his rancid smelling sidekick.

"Alright," she said, "I'll do it."

Grinning, Bormann lifted her off the ceiling hook and unlocked her handcuffs. He waited for a few moments whilst she painfully worked the feeling back into her sore arms even going so far as to massage the bunched muscles in her shoulders. Once she had the circulation flowing she turned to face him.

"Ask me nicely," he said.

Slowly, Cassie raised her hands to his shoulders pressing her belly and breasts closely to him, "please take me, Gunter," she murmured, nuzzling his mouth with the tip of her nose, her tongue flickering out to part his lips, "please honey, I want to serve you and feel you inside me so bad."

Despite himself Bormann groaned. He had to admit that this bitch was a class act. She had a way of making a man want her absolutely and, per- haps more importantly, making a man like him want to abuse her soft pale beauty, to demean her and crush her proud spirit. He inhaled her odour. Jesus, even her days old sweat smelled like perfume. Greedily he returned her kiss, mashing her lips with his, savouring the taste of her tongue in his mouth and the feel of her long fingers running over his closely cropped scalp.

Even though he knew she was only pretending to want him and would cheerfully have stabbed him had she the opportunity, the sound of her stuck-up English voice begging him for sex was intoxicating. He walked the length of the boat to his stern cabin with the naked creature follow- ing meekly behind. Once there he sat in his chair and watched her as she showered and brushed out her long dark hair, marvelling at her pale green-eyed beauty.

Then, at his direction, she cleaned his cabin from top to bottom, scrubbing the floor on her hands and knees. Afterwards, she cooked for him and when they had eaten she washed the dishes.

Cassie knew that Bormann was deliberately seeking to dominate her by forcing her to perform menial tasks and wait on him in a crude effort to break her will. The problem was he was succeeding. As she completed cleaning up the tiny galley, she could already feel the excitement grow- ing in her belly. It was late and he would soon expect to fuck her and in- credibly she had to admit to herself that she was becoming addicted to the sort of rough, uncompromising sex she had been subjected to over the past week.

Returning to his cabin, Cassie blushed as Bormann's hard grey eyes raked over her naked body, and her blush deepened as she felt the juice start to flow into her vulva. A deep sexual flush bloomed over the wide globes of her breasts and down over her gently curving belly, as her breathing deepened and clean sweat began to trickle from her armpits.

Bormann stood and unbuckled his belt, allowing his pants to fall to the floor he was wearing no other clothing. Now it was time for Cassie's eyes to rake over the muscular slaver's broad, hirsute frame, noting the slabbed muscles of his chest and belly, his massive arms and strongly muscled legs.

And then there was his monstrous veined cock, already firmly erect and quivering. Cassie felt her legs move forward almost with a will of their own dragging her toward him and then she was sinking to her knees, her mouth falling open to nurse the painfully swollen glans, lapping off the pre-cum that she found there.

Bormann wound his hands into her long dark tresses and rocked his hips back and forth, groaning with pleasure as she slowly extended her neck to allow him into her gullet. With one hand she cupped his heavy scrotum, rolling his stone hard balls in her palm, milking them. With the other she stroked his buttocks digging her fingertips into the muscled flesh and then pushing her middle finger into his sweated anus making him grunt and hunch forward his sudden orgasm taking him by surprise.

Cassie held him tightly as his hot spunk flew into her mouth, sucking greedily, ensuring that she got every drop of the precious load. When he had finished Bormann pulled himself out of her mouth and allowed her to lick him clean. Once she had finished, she picked up his broad belt with which he had leathered her on the first day and handed it to him. Then she knelt on the narrow bunk spreading her thighs and leaning back with her arms crossed behind her back exposing her belly and breasts to him.

Bormann smiled broadly as she assumed the position of total vulnerability and submission.

"You know what I need," she whispered to him hoarsely, looking at him through heavily lidded eyes.

Inside her head, Cassie's mind was a whirling maelstrom of confused thoughts and desires. When he had offered her the chance to serve him in his cabin she told herself that she had agreed simply to get out of her cell, but having spent the evening serving this terrible man, the urge to demonstrate her complete sexual compliance was as overwhelming as it was inexplicable.

Bormann wound the end of the belt tightly over his knuckles and then lashed the supple leather across her belly with a crack, instantly leaving a broad red stripe on the heated flesh. She grunted harshly "Uhnnn," increasing the arch of her body, watching him, her green eyes moody with desire.

Bormann brought the belt down in his familiar criss-cross fashion, working from the tops of her full breasts, over her belly to complete the hard dozen on the tops of her spread thighs. At each bite of the leather she grunted sharply through gritted teeth, tears slowly rolling down her cheeks. Within her throbbing belly the white heat of desire churned and roiled spreading out to further harden her aching nipples and fill her sex with boiling love juice.

As soon as he delivered the last stroke Bormann threw down the belt and jammed his fingers into her crotch making her scream out in ecstasy as he invaded her soaking sex, his wide thumb crushing down on her erect stamen. And then he was pushing her on to her back and ramming his again iron hard cock into her, bringing her to orgasm instantly, as she unfolded her arms and legs to clutched at him frantically, her mouth wide and panting as they thrust their loins together with all of their combined strength.

After he had spent himself in her for the second time she crawled up on to his sweating belly and took his fading cock into her mouth. Cassie rolled the heavy, flaccid flesh with her tongue, nursing the purple head, her hand clenching around his scrotum firmly rolling his balls in her small palm as she slowly sucked him back to full hardness.

Enjoying the feel of her hand round his sack and her gently sucking mouth on his glans, Bormann groaned as his manhood began to stir for the third time. He marvelled at the sexuality of the woman as she mounted him, reaching between her thighs she clasped her hand tightly around the base of his cock squeezing the shaft to force him to erection.

Cassie groaned long and hard, smiling as she sank down, impaling herself on his meat, gasping with pleasure as Bormann caught her nipples between his fingers and pinched the engorged, umber flesh, extending the thick teats as she began to pump her lavish hips above him.

Finally, she sped her frantic thrusting as he began slapping her large breasts back and forth with his hard palms. She groaned through clenched teeth as the pain-pleasure mixture filled her flesh and flooded her sex with liquid heat, her juices running out of her crotch to soak his shaft and balls.

For the next several days the boat chugged up river, rarely passing any other traffic in the increasingly isolated hinterland. Each morning Bormann returned Cassie to her cell, always shackling her in painful, unyielding postures designed to ensure that each evening when he came to the cells she begged him for release, promising to cook and clean for him and most of all to fuck him.

As each pleasure-pain filled night came and went Cassie found herself sinking deeper and deeper into the cauldron of sado-masochistic pleasure that was her new life with the slave master, Gunter Bormann.

At the end of the second week, both Cassie and Sandrine were brought on deck together.

It was the first time that Cassie had seen the French girl since she had begun sleeping with Bormann and the change in the girl's appearance was shocking to say the least.

Sandrine's already slim body had lost weight, with her ribs plainly visible under her skin, which was covered in many, deep crop welts. The pretty face also bore a number of cuts and bruises where she had been slapped and punched. Both her breasts were dreadfully bruised and swollen and the marks left on her nipples by Marco's sharp teeth were plainly evident.

Despite her own body bearing the tell-tale marks of Bormann's ire, Cassie thanked God that he had preferred her as his bed partner otherwise she would have been left in the cells to endure the far more vicious treatment meted out by the vindictive mate.

"Okay ladies," announced Bormann stepping out of the wheelhouse, "this is as far as your cruise goes, so move your fannies on to the jetty sharpish, you've got some liquor to haul."

Both girls moved hurriedly to obey, neither wanting to feel the bite of the braided crop he dangled in his wrist. Even though Cassie had recently begun to enjoy the feel of leather on her skin, she was under no illusion that without the anaesthetic effect of deep sexual arousal, her flesh would burn just as fiercely as any one else's under the crop. Despite their nightly sex sessions, Bormann had shown absolutely no sign of softening toward her whatsoever. Still chaining her into tortuous positions during the day and cropping her for the slightest infraction of his arbitrary rules.

Waiting on the jetty for them, Marco tucked a heavy wooden liquor cask under each of their arms gleefully taking the opportunity of tweaking both girls' nipples before driving them down the jetty with a swift kick in the buttocks apiece.

They followed a well-trodden track that disappeared off into the dense rain forest and for the first time Cassie noticed that Bormann carried a heavy pistol at his belt and a short carbine in the crook of his arm.

As they walked, the casks became heavier and heavier in their arms, making their muscles burn and cramp with the dead weight, but neither girl dared let a cask drop nor slow her pace for fear of the crop coming along behind.

Presently, the track widened out to reveal a ramshackle building standing in a small clearing. As the small group approached, a man emerged from the entrance. He was immensely obese with long black curling hair and a week's growth of beard covering his swarthy face. He wore a pair of soiled baggy pants and a grubby vest stretched over his incredibly bulging guts. Recognising Bormann he waived, smiling broadly as he ambled forward the wattles surrounding his chin wobbling as he moved.

"Hello Gunter, it's good to see you again," he said in thickly accented English. "I see you've brought our supplies and some new mules to carry them, eh!" He looked appreciatively at the women, sizing them up with pursed lips and quick black eyes.

Bormann slapped the huge man on the back, "your usual order Raoul," said Bormann, "delivered direct to your door, as always, and two prize sows for you to groom and fatten up for His Excellency's pleasure."

Bormann followed the swaying Raoul into the building, impatiently motioning the women to follow. Once inside, Cassie's eyes took several moments to become accustomed to the dim light after the brightness of the trail.

Looking around, she saw a number of locals hunched over their drinks, the men nudging one another and grinning as one-by-one they became aware of the two nudes.

"Okay sluts, step over to the bar and hand over the liquor," barked Bormann, cruelly punctuating the order with a crack of his crop across Cassie's hunched shoulders.

The hapless girl lurched forward, biting her bottom lip to stifle the pain, determined not to let the room full of men hear her scream. Standing behind the makeshift bar a man identical to Raoul in every way, even down to his grubby pants and vest waited to pull the heavy kegs from their dead arms.

"It's good to see you Manolo," said Bormann pumping the huge paw the barman offered.

"It's been too long, Gunter," agreed the fat man, stowing the kegs before pouring Bormann and Marco a cooling drink.

"More bitches for the Senator eh " he asked, twitching his head in the women's direction.

"More bitches for His Excellency and more meat for you and your brother to make use of," confirmed Bormann.

The fat man grinned, showing his crooked, tobacco stained teeth.

"I'll put them out back, then we can talk business," he said, rounding the bar sideways so as to accommodate his massive bulk. He grasped the girls by their upper arms making them writhe and twist at the crushing power of his grip.

"It's no use struggling ladies," he grinned, as he dragged the two helpless females easily toward a small door in the back of the room. "I've been known to crush a croc's head with these hands." He pushed the two through the doorway kicking the door shut behind him, then clicked on a naked light bulb, revealing a small, square windowless storeroom devoid of furniture.

Cassie's heart sank when she saw the varied assortment of shackles and chains hanging from nails in the crumbling plaster walls. Oblivious to the women's feelings, Manolo selected several items and quickly shackled Cassie's hands behind her back, pulling her arms painfully up to a ceiling joist and suspending them by a length of chain.

Cassie fought back the urge to wretch as the obese man loomed over her, his rank body odour thick and cloying in her nose. Next he crammed a filthy rag into her mouth and tied it in place with another strip of cloth.

After dealing with Sandrine in the same manner, he clicked off the light and went out, the sound of a heavy bolt shooting home like a gunshot in the tiny room.

For the rest of the evening Bormann, Marco and the fat twins sat eating and drinking, exchanging news from both ends of the river and conversing in raucous tones. Eventually, the local patrons dispersed to their homes leaving the four to talk privately at last.

"So what about the bitches, Gunter," asked Raoul, reaching under his immense paunch to scratch at his sweating crotch.

Bormann accepted another fat cigar from Manolo.

"The same deal as always," he said leaning back in his chair, emptying his shot glass, "you keep them here for a week or so while Marco and me go on up river to sell the others. You feed the bitches up, get plenty of fat on them, keep them out of the sun so that their skins whiten up and no whipping - I want them unmarked for His Excellency's inspection. Let them sleep in a soft bed for a couple of days to get them loosened up again." Bormann grinned slyly. "Maybe rub some coconut oil into them to soften the skin."

"What about the cost of the feed All that milk and eggs cost a lot," grumbled Raoul.

Bormann waved his cigar dismissively, "you know as well as me you'll make fifty or sixty times the feed costs from the paying customers. Once word gets around that you've got two new European whores upstairs, this place will be full to bursting. Just make sure the punters know not to damage the goods," he growled meaningfully.

The twins nodded their understanding whilst smiling broadly at each other. They hardly needed to hear Bormann's instructions they had performed this same service for him many times over the years and were quite expert at putting the bloom back into the traumatised females that Bormann brought up river.

The next morning, Raoul took Cassie out back and allowed her a bucket of water to sluice the sweat and grime of the trail from her body and hair. When she had finished he led her upstairs and pushed her into a small bedroom with heavily shuttered windows that allowed in only a few desultory shafts of sunlight into the dim chamber. The obese twin padlocked a broad leather collar to her neck that was attached by several feet of chain to the metal bed frame.

Presently he brought her a pitcher of water and a large bowl of slop that smelt like heavily creamed, sweet porridge and half a loaf of dark bread.

"Okay here's the deal," he said, wheezing heavily after his two trips up the stairs, "you can drink as much water as you want and you eat everything I bring you. Anything you leave, I ram down your throat with my cock. You sleep in the afternoon and in the evening you rub this coconut oil all over your body. Then me a Mano we're gonna start sending a few paying customers up here, all select guys, and you're gonna let them do whatever they want. If you give us any trouble you get tied to the bar downstairs and the patrons get to fuck you for free."

He paused to let the threat sink in.

"If you're a good girl you maybe only have to fuck five or six guys a night. The last time I had to tie a bitch up to the bar the stag line was out the door and she must have humped fifty field hands before she passed out."

Raoul pushed the bowl of slop into her hands.

"Eat up bitch."

Cassie sat on the bed stunned into silence. This moron actually expected her to prostitute for him and his foul brother. Was this why she had been brought all the way up the Amazon, to live as a whore in this backwater hell hole Desperately she tried to think of something to say that might change things, but when she looked into Raoul's unyielding black eyes she knew that there was nothing at all she could say to alter her dreadful situation.

Cassie swallowed hard, the tears springing into her eyes as her bottom lip began to quiver. She felt very close to loosing what tiny vestige remained of her self-control. Slowly, her hands shaking feverishly, she took the proffered bowl and began to shovel the thick, sweet tasting meal into her mouth with her fingers.

Raoul placed the bottle of coconut oil on the nightstand, turned and ambled out of the room, locking the door carefully behind him.

For the rest of the afternoon, Cassie lay on her bed trying to pass the time by dozing. But even though she was desperately tired from hanging in the stockroom all night, the awful prospect in store for her that evening kept her clamouring mind from escaping however briefly into sleep.

Later, Raoul, or was it Manolo, she really couldn't tell the difference between the obese twins, came to her room. Cassie swung her legs to the floor trying as best she could to conceal her nakedness from his dark glittering eyes.

"Supper," he grunted, pushing another bowl of slop into her hands. "Finish that up quick and then use the oil, we've got customers." Before leaving he unlocked the window catches and threw back the shutters to allow some light and air into the stuffy room.

Next door she could hear the muffled sound through the thin wall of him instructing Sandrine in similar fashion and then the sound of crying and finally the sound of slapping as he chastised the distraught blonde.

After she had forced down the bowl of sweet slop, Cassie rubbed the coconut oil all over her body and sat back on the bed awaiting the first of her customers. As an after-thought she poured some more oil into her palm and massaged it in to her vulva.

She had spent most of the day trying to get herself into a frame of mind that would help her to get through this nightmare and still retain her sanity. But most of all she knew she was desperate to avoid the public punishment that Raoul had threatened her with earlier.

Nevertheless, Cassie's heart sank as she heard the sound of footsteps on the landing outside and then the door was opening and a black man of about fifty stood in the doorway. His eyes darted around the room, quickly settling on her as he slammed the door behind him and came to the bed.

Cassie swallowed her revulsion and attempted a weak smile, but the man was already staring intently at her sex as he unzipped his pants.

Quickly, he climbed onto the bed, his coarse hands reaching out to grasp her thighs and pulling her roughly toward him. He showed no inclination to speak to her, nor to indulge in foreplay of any sort. He simply knelt between her legs and roughly jammed his hard cock into her. Cassie gasped as he forced his manhood into her unprepared sex, immediately beginning to thrust as hard as he could, his face buried in her shoulder.

Even with the help of the oil she had earlier used to lubricate her labia the pain was intense as he tore into her tender vagina and she was greatly relieved when after only a dozen stokes he suddenly spasmed and spent himself quickly.

The man climbed off her and pulling on his pants was gone as quickly as he had arrived, leaving Cassie to lay in stunned silence on the bed his rapidly cooling spunk running slowly out of her raped sex.

Cassie deliberately did not keep count of the many similar visits she received that night. All of the men were blacks of various ages and all of them were completely disinterested in her as a person. Each simply mounted and pumped her until he ejaculated, merely using her as a receptacle. By the end of the night, she lay spread out lifelessly on the bed, her body drenched in sweat, her exhausted limbs lying slackly apart, a huge quantity of ejaculate running freely from her swollen, abused sex.

Her last customer that first night was a powerfully built Negro in his early twenties. As soon as he came into the room he stripped off his shirt and trousers. In the moonlight she could easily make out the man's huge arm and chest muscles and as he approached the bed her eyes were transfixed by the incredibly thick sex that reared up to his navel.

He sat beside her on the narrow bed stroking her hair and crooning to her in soft tones. He smelt strongly of tequila and she guessed that he was very drunk. His hands went to her breasts, gently kneading the wide globes and rolling the dark nipples before he scooped the lush flesh into his hot wet mouth and sucked until the thick teats hardened and began to ache, wringing a reluctant groan of pleasure from the slowly squirming woman.

With his huge hands he lifted her buttocks into the air and presented her soaking sex to his face, inhaling her essence before plunging his mouth into her crotch. The incredibly gentle giant patiently soothed the heated flesh with his mouth working the tip of his tongue into her labial petals and slowly erecting stamen. Cassie felt her belly swell with lust as her need grew and juice flowed into her ravaged vagina.

Grateful for his gentleness, she ran her fingers through his crinkled hair massaging his scalp as he in turn massaged her sex, and slowly drew him over her body, opening her thighs and guiding his huge cock into her throbbing cunt, clasping his slim hips between her thighs and pulling him in to her body.

For the first time tonight, Cassie was grateful for the incredible amount of spunk already within her sex, as it eased the passage of the Negro's giant phallus. Slowly she began to pump her hips up to meet his long, gentle thrusts wrapping her legs around his and locking him in to her.

Without hesitation she accepted his lips on hers and sucked his long tongue into her mouth groaning, as he invaded her throat. She felt her orgasm begin to grow deep within her ravaged vagina, swelling outward to engulf her whole belly as she encouraged him to speed his thrusting, pumping her hips up harder to meet him.

Suddenly he arched his magnificent torso and thrust deeply into her, lifting her off the mattress, supporting her in his huge arms, shuddering as he shot his spunk deep into her hotly sucking sex, triggering her own orgasm as she hung quivering in his supportive arms.

For the next few days things continued in much the same vein.

In the early morning she was taken out back and allowed to wash in a bucket under the watchful eye of one of the twins. They fed her three large bowls of the richly sweetened slop every day and she soon noticed that she was putting weight on to her breasts and buttocks and that her belly was becoming deeply rounded, replacing the weight she had lost on the trip up the river.

The rest of her time she spent chained to the bed in her darkened room awaiting the evening session and it was during this time that she decided on a plan of escape.

At the very end of each night the gentle giant' came to fuck her when he had drunk enough tequila to give him the confidence he presumably lacked with women when sober. It quickly became obvious that the big black was totally besotted with her. His treatment of her was in direct contrast to the others, who merely used her as a receptacle to ejaculate into.

Cassie had to admit to herself that after two weeks of being beaten and raped by everyone she came across, his gentleness was greatly comforting and this had the added benefit of making the task of seducing him all the easier.

She had read somewhere once that prisoners held by terrorists greatly improved their chances of survival if the were able to form a close personal relationship with their captors, or, in this case, her customers. Juan, as she learned he was called, was the village blacksmith and visited the cantina every night to drink and when he was drunk enough, to use the local prostitutes working upstairs.

Cassie quickly realised that Juan was a shy and frankly dense young man and as they made love, she began to talk to him in her soft, halting Portuguese, learning about him and his village, telling him about herself.

When she judged that he was ready, she told him she was in love with him and begged him to help her escape so that they could run away to the coast and be married. Juan readily agreed, happily believing Cassie's beguiling tale of being the daughter of a rich industrialist who would welcome him as her husband to be, and richly reward him for rescuing his beloved daughter. She had few qualms about tricking the simple minded blacksmith in this fashion, she honestly believed that her present position was extremely perilous and as such it easily justified seducing and deceiving Juan, whom, she told herself, would, in fact, be amply rewarded if ever she made it safely home.

The next morning, the twins surprised Cassie and Sandrine by allowing them two buckets of water each to wash themselves with, even going so far as to provide them with block of soap and a comb. After they had finished bathing, they were led back inside where Cassie was stunned to see Bormann leaning against the bar.

"Come in girls," called the slaver, waiving his arm, "you two lazy sluts have kept His Excellency Don Alvarez waiting long enough already."

The two women were pushed into the centre of the room to stand in front of a devastatingly handsome man who looked to be in his early to mid thirties lounging carelessly in one of the rickety bar chairs with an air of supreme insouciance.

The newcomer was immaculately dressed, his cream tropical weight suit and pale blue silk shirt accentuating his smooth tan and dark, slightly waving hair. Cassie felt herself blush deeply as the elegant man's warm brown eyes slowly wandered over her voluptuous body.

"As I told you Excellency," said Bormann, "two absolute beauties, the very best merchandise available. The blonde slut is French and the brunette is English. Very posh too," he laughed, mimicking an upper class English accent, "and both of them, as you can see, in the very best physical condition."

Cassie noted with amazement the obsequies tone in Bormann's voice and the respectful silence of the twins standing to attention in the shadows. Whoever His Excellency Don Alvarez was, he apparently possessed enough chutzpah' to impress even these inhuman pigs.

The man beckoned Sandrine with a small movement of his hand and the blonde girl instantly moved forward to stand within a foot of him. He made a small turning motion with his index finger and Sandrine obediently rotated slowly under his gaze.

"How much " he asked, his voice quiet yet direct.

"Thirty five thousand U.S," said Bormann without hesitation. "The usual fee for her type and quality of animal, Excellency."

"Very well."

Cassie's blush of embarrassment deepened as the darkly handsome face turned to regard her. Ordinarily, she would have relished the prospect of receiving this beautiful, urbane man's attention, but fully clothed in her best finery and after having spent three or four hours on her hair and makeup. Not here, naked, in this filthy place, in front of these three unspeakable pigs.

Once again, the manicured finger beckoned and she advanced to stand in front of his chair. Despite having been without clothes for over three weeks, Cassie became acutely aware of her nudity, as he ran his soft palm up her thigh, turning her with gentle touches of his fingers on her hips.

He stood up, coming very close to her, examining her face, eyes and teeth in detail. She could smell his sophisticated cologne, which made the earthy smell of her own body all the more embarrassing.

"Speak, I want to hear your voice," he said to her. "Say your name."

"Cassandra, my name is Cassandra Elspeth Ward."

He nodded slowly, lifting the thick, dark fall of her still damp hair, as if weighing it. His fingers caressed her nipple, making her gasp at the sudden intimacy, rolling the delicate tissue until it began to tumesce, causing her to bow her head and bite her lower lip in shame.

"This one really likes to fuck, Excellency," said grinned Bormann. "She's a real hot arse, especially after she's been tied up for a while."

Cassie groaned inwardly at hearing herself described like a common whore, but then wasn't that her occupation now She cringed at the thought that this man must know what she did here, even if it was against her will.

"How much " was all he replied.

Bormann hesitated, "this one's really special, it's not everyday you get a real classy looker like this bitch." Bormann added his ultimate sales pitch "She really does enjoy the feel of the whip, it really makes her pump her arse."

"How much " the tall man persisted.

"Sixty thousand."

"That's a great deal more than I've ever paid before," the man said, a steely edge coming into his voice.

"I can get that from Gonzales further up river," Bormann asserted confidently, "he likes her sort."

"That ignorant, Spanish pig," sneered the man distastefully, "he would whip her to death inside a week."

He sat down again, pulling her forward to stand with her legs astride his closely spaced knees, his hand went into her crotch, fondling the petals of her labia and expertly searching out the tight bud of her clitoris.

Cassie groaned as his expert fingers brought her to instant readiness, her flesh quickly heating up and becoming engorged, as he gently masturbated her. She guessed what he was up to, looking to see how rapidly she could climax, testing Bormann's sales pitch in the only sure way.

Again Cassie groaned, sliding her bare feet further apart on the dusty floor, parting her legs and pushing her belly gently toward him. Now she knew exactly what he was doing and why, and for some inexplicable reason she desperately wanted to prove herself to this beautiful man.

He smiled as he sensed her willingness, his rapidly moving fingers spreading her hot juices over her sex lips, working his hand into her hot sucking chasm, feeling her fluttering muscles clutch at his fingers tips as he stimulated her for several minutes, his concentration intense as he worked on her.

Much to her chagrin she was moaning loudly now, her wide hips pumping rapidly to the beat of his fingers, her head thrown back with abandon as she panted, her breath rasping harshly in the otherwise silent room.

At a nod from Don Alvarez, Bormann stepped forward and swung his crop in a blistering arc to land across her thrusting buttocks, once, twice, thrice.

Cassie gasped in shock and sudden ecstasy as the incredible heat and pain flashed into her loins, boosting her already burgeoning orgasm and sending her folding to her knees as she climaxed, crying out at the intensity of the pleasure as her scalding juices flooding out on to her quaking thighs.

She knelt for what seemed an eternity in front of the man, her head bowed, shoulders and chest heaving with the strength of her passion.

After a few moments, he took hold of her by the chin and tipped her head back to look into her tear filled eyes. "She is absolutely exquisite," he breathed, so quietly that only she could hear and for some reason she could not fathom his words rolled over her like a divine benediction.

"I'll take her at fifty-five thousand dollars," he announced decisively, carefully drying his fingers on a maroon silk handkerchief. His tone telling Bormann that the negotiations were concluded. "I'm flying down to the state capitol after lunch I'll be back the day after tomorrow in the early afternoon. Have them both ready at the strip they'll fly up to the Fazenda with me."

He looked pointedly at Raoul and Manolo. The cultured voice suddenly cracking out like a bullwhip. "No more use is to be made of them."

The obese twins immediately nodded their understanding from the shadows. "Si Excellency," they chorused together.

Sitting alone, chained to her bed once again, Cassie tried to pick her way through a tangle of conflicting emotions.

Tonight was the night she had planned to escape with Juan after the bar had closed. But her immense relief at not having to service the fat twins' customers any longer was tempered by the knowledge that her blacksmith lover would not be able to come to her to receive his final instructions. She could only hope that the plans she had already explained to him would stick in his painfully slow mind.

And then there was her new owner'. Cassie could hardly deny that being bought, apparently for a record price by such an attractive and obviously powerful man, was an amazingly strong aphrodisiac.

The truth be known, she had revelled in his treatment of her, shocking herself at the sensuous feeling of achievement she had experienced in passing his test of her sexuality. She wondered what it would be like to give herself willingly to such a man as this Don Alvarez. A man who would undoubtedly want to develop the dark pleasures she had so recently been introduced to and, she admitted to herself, which she had now begun to crave.

Nonetheless, she told herself, she could not give up the chance of getting away, especially as in two days time she was due to fly deeper into the wilderness with the mysterious Don.

The hours dragged by as Cassie waited for the bar to close and the obese twins to close up shop.

Eventually, the last customer staggered out of the door and the place gradually became quiet and Cassie began to keep a nervous watch for

Juan from the open bedroom window.

As luck would have it there was no moon and so the blackness outside was almost totally complete. After what seemed like an eternity of waiting, the blacksmith loomed out of the dark and quietly placing a ladder up against the side of the building he climbed up into the room.

Cassie was anxious to be away, but Juan, who smelled strongly of alcohol, was clearly intent upon having the sex he had been denied earlier in the evening. He pulled her to him, seeking out her mouth with his thrusting his tongue between her lips his huge hands roaming over her lush buttocks as he squeezed her hungrily.

Cassie squirmed out of his grasp, urgently whispering for him to wait.

"Not yet Juan," she hissed, "wait until we get to your place and then we can do it all night." Juan groaned, allowing her to disengage his hands from her nudity with obvious reluctance. He pulled a set of bolt croppers out of his belt and motioned for her to kneel down, searching with his fingers for the padlock on her collar.

The sound of the jaws snipping through the steel sounded like a pistol shot in the silence and they both froze for several heart stopping seconds, listening for any sounds of alarm. No one stirred and after what seemed like the longest minute of her life, Cassie pulled the leather collar from her neck with considerable relief, at the same time motioning Juan toward the window.

The pair quickly made their way down and then ran the half-mile to the outskirts of the village where Juan lived in a small shed behind his forge. Once they were safely inside, Cassie slumped down on to the old wheezing bed, her heart pounding like a sledgehammer from the excitement of the ordeal. Each step of the way she had expected to hear the cry of alarm raised behind her and to be dragged kicking and screaming back into the twins' hellish brothel.

But Juan seemed to harbour no such fears as soon as the door was closed he immediately ripped off his pants and stood naked in front of her, his rampant cock swaying in front of her face.

Cassie was desperate to get further away from the area before dawn, but she knew that she would never be able to persuade Juan to go anywhere until they had had sex. He was in a state of advanced arousal and she knew that if she was ever going to be able to get him to help her put more distance between her and the village she needed to cool him down and quickly. She reached up and clasped his big face, pulling him down to the level of her crotch, opening her thighs to him. Juan didn't need any further invitation. He thrust his tongue deep into her soft beaver, lapping at her like a dog, soaking her with his saliva, drawing her lips into his mouth and hungrily feeding on the succulent flesh.

Cassie relaxed back on the bed, trying to calm her nagging fear of imminent discovery and her frustration at the delay in getting further away.

She closed her eyes, trying to concentrate on her own arousal, imagining that it was the handsome and cultured Don Alvarez licking her sex. She immediately felt the heat blossom in her belly as she visualised her new owner, her juices instantly beginning to flow hotly as she replayed the events of the morning in her mind.

Juan ran his face over her sweating belly plunging his tongue into her deep navel, sucking on her suddenly engorged nipples, as she reached down and guided him into her heat, bucking her hips sharply to settle the cock deeply within her. She groaned as she fantasised that it was Don Alvarez firmly shafting her. Shivering as she remembered the feel of the crop on her arse as he had frigged her, she quickly began to climb the slope toward her orgasm at the mere thought of the darkly handsome Senator. Cassie reached between their bellies and grasped Juan's massive balls, she squeezed them cruelly, the pain making him rear and gasp as she mercilessly milked them of their heavy load.

Juan began to pump his hips faster, gathering up and spreading her thighs wide with his massive forearms. He slammed into her sopping vulva with his full length, battering her cervix, making her expel a noisy grunt with each monumental thrust.

Cassie groaned through gritted teeth, not wanting her cries to be heard outside of the tiny shed as she shuddered through her long climax under the madly plunging blacksmith.

She gasped with pleasure as she received his scalding spunk deep within her vagina, the molten hot liquid mixing with her own juices, the thick sexual flux being squeezed out of her sex and on to inner thighs by the blacksmith's enormous girth.

The couple lay panting together on the bed for several minutes, Juan finally rolling off her and beginning to snore softly as the combination of alcohol and his long awaited climax took their toll.

Rousing herself with difficulty from her own post-orgasmic stupor, Cassie slowly eased off the bed to stand looking down at the slumbering blacksmith.

She was reluctant to wake him, as he would probably only want sex again and in any case he was obviously the worse for wear, having spent the evening stoking up on Dutch Courage back at the bar.

Whatever happened, she reasoned, the hapless blacksmith would be far better off if she left him sleeping. He would soon find another whore to fall in love with and perhaps Bormann and the twins would not discover his part in her escape.

Her mind made up to go it alone from here on in, Cassie quickly slipped on Juan's massive shirt, which covered her almost down to her knees. She grimaced wryly as she realised that it was the first time she had worn a stitch of clothing in over three weeks.

Quietly, she padded to the door and without looking back, slipped out into the night.

Cassie had no set plan of escape in mind as she trotted fretfully from shadow to shadow through the sleeping village.

Other, that is, than to find some way, any way, of putting distance between herself and the bar before morning, when the twins would discover her disappearance.

She had no doubt that they would instantly begin to scour the immediate area for her and that the locals would be willing helpers in any such search. For that very reason she did not feel that she would be able to count on anyone's help here in the village, not least because half of the local men had likely been her clients over the course of the past week. After spending a fruitless hour scouting the small settlement, she sat huddled in the shadows slowly becoming more and more fretful.

There didn't appear to be any obvious means of getting further away, other than on foot, and without shoes and alone she did not see how she could possibly bring herself to venture down the forest track in the darkness with its inevitable plethora of prowling night creatures.

She sat gnawing at the inside of her cheeks for long minutes, agonising over her options, which at the moment appeared to be confined to returning to her room over the bar and putting herself back into the hands of the slavers, or going back to wake Juan and somehow forcing him to help her get away.

Just as she was about to walk out of the shadows for another desperate look around, an ancient water truck came clattering into the small square and stopped beside the village cistern. She waited with baited breath while the lone driver jumped down from the cab and began to busy himself connecting up the pipe and filling the communal tank.

This was her ticket out of here! This truck must visit a number of villages during the night before returning to a depot somewhere. Somewhere far enough away from here so that she could not be found, at least not until she got a telephone call through to the authorities.

After ten minutes or so the driver re-wound the hose and climbed back into his cab. As he revved up the old diesel engine, Cassie threw caution to the winds and sprinted out of the shadows and across the small square. Nimbly she hopped up on to the back of the truck as it began to move off, clambering up the narrow steel ladder on to the top of the tanker, where she pressed her body flat, clinging on to the grab rails as the truck thundered out of the village.

The tanker visited three more villages during the early hours, with Cassie hanging on for dear life as the ancient vehicle plunged and rocked madly down the unmettled forest tracks. At each stop she sought to make herself invisible, pressing herself down into the cold metal as the driver dismounted to transfer the water.

Shortly after leaving the last village, the truck slowed and pulled off the narrow road into a passing place. Cassie again flattened herself into the steelwork as the driver got down from the cab. She heard his feet crunching on the ground as he walked around the truck, freezing in terror as his voice called out to her.

"Come on down from there, and slowly, I have a gun."

Cassie looked about desperately for an escape, but the driver had stopped in the middle of nowhere. The menacing blackness of the forest edge came right up to the roadside, hemming her in with a primeval fear of what lay beyond. Shivering with fright she slowly crawled down the ladder and dropped reluctantly to the ground.

"Come around to the front and stand in the lights," the driver instructed tersely.

Carefully, Cassie picked her way forward to stand as he had ordered.

"What were you doing up there " he demanded.

"I needed to get away from one of the villages you stopped at," she replied, shielding her eyes with her hand, trying vainly to peer through the beams at him.

"Riding on the Water Company's truck is not allowed, it's not a bus."

Cassie tried desperately to think of something sensible to say, to somehow gain his sympathy, but could only blurt out lamely, "I-I had to get away from some men who were going to hurt me. P-please, I meant no harm, couldn't you help me " She was pleading now. "I need to get to a town."

"If you ride, you have to pay," came the voice, somewhat less harshly.

"I don't have any money, everything was stolen from me."

"Then you will have to walk, I can't carry passengers for free," said the voice accenting the last word artfully.

"No! please, don't leave me out here alone," Cassie begged and then, sensing the inflexion in his voice, "I-I'll d-do anything if you'll take me with you."

There, she'd said it, in the full knowledge that she was stepping over a very dangerous line. She waited, trembling as he considered her words.

"Take off the shirt, I want to see you naked," the voice said suddenly thickening with lust.

Blinded by the harsh lights and unable to see the driver standing behind the beams, Cassie was astonished to feel her belly heave and her nipples blossom at the prospect of showing her naked body to this stranger.

Not for the first time over recent days she was suddenly experiencing a powerful sexual thrill at the notion of being at the total mercy of a dominant male. Her heart began to pound in her chest as she slowly reached up and began to undo the buttons of her shirt one-by-one, finally shrugging the garment from her shoulders to stand nude.

After a moment's silence, she bent one knee and pushed it slightly forward at the same time arching her foot and twisting her hip toward him, sucking in her stomach and provocatively thrusting out her large breasts.

There was a very long pause, during which time she felt the juices start to slowly trickle within her.

"Alright, I'll take you," he said, and then somewhat breathlessly, "you've got the fare."

Pausing only to collect her shirt, Cassie stepped through the light beams and allowed the driver to assist her up, his hand going under her shirt and clasping her well-rounded buttock as he boosted her into the cab.

Once inside, her saviour cut the main beams and clicked on the dim interior light showing himself to be a swarthy, unshaven man in his late thirties heavily built with broad shoulders and avid brown eyes.

As Cassie watched him quickly shuck off his clothes, his intention to rape her obvious, the now familiar heat began to bloom in her belly to spread like a tidal wave into her loins making her already warm fluids roil. She felt the sweat break out under her arms and in her cleavage as the last of his clothes came off to reveal a large, erect cock jutting up from his darkly haired crotch.

Cassie expelled a soft sigh as she beheld his painfully erect manhood. At that instant, she made the conscious decision that she would fornicate with him willingly. As she did so, it was as if a great weight was suddenly lifted from her shoulders, and inexplicably, all of the gut-twisting nervous tension that had built up over the last few hours simply melted away.

The driver reached out to cup her wide breasts, his work calloused thumbs manipulating her hardening nipples, rubbing the broad areolas, his large hands crushing the pale bowls of her breasts, kneading the sensitive tissue until Cassie moaned and arched her spine to force herself against his clutching fingers.

Sliding across the seat toward him, she reached out to take his hard

74

cock in her soft palm, rolling back the foreskin from the purple glans, slowly pumping the dark skinned shaft until he gasped and cruelly tweaking her nipples in return.

Cassie cried out shrilly as the pain seared through the sensitive flesh to heat her already fevered breasts further, her hand pumped his stiff meat faster as insane desire flamed in her dampening sex.

"Suck me," he demanded coarsely, spreading his thighs he grasped a handful of her thick hair and pulled her head roughly into his crotch.

Cassie wrinkled her nose at the smell of him. He had been working for eighteen hours in the tropical heat and the musk rising from his balls was tangy and thick with pheromones, filling her sinuses and making her dizzy with his masculine stench. She moaned as he forced her face deep into his crotch, and the big man hunched his hips forward so that she could suck his balls into her hungry mouth.

Cassie revelled in their salty taste, rolling the heavy plums in her mouth, flogging them with her tongue, sucking hard on them until he grunted, arching in exquisite agony.

Next, she ran her tongue up the length of his shaft, opening wide to take in the bulging head, nursing the swollen flesh in her deliciously suckling mouth.

Panting, the sweating driver held her tightly by the hair pumping her face up and down on his shaft with his huge arms, gasping in surprise as she took him deep into her well-practiced gullet.

Suddenly desperate to fuck this amazing women who had come to him out of nowhere, he cried out, "get on your back, puta!" and pulling his iron hard sex out of her mouth, he threw her sweating body across the bench seat.

Sharing his urgency and electrified by his use of the uncouth epithet puta', Cassie spread her thighs and hooking her hands behind her knees she stretched herself wide for him. She hissed sharply as he plunged his iron hard cock into her right up to his saliva soaked balls.

The driver grasped the grab handle above the door to give himself extra purchase as he slammed in and out of Cassie's soaking cunt. His breathing came out harsh and ragged through gritted teeth as he strained mightily above her, flexing himself forward from his hips, his foot jammed against the engine housing as he banged away at her for all he was worth.

Cassie was now completely consumed by her need for rough sex.

She arched her back into a tight curve and craned her neck so that she could take one of his thickly haired nipples into her mouth, laving the brown nub with her tongue and nipping at it with her sharp teeth.

The driver grunted volubly and increased his frantic thrusting, his belly convulsing as she used her vaginal muscles to grip his shaft, swelling his manhood even further as he began to climax with his lips drawn back from his teeth. He spasmed hugely, releasing his copious seed into her, the scalding liquid rushing in a churning torrent up her vaginal canal and boiling against the entrance to her womb.

Cassie clasped her arms around his shuddering trunk, mashing her sweat slicked breasts to his hirsute belly, desperately sucking at his cock with her sex muscles, bucking her hips against him until her own orgasm rolled over her like a thunderstorm, wracking her body with raw lightening bolts of electrifying pleasure. She writhed in a miasma of intense sexual pleasure, which rendered her oblivious to the man's rancid breath as he covered her gaping mouth with his thick lips.

Allowing her own mouth to fall open, Cassie welcomed his thrusting tongue, sucking hard as it writhed obscenely inside her sweet mouth as the final flashes of their orgasms faded away.

The tanker driver called at two more villages before dawn with Cassie hiding on the floor of the cab, whilst he got out to transfer the water. And twice more, he pulled over in the early morning darkness to spread her across the old leather bench seat and fuck her yielding, endless fecundity.

Cassie felt an immense weight lift from her shoulders as she stepped down from the cab and walked the short distance to the Federal Police building.

Now she was free to could tell the dreadfully humiliating details of her ordeal to someone in authority and let the full force of the Law descend upon the odious Bormann, Marco, Abdullah, the hideous twins and His Excellency Don Alvarez - whoever the hell he was.

The desk officer, a huge mulatto from the hinterland, looked dubiously at her when she asked to see the Chief of Police, dressed as she was only in Juan's oversized shirt and barefoot, but she insisted that as a British passport holder she would only make her extremely serious complaints to the senior officer present.

The big mulatto quickly became bored listening to the stupid white bitch's strange English accented Portuguese and shrugging disinterestedly, led her the down a passageway to a door marked Commandant'.

There was a meaningful delay after knocking before a gravely voice called, "enter."

Upon first inspection, the Commandant was a harsh, but authoritative looking man, who rather disconcertingly put Cassie in mind of Bormann.

Nonetheless, he listened politely to her story from start to finish without expression, nor interruption. When she had finished speaking the policeman sat looking at her for a long time, his mind turning over she knew not what.

Conscious of her scruffy and dishevelled appearance, Cassie shifted uneasily in her chair. She was acutely aware that having had sex four times in as many hours in the stifling tropical climate, that she stank to high heaven. As discreetly as possible, she crossed her legs and endeavoured to keep her thighs pressed tightly together.

Eventually the Commandant lent slowly forward clasping his large hands together on the top of the desk.

"Signora Ward," he began sonorously, "the charges you make are extremely serious and, if well founded, will undoubtedly result in me having to take some very firm action. However, in a matter as grave as this I will need to communicate with my senior officers at headquarters, not least because one of the men you have mentioned, His Excellency Don Ramon Jesus y' Alvarez, is a distinguished member of the State Legislature, as well as a local land owner of some repute." The Commandant paused to smile reassuringly at her. "But this should only take me an hour or so at most and then I will be in a position to tell you what action I will be taking."

Cassie let out a huge sigh of relief as the policeman finished speaking. "Thank you, thank you so much," she gushed, almost wanting to hug him as he rose from his desk and led her to the door with a supporting hand on her elbow.

"Perhaps you would like to lie down," he suggested solicitously. "You must be very tired after your ordeal. I will send for you when I have news."

Cassie readily agreed that she was, indeed very tired and gratefully accepted the offer of a blanket and the use of a couch in the empty waiting room.

The exhausted girl was awoken by the big mulatto Sergeant standing over her, shaking her roughly by the shoulder. "Come with me," he said abruptly, beckoning her to follow.

Cassie climbed wearily to her feet, shaking her head to clear the thick fog of sleep from her mind. She was desperately tired and the brief catnap seemed only to have increased her exhaustion. To her surprise the Sergeant led her not to the Commandant's office as before, but down a series of confusing passageways, the cement floor becoming cold on her bare feet as they descended into the bowels of the building.

Far too late, Cassie began to realise the danger as the Sergeant stopped before an open doorway and gestured for her to enter. She hesitated in the passageway trying to peer into the room without actually entering.

"Come in Signora," called the Commandant. "I have some news for you about your kidnapping friends."

Slowly she stepped into the cold grey room her heart suddenly thumping in her chest with alarm. Looking around she saw the Commandant sitting behind a heavy wooden table. In the corner there was an old iron bed frame and in a side room she could make out a large bathtub filled to the top with water. She flinched as the Sergeant slammed the door behind her and when she turned she saw another man, a corporal, lounging indolently against the back wall picking his teeth with a matchstick.

The Commandant cleared his throat before speaking in a tone pregnant with suppressed menace, "you may be interested to know that while you were snoring like a sow in its sty, I was able to contact your owner, His Excellency Don Alvarez at his home in the State Capitol."

"What!" incredulously.

"I should tell you that His Excellency is personally affronted that you have rejected his benevolence in purchasing you from the trading post yesterday."

The Commandant paused, savouring the look of disbelieving horror slowly dawning on the perfectly formed face in front of him. The Commandant could well understand why the Senator had been most specific in his instructions as to the prisoner's treatment and care.

"His Excellency will be flying back upcountry tomorrow afternoon and has asked if you would be good enough to meet him at the airstrip as arranged."

Cassie shook her head from side-to-side, not wanting to believe what she was hearing. Tears began to well in her eyes and her breathing faltered as she tried to make sense of what was happening to her. "I-I d-don't understand," she stammered, "why are you doing this to me you're supposed to be a policeman, you're supposed to help me, these men are criminals."

The Commandant laughed quietly, delighting in her obvious confusion and fear. "Things go somewhat differently here in the interior." He grinned over her shoulder at his henchmen. "We are not like the guards at your Buckingham Palace."

Cassie heard the Commandant's men snigger nastily at their boss's joke. She spoke again, her voice weak and tremulous, "what are you going to do with me "

The Commandant nodded reasonably, as if her question was worthy of an answer. "His Excellency has asked me to explain' to you the mistake you have made in rejecting his ownership. He would like you to be very clear about this before you meet him tomorrow, so that you will not be tempted to make the same error in the future."

All of a sudden his expression hardened and his voice lashed out at her, "strip off that shirt, bitch!"

Cassie was overcome with a feeling of total despair as she realised that she had escaped from Bormann and the twins only to walk straight into the hands of people even more dangerous. People who were not only beyond the Law, but who actually were the Law! As she looked into the Commandant's vulpine face she knew with absolute certainty that the explanation' he was about to inflict upon her would be far worse than anything she had experienced thus far. Against her will, she felt her belly tighten and her nipples begin to stiffen as the awful realisation dawned that she was completely at the mercy of these insane men.

Again the Commandant's voice lashed out. "I said strip off, bitch, we want to see you naked!"

Cassie sensed, rather than saw the two henchmen step in close behind her. Cold sweat began to trickle slowly from her armpits, as with infinite slowness, she raised her trembling hands to open her shirt and the three men came very close to surround her as the heavy material slowly slipped to the floor.

The Commandant ran his hands up over the ripe swells of her hips stroking her soft skin, before pressing his hard fingers into her quivering belly.

Cassie gasped as he bent to take the broad cone of her nipple into his mouth, suckling until the stalk became fully hard. Despite herself Cassie whimpered as the warmth of his mouth invaded her flesh to make her sensitive breasts swell.

Shamefully, she hung her head. Closing her eyes to block out the sight of what was being done to her, whilst deep down she fought desperately to contain the dark arousal growing in her core, as her faithless vulva began to slowly pucker and run with juice.

Without warning, the Commandant bit down hard on her throbbing teat making her scream and lurch backward only to be caught in a vice like grip by the Sergeant. His massive hands grasped her upper arms, holding her still while his superior alternatively sucked and bit at her succulent nipples. Working away at her flesh until she began to groan and twitch at the confusing blend of sensual agony sweeping through her body.

Then, as her torment grew to an almost intolerable pitch, "Stretch and spread her. I'll start with a whipping," he rasped huskily.

The two assistants quickly shackled Cassie's ankles to widely spaced rings in the floor and fastened a steel spreader bar between her wrists. They hooked the bar up to a pulley block and hauled her feet off the ground, making her cry out in pain as the tendons in her arms and legs were extended into tight cords.

The Commandant took a four-foot long cat o' nine tails from the Corporal and began to swish the evil looking flails back and forth in front of the terrified girl, who began to sob in panic. "P-p-please, I-I'm sorry for running away," she spluttered. "I'll n-never d-do it again, p-please, I promise."

The Commandant nodded. "That's good, but just to make sure you remember. …" His arm flashed out to bring the cat screaming around his head the flails spreading out to impact across her shoulders in a blow that took the breath out of her lungs, her pale flesh instantly displaying nine livid wheals.

Cassie howled, vibrating in agony against her restraints, her spine arching into a tight bow as the brutalised nerve endings transmitted the full effect of the strike to her brain a split second later. And then, before she had chance to draw another breath, the cat was coming round again, this time across her taught buttocks. The wicked tails curled over her hip and bit into the soft flesh of her pale belly.

The Commandant kept up a slow rhythm, picking out a fresh piece of skin with each devastating stroke. Making the demented girl jerk slack mouthed at every touch of the leather on her soon to be sweat soaked skin.

Halfway through the flagellation the Commandant paused while his subordinates sluiced her down with buckets of ice-cold water, stimulating the red-hot flesh and preventing her from fainting. Then the Commandant began again, this time targeting her heavy breasts, scorching the pale globes and tumescent nipples, laying down a tiger stripe pattern across her flesh as the insidious leather burned its way down across her belly and thighs.

By the end of the flogging Cassie hung exhausted from the spreader, head lolling limply, her body and hair dripping with sweat. From her shoulders to her knees her inflamed skin glowed in an angry coalescence of crimson wheals.

She was barely conscious by the time they took her down and dragged her to the side room and plunged her into the waiting bath, holding her body beneath the freezing surface as she convulsed with the sudden cold shock her chest bursting for air.

Time and time again they submerged her madly thrashing body, holding her under the surface for what seemed like an eternity to her oxygen starved brain, only to pull her out at the last moment, her mouth gaping wide like a landed fish, her breath coming in great whoops as she sucked in huge lung-fulls of air.

"Bring her to the table," ordered the Commandant, at the same time stripping off his shirt to reveal a taughtly muscled chest.

The henchmen dragged her coughing and spluttering from the bath and frog marched her gasping and staggering back into the room forcing her belly down on to the tabletop. Cassie lay shivering, her heaving breasts splaying out to either side as they held her with her crotch jammed firmly against the table's edge.

Then he stepped in between her thighs, forcing them apart with his knees he roughly parted her labia with the silver pommel of the cat, making her grunt "Uhn, Uhnnn, Ahhhhhh".

And then he forced her to rear up gasping as he penetrated her vulva and pumped the thick plaited length of the haft into her half a dozen times, before pulling it out to examine the glutinous yield coating the leather.

"It seems the whore enjoyed the lash," he laughed cruelly to his men, at the same time pulling open his uniform pants and liberating a large veined cock, "well, now she can give us all some enjoyment."Again Cassie grunted loudly, "Uhnnnn," as the Commandant thrust his fat cock into her wet sex and began slamming his hips up against her blazing arse cheeks.

The pain of the comprehensive whipping had now transformed itself into an all over burning sensation that made Cassie's entire body glow with an incredible sexual heat that filled her belly and made her love juices boil into her sex.

Once again, Cassie found herself being sucked down into a whirling maelstrom of intense sexual arousal at the hands of these cruel, dominant men. Slowly, she raised herself on to her elbows, taking hold of the table edge with her hands bracing herself against the rapid thrusting. Her breath hissed between her teeth as her engorged nipples slapped and scraped across the rough wooden table top as he continued to thud into her buttocks.

Cassie arched her back, helpless to prevent herself from pushing her buttocks high into the air to grant him better access to her slick, gaping sex.

"Mother of God this slut is hot," panted the Commandant to his men, "look at her raise her arse for me," and then. shouting to the Sergeant, "give it to her in the mouth."

Cassie knew what to expect. She licked her lips and prepared herself as the big mulatto Sergeant ripped off his shirt, pulled open his uniform pants and took out his huge black cock, the smooth wide head already thickly coated with seminal fluid. She stretched her mouth wide as he clapped his massive hands around her face and drove himself into her, sliding over her tongue and into the top of her gullet in one smooth thrust.

Behind her, she could hear the Commandant's breathing begin to labour as he neared his climax, his rapid thrusting becoming erratic as he leaned back, his hands pulling her hips back with him.

In front, the Sergeant had begun to pump himself energetically in and out of her gullet, holding her face tightly to his belly.

Cassie's own excitement was intensifying to fever pitch as her shuddering body was stretched between the two madly fucking men. Moaning loudly she sucked and laved the Sergeant's cock avidly with her mouth, whilst at the same time using her vaginal muscles to clutch wetly at the cock battering her soaking sex. Her mind whirled as she fought to understand and contain the strength of her arousal. All of the pain and terror, which she had been subjected to only minutes before seemed to have come together to form a huge, burning knot of lust in her belly.

Once again, Cassie found herself responding to the heady drug of pain and sexual domination, as she had begun to do with inevitable, increasing ease over recent days.

One part of her mind still wanted to hide in shame as she imagined the spectacle her arched, sweating body must be giving the men around her. But another, ever growing, stronger part of her needed to display her sexuality to these same men and this she did by straining her buttocks up to meet the Commandant's mighty thrusts and lunging forward to swallow the Sergeant's manhood deep into her gullet.

Her only coherent thought to give herself totally to both men.

The Commandant's orgasm finally overwhelmed him and he shot his semen deep into her belly in a stream of scalding fluid that instantly precipitated Cassie's own orgasm.

Her vaginal walls contracted spasmodically at the feel of the inrushing semen to milk the final, few spurts from the groaning policeman, as at the same time she gratefully accepted the Sergeant's copious load into her sucking mouth and throat.

No sooner had the Commandant withdrawn himself than Cassie felt the Corporal rush to insert his hardness into her sopping sex. His eager hands reaching out to grasp the heavy flesh of her splayed breasts as he began to thrust himself desperately into her heat.

Cassie sighed regretfully as the Sergeant withdrew his now exhausted member from her mouth, hesitating just long enough to allow her to lick the final drops from the bloated glans, which to her shame she did willingly, straining her neck forward to prolong the final seconds of contact with his huge dark sex.

Cassie's orgasm once again bloomed deep within her belly, the earthy sound of her grateful grunting filling the room as the Corporal discharged himself into her, his thick spunk flooding into her sex before running out to trail with the rest of her juices in thick rivulets down the insides of her shaking thighs.

Cassie lay for a long time across the sweat-stained table, her lungs heaving as the last powerful tremors of her orgasms echoed deep within her belly. As she lay with her eyes closed, listening to the sounds of the men moving about the small room she realised to her absolute shame that she was desperate for more sex and knew that she would have gratefully welcomed any one of the three policemen mounting her again.

However, Cassie was abruptly shaken out of her lustful reverie when the Sergeant and Corporal once again took hold of her arms and pulled her roughly to her feet. She opened her eyes and experienced a brief thrill when she saw that all three men were now completely naked, their sexes hanging dark and heavy between their thighs as they crowded round her.

However, her terror quickly resurfaced when she realised that she was being pulled over to the old iron bed frame, not for more sex, but for more punishment, as she was quickly spread eagled face down on the naked springs with her hands and ankles hand-cuffed to the four corners of the old iron frame.

"P-please", she whimpered, "d-don't hurt me anymore, I'll do anything, you can fuck me all you want, but p-please just don't hurt me anymore".

The Commandant laughed shortly, black eyes roaming over her body his pupils dilated and heavy with lust. "Oh don't worry bitch, we'll fuck you some more alright, but first another lesson to make sure you remember not to defy your masters."

Cassie opened her mouth to protest, but this time the Corporal was waiting to force a large leather ball gag into her mouth. The girl choked at the foul tasting wad as it was rammed deep into her mouth spreading her jaws wide and crushing her tongue back into her throat. With the broad leather straps securely buckled behind her head she was effectively rendered completely mute.

"My apologies for the gag," said the Commandant insincerely, "but this part of the treatment usually makes the customers scream so loud they can be heard in the street and we don't want you disturbing the peons on their way to work now do we "

Cassie had enough slack in her regulation police bracelets to allow herself to rise up on to all fours, the steel bedsprings cutting painfully into her palms and knees as she did so.

The ball gag that prevented her from speaking also prevented her from closing her lips or moving her tongue and as a result the saliva was beginning to run out of her mouth and drip from her quivering chin in thin, waving strands. She rolled her eyes and tossed her head from side-to-side in a plaintive effort to plead with the three men, each of whom stood looking down at her with a mixture of greed and cruel excitement etched on his face.

Cassie knew, as she looked into their avid, sexually ravenous expressions, that there was nothing she could do to alter the course of what was to come. And at the moment of this dreadful realisation the beautiful English girl once again felt the dark stirrings of her perverted lust thrash like a burning serpent deep within her belly as fresh juices slowly began to trickle into her pouting vagina.

The Commandant opened the front of a stout wooden cabinet fastened to the wall behind her and uncoiled a pair of wires which he fastened to Cassie's already turgid nipples with strong crocodile clips.

The sharp, spring-loaded teeth bit into the sensitive tissues, causing her to moan through her nose at the sudden pain. Scarcely had Cassie accepted that discomfort before another pair of clips was attached to the delicate folds of her moist inner labia. Again making her yelp and switch her wide hips, but the Sergeant simply held her haunches immobile in his massive hands whilst his superior fitted the last clip to her wildly fluttering flesh.

The Commandant flicked a switch and Cassie heard the low hum of a transformer start up within the depths of the cabinet hidden behind her.

"Now bitch," he said, coming to stand in front of her, "His Excellency Don Alvarez requires you to put all further thoughts of escape from your ungrateful whore's mind."

Cassie shook her head, her dark mane flying about wildly as she tried desperately to scream around the gag. Her stricken eyes followed the wire trailing from the cabinet to the small box with a single black button nestling in his outstretched palm.

The policeman paused whilst Cassie's wide staring eyes drank in the entire scene, including the now fully erect penis standing up against his hirsute belly. Only when he was sure that she fully understood what was about to happen to her, did he bring his thumb down upon the contact.

The surge of raw power exploded simultaneously in the most sensitive and delicate tissues of Cassie's body.

The lightening shock drove the air from her lungs and paralysed her larynx as every muscle went into spasm, instantly catapulting her body up into an impossibly steep arch with her shoulders and buttocks raised almost to the vertical.

Cassie quivered on the bed, her fingers fastened around the wire springs like talons and the tendons in her neck, arms and legs standing out like corset stays, as the electricity sizzled its way through every part of her quivering musculature.

The Commandant stepped closer, staring enraptured into the girl's tortured face as her head snapped backward and her desperate green eyes grew huge and bulging. He nodded delightedly, as her full red lips curled back to reveal her teeth clamping down on to the gag, her canines and incisors cutting deeply into the tough leather with the huge force of the bite reflex.

For a long moment the Commandant held her there, marvelling at the living sculpture stretched out before him. His eyes widened as Cassie's bladder suddenly emptied involuntarily, her golden urine splattering down through the bedsprings to run unchecked across the cement floor and into the room's large central drain. He cut the power reluctantly, allowing Cassie to crash back down on to the springs, her slack body shaking and twitching as the residual effects of the electricity slowly dissipated.

She groaned through the gag as the pain in her nipples and labia throbbed incandescently, the agony spreading in waves throughout her entire body to further saturate her already drowning senses.

Unable to move for the shock and mental confusion, she could only lie there gasping through her nose, saliva drooling freely from her wide stretched lips, perspiration dripping out of every pore as her whole being seemed to implode into a tightly coiled core centring upon her aching nipples and sex. Both sets of organs felt massively engorged and sensitive to her stunned and agonised senses.

The Commandant allowed her only a few second's respite before pressing the button and once again force her spine to snap into another impossibly tight arc. But this time, he reduced the power output after a few moments and increased the frequency of the jolts.

Always he contrived to keep the girl up on her hands and knees, her trunk beginning to flex in and out as her hips and shoulders alternatively contracted and relaxed to the rhythm dictated by the humming machine.

As the torture proceeded, the electricity scorching through Cassie's nipples and labia soon began to transform itself into a deep throbbing need that burned throughout her entire body. The power causing her belly to shudder uncontrollably and her roiling juices to flood out of her cunt and her aching teats to harden and extend hugely.

Cassie sobbed helplessly into the gag as her hips were forced to pump in and out as her stomach muscles spasmed helplessly in time to the insidious electrical impulses.

Seeing the petals of her vaginal lips gaping wide open and glistening with her freely running juices, the Sergeant took a wooden baton from a wall rack and screwed it roughly into her sopping vulva, causing Cassie to snort and grunt in surprise as she was forcibly invaded.

Nonetheless, her hypersensitive vaginal walls instantly clamped down around the smooth wood, the electrically excited muscles grasping and sucking its welcome hardness deep into her sex chasm, until only the leather bound handle remained visible extending out between her thrusting haunches. Now the Commandant increased the frequency of the jolts still further, sighing with perverted pleasure as Cassie's sweat drenched body began to move faster, hunching up and down as if she were madly fucking an invisible lover lying on the bed beneath her.

The Commandant handed the control box to the Sergeant. "Keep the little trollop going like that while I get the whip," he ordered, his voice thick with barely suppressed lust and then turning to the hovering Corporal, "get a couple of buckets of water from the bath and cool her down".

The Corporal returned a few moments later to dash the freezing liquid on to Cassie's heated flesh, sluicing away the oily sheen of sweat coating her burning body.

In her tortured state, Cassie barely felt the added stimulation. Her whole being was now in a state of complete sexual turmoil as the incredible heat in her sex demanded only that she fuck the thick wooden baton embedded deep within her.

The irresistible electrical charges forced her vaginal muscles to contract with incredible force around the truncheon and made her clitoris erect into a stone hard bud that protruded from its protective hood to stand raw and vulnerable between her spread thighs.

And it was to this part of her anatomy that the Commandant next turned his cruel attention. Cruelly, he slashed the leather falls of the cat upward into her hopelessly exposed groin over and over until the helpless girl was driven into the first of an unending stream of towering orgasms, as her body continued to buck and writhe atop the creaking bed.

Seeing that Cassie had finally crossed over into a state of orgasmic delirium fuelled by the pain and electrical energy, the Commandant began to flog the cat across the soaking flesh of her back and buttocks, bringing the skin once again to a feverish crimson glow.

Each of the torturers now stood with an enormous erection, their faces alight with cruel desire as their manic eyes drank in the sight of the helpless girl responding so eagerly before them.

Then, at a signal from the Commandant, the big mulatto Sergeant reduced the power setting, leaving just enough energy running through Cassie's sexual parts to keep her muscles twitching and her hips still pumping involuntarily back and forth.

Taking hold of the baton handle protruding from between her buttock cheeks, the Commandant began to twist it slowly in her soaking maw, stroking it relentlessly back and forth until Cassie screamed into her gag, the sound of her anguish coming out as a strangled gurgle as her loins exploded with indescribable pleasure sensations as the cock like object stimulated her core in the way she needed most.

Unable to communicate in any other way the girl was reduced to simply nodding her head back and forth between her peaked shoulder blades, pleading with him to continue as yet another crushing orgasm rolled over her.

"This slut is hotter than all the whores in Hell," chocked the Sergeant hoarsely.

"Si," grinned the Corporal breathlessly, "we've never had one this good before, eh Comandante "

By way of answer, the Commandant slowly slid the surrogate phallus out of Cassie's gaping vagina, grinning wolfishly at his comrades as the girl pushed her shaking buttocks backward, desperately searching for the suddenly withdrawn tool, moaning and snorting her disappointment through wildly flaring nostrils.

The Commandant tossed the baton away and moved close to her rear, his penis stiffly erect and glistening - waiting.

"Reduce the power to minimum setting," he said thickly, and once the dial had been set, he slowly slid his iron hard cock deep into Cassie's sex in one fluid motion, gasping ecstatically as the minute electrical charge was conducted down the length of his shaft directly into his prostate.

It took only a few moments of rapid thrusting for the combination of Cassie's intense vaginal contractions and the pulsating electricity to trigger his orgasm and then the Commandant was roaring like a bull, the climax crashing through his belly as he pumped his copious seed deep into the once again helplessly bucking girl's belly.

As soon as he withdrew, he was instantly replaced by the hugely endowed Sergeant and then, in turn, by the sweating Corporal.

And so it went on for a further two hours with the three men taking turns to plunder their victims fluttering sex. The pulsating charges flowing through Cassie's body rekindling their waning erections and prolonging their ability to shaft her until her own orgasms drained her so deeply that even the surging electrical currents and the sting of the cat could not revive her exhausted body and she fell twitching and unconscious on to the harsh bare springs.

Sometime around midnight, the Commandant returned to the chamber and went to stand in front of Cassie who was once again suspended from the ceiling, her wrists and ankles spread wide so that she stood awkwardly on the balls of her feet.

She had been hanging since they had finished with her around midday and her entire body ached where the muscles and sinews had been stretched and twisted beyond belief by the insidious electrical charges the policemen had used upon her to such devastating effect.

The Commandant's liquid black eyes roved slowly over Cassie's tortured body, noting the way her musculature twitched and rippled as she constantly sought to adjust her position by minute degrees in order to ease her myriad aches and pains.

Her flesh glowed redly in a sea of individual wheals that covered her body back and front from shoulders to knees and down across her full breasts and gently curving belly. She flinched involuntarily, moaning around the soggy leather gag as he slowly stroked his left palm over her hip, re-kindling the searing heat in her recently flogged flesh as the abused nerve endings once again flared to his knowing touch.

She whimpered as the fingers of his right hand cupped her hugely swollen and bruised pudendum, his index and middle fingers easily slipping between the slackly gaping labia to slide deeply inside, gently massaging the battered tissues whilst his thumb pressed down on her already rising stamen.

Cassie's mind reeled in horror as her bruised and painfully throbbing nipples began to tumesce and the serpent of desire once again raised its head deep within her belly, springing juices into her vagina and humid warmth into her armpits.

The Commandant sensed her helpless yet immediate response, and smiled into her anguished eyes, enjoying the mixture of fear, confusion and lust he saw reflected in the deep green pools.

"I can see why His Excellency places such a high price on you," he murmured softly, "never have I seen a woman more beautiful," and pausing for a moment he grinned lasciviously, "nor one so totally ardent."

Spellbound by his coal black eyes, Cassie did not even attempt to deny the feelings this terrible man's insistent fingers were generating within her now soaking sex.

Ever since she had regained consciousness to find herself once again hanging from the ceiling her arms and ankles shackled to the punishing spreader bars, Cassie had had to battle against the incredible aching sensual weight left in her plundered womb by the combined effects of the flogging, electrical torture and rape she had been put to that morning.

Throughout the day, her raw nipples and labia had continued to throb and sizzle with phantom impulses, as her traumatised flesh remembered the cataclysmic sensations to which it had been so cruelly subjected.

And as had happened so often over recent days, Cassie had had to come to terms with the incredible sexual pleasure her body had derived from the experience of bondage and torture at the hands of monsters such as Bormann, the twins and now, these terrible Federales. So, it was with a feeling of profound shame coupled with immense relief that she heard the sound of the Commandant's zipper being lowered, as he liberated his once again rampant erection. Seemingly without conscious thought, she stretched her thighs wider and hunched her pelvis forward as the man began to push at the moist entrance to her sex with his distended glans.

The Commandant reached up and undid the buckle of her gag and pulled the sodden ball out of her mouth. Cassie worked her mouth and stretched her cramped jaws, before allowing him to cover her lips with his, gasping loudly into his mouth, "ahhhhhhhh," as he thrust his cock fully into her trembling interior.

Cassie welcomed his hungry tongue as it slipped in between her teeth and writhed in her mouth, her own tongue quickly responding as their bodies rocked back and forth in the centre of the silent room.

The Commandant brought his hand up under her breast grasping the swollen bowl in his large hand, kneading the flesh and making Cassie groan again into his mouth as his thumb crushed and pinched the hard umber tip.

With his other hand, he wound a thick twist of her hair into his fist and pulled her head backward until her neck was tightly arched. Then he placed his wide-open mouth over her Adam's Apple and sucked greedily at the pale, soft flesh of her throat before bending to lap at the broad, dark cone of her right nipple.

As the policeman sucked the distended flesh deeply into the wet heat of his mouth, he again wrung a long gasp of pleasure from Cassie, as he continued to rock back and forth between her shaking thighs. In her spread and tightly arched position balanced on the balls of her feet, she could only stand helplessly whilst the Commandant suckled at her breast. Her only movement was the rippling of her vaginal muscles as they spasmed rhythmically along the length of his slowly pumping cock, clutching at him and sucking at his veined hardness.

Cassie was panting now, the strain of maintaining her posture and the massive sensations thundering through her belly and breasts making her head swim. She moaned as he swirled his rough tongue over the bowls of her breasts, lapping greedily at the abundant flesh before once again sucking one of her long, thick teats deep into his mouth. She steeled herself for what she knew was coming, her mind suddenly reeling at the shocking realisation that she needed the extra' that she knew he was about to give her. Thrusting her hips forward another fraction of an inch and clamping her aching vaginal muscles tighter around his swelling cock, she couldn't wait any longer.

"M-my nipple, bite it!" she begged sobbing, "p-p-please, I need it now."

The Commandant was eager to comply and immediately closed his sharp, white incisors on the stone hard tumescence, grunting out his own pleasure as the girl bucked and screamed into the air, "ahhhhhhh, oh God! yesssss!"

Cassie's cries quickly turned to moans of pleasure as the incredible sensations rushed through her breast flesh, to plunge down into her roiling belly and trigger her climax, making her tightly suspended body vibrate as the love juices fell from her in scalding torrents, drenching his shaft and trickling out on to their coupled thighs.

The policeman released his grip on her hair, took hold of her hips in his hands and began to thrust wildly into her, punishing her inner thighs with the force of each impact, as his hard, narrow hips battered her hopelessly spasming body. His own climax shattering in its intensity as her cunt deftly sucked the semen out of his plunging cock in searing waves that left him hanging on to her, his face buried in her heaving, sweated cleavage.

Cassie watched the Commandant tuck his sated member away and zip up his pants through eyes still dark and heavy with lust. Her breathing had begun to return to normal and the sweat that had covered her body moments ago had cooled so that now she shivered in the dank atmosphere.

However, between her legs, her sex continued to throb and her juices continued to trickle out of her gaping labia the swollen vermilion folds hanging open like the petals of a storm-drenched rose.

The Commandant returned her smouldering gaze.

"Do you understand the perils of running away now, bitch " he asked her softly.

Cassie nodded, "y-yes, I won't ever do it again," she promised her voice barely more than a whisper.

"His Excellency is a very private man and whilst he is known throughout the state as a rich and successful businessman and politician, or perhaps because of it, he values and guards his privacy very highly. And so I must now teach you a final lesson upon this very subject."

Cassie felt the seemingly bottomless need in her belly suddenly recede only to be replaced by a feeling of stark terror as the policeman continued on. "When you arrived here you made certain outrageous allegations concerning His Excellency, which, if repeated often enough outside of this building might conceivably cause him some embarrassment. This sort of slanderous gossip, you understand, must be stamped on. His Excellency is a much loved and respected benefactor to many people here in the interior. He built the local hospital and school and has been personally responsible for many other civic improvements. My brother,

Herve, is the general manager at His Excellency's Fazenda, where you will be going tomorrow. Why, I myself owe my own position here as Federal Police Commandant to His Excellency, who is also President of the State Police Authority."

He came very close up to Cassie's face so that their noses were almost touching, his eyes slitted and menacing transfixed her wide, green ones, "so you see, you stupid English cunt, no-one is going to listen to the ramblings of a common whore like you around here."

"I p-promise I w-won't say anything t-to anyone again," Cassie choked, her mind madly searching for anything she could say to put off the final lesson' he had in mind. "I-I didn't understand before," she stumbled, "I m-mean about how important a person he is."

The Commandant reached out to press a call-button on the wall. "I'm pleased you understand," he said smiling, "but we still need to," he paused for a moment, as if searching for the right phrase, "to reinforce your understanding," he finished with a sinister, vulpine grin.

Cassie shrank inwardly as the big mulatto Sergeant came into the room.

"Open her mouth and keep it open," snapped the Commandant.

Cassie struggled ineffectually in her chains as the Sergeant moved out of sight behind her.

"Please," she stammered, "you don't need to do anything more to me, I understand, believe me, I won't say anything to anyone, I beg you." Her pleas suddenly turned into an anguished howl as the Sergeant walloped her across the backside with his massive palm and then, as she opened her mouth to scream at the stinging blow, he grasped her face with his leather gloved fingers and pulled her jaws apart until she thought they would crack.

Moving with slow deliberateness, the Commandant reached into her mouth with a pair of long pliers and grasping her tongue, pulled it out and down to the level of her chin. In his other hand he held a strange looking claw-like tool with a large yellow plastic card clearly marked "AZ", hanging from it, which he now brandished in front of her horrified eyes.

Ignoring her strangled, choking cries he said to her, "this is a little gadget I got from my brother up at the Fazenda, they use it to label the cattle there, you know the sort of thing, those coloured I.D. tags they fasten to the cow's ears, so they know which is which - in case they wander off somewhere they shouldn't." His words turned to laughter as he saw the dreadful realisation dawning in her terrified eyes.

The Commandant continued, "Don Alvarez was most particular in his instructions about not marring your beauty, so I cannot fix this through your ear like my brother does with the cattle. But this way, serves two purposes, we label you and we shut you up all in one."

And so saying, he pulled Cassie's tongue into the jaws of the tool and compressed the grips, punching a thin stainless steel spike down through the centre of the soft flesh. Each end of the spike was automatically secured by a thin nylon grommet so that it was prevented from coming out and neatly affixed the yellow plastic ID tag to the top of her tongue.

The Sergeant let go of Cassie's face and as her head sagged on to her chest, a thin stream of blood mixed with saliva ran out of her gaping mouth.

The girl issued a tortured scream from the back of her throat as the fire-like agony consumed her mouth, which she found she could not now close due to the thick plastic label fastened to her rapidly swelling tongue. The tag also prevented her from retracting her tongue, or closing her lips and Cassie sobbed as the dreadful thing flapped obscenely in front of her face.

Cassie drifted in and out of consciousness as the shock and pain of what had been done to her overwhelmed her senses. Senses, which barely registered, as the two men took her down from the ceiling and laid her on the cold cement floor.

Through the cloying mists of her stupor Cassie felt her arms being bent and twisted and then the feel of rough cloth on her skin as they slipped her into a restraint jacket and cinched up the various straps, binding her arms tightly across her chest, fastening her wrists behind her back, and then they were rolling her over and she felt her body bend somewhat, as the thick crotch strap was pulled tight between her thighs and buckled at the small of her back.

Finally, she felt herself being lifted and carried a short distance and then as if from a great distance she heard the clanging of a metal door. After many minutes her addled brain realised that she was alone at last and presently she drifted off into a deep and bottomless sleep.

Sometime the next day, Cassie was rudely awoken by the Sergeant and Corporal entering the tiny cell and roughly dragging her to her feet, where she stood tottering and stooped. The heavy-duty restraint jacket prevented her from straightening and cunningly transferred any attempt at upward movement to the thickly stitched canvass gusset strap passing between her thighs.

Once she was on her feet the two federales quickly hobbled her ankles with a short length of chain, which snagged painfully as she staggered between them and threatened to trip her as she was marched through the dank cell block and out into the rear yard where the Commandant was standing by the open rear door of his Jeep.

After spending so many hours in pitch darkness, Cassie could barely open her eyes in the bright sunlight and she knew she must make a frightful sight as she stood hunched and trussed, with her long hair hanging matted and dishevelled over her face and the hideous yellow plastic cow label stretching her blood stained lips and tongue grotesquely.

The Commandant barely looked at her as the huge mulatto Sergeant slipped his hand beneath the heavy belt circling her waist and hoisted her one handed into the back of the truck.

Both men pointedly ignored Cassie's anguished cries, as the thick gusset strap sank deeply between her legs, cutting into her raw sex lips and burning the delicate bud of her anus. Once she was inside, the Sergeant threw a tarpaulin over her and slammed the door shut.

With a casual salute the Commandant started the engine and drove the truck out of the yard and into the traffic.

Cassie lay moaning miserably under the musty smelling tarp. Her tongue felt incredibly swollen and excruciating pain lanced through the tender flesh every time she tried to swallow, or move any part of her face.

The cow label stretched her mouth almost from ear-to-ear making her jaws ache from the constant gaping and she had to fight constantly to keep her tongue partially extended otherwise the steel spike holding the label threatened to further tear the aching tissue. Her whole body seemed to be a mass of aches and pains from the savage stretching and flogging she had suffered and even now her nipples and labia, which had borne the brunt of the punishment on the iron bed, felt heavy, distended and filled with a constant dull ache.

Soon the truck left the town behind and as she lay listening to the rumble of the wheels on the roughly surfaced road, Cassie recalled the last time she had been trussed up and locked in the back of a vehicle being taken God knows where'.

But that had been at the beginning of this nightmare. How long ago was it exactly She searched her memory and tried to figure the exact number of days, but so many things had happened and her sleep pattern had been so badly disrupted that she had lost track of time.

It felt like months, but it could only be a two or three weeks. A week on the boat with Bormann, a week with those two fat pigs at the trading post, she could not bring herself to call it by its real name – the brothel. And then yesterday and today at the Police Station. What was that A little over two weeks, maybe sixteen days.

What would her friends be thinking By now her disappearance would be well known. Inquiries would have been made at her apartment, at the Racquet Club and at work, but Bormann had been thorough and she knew that no one would be looking for her this far into the interior. And what if they did Don Alvarez virtually owned this part of the country, what had the Commandant said He was the President of the State Police Authority, the man who had given him his job. The man who built hospitals and schools and probably employed most of the locals in one way or another.

Cassie knew that she was beaten. The terrible punishment she had received for even attempting escape meant that she would never dare try again. And even if she did get away, how could she avoid the Police and make her way hundreds of miles down river, without money, or clothes

Presently, she felt the truck turn off the road and bump across a stretch of grass and then she could hear the dull throbbing of an aircraft's engines getting closer. She was at the landing strip. Where her owner was waiting to fly her even farther up-country, so far away she knew she would never get out.

The truck came to a stop. Cassie heard a brief shouted conversation above the sound of the plane's engines and then the rear door was wrenched open and the Commandant reached in to haul her out from under the tarp with the help of a plump, middle-aged man dressed rather incongruously in a morning suit.

Cassie was led staggering between the two of them across the grass to a small, but expensive looking twin-engine Cessna. In the rear of the cabin sat the French girl, Sandrine. She sat with her head bowed, staring fixedly at her knees and in the pilot's seat in front of her Cassie saw the patrician profile of Don Alvarez talking into his radio and smiling, as he exchanged polite pleasantries with the unseen air traffic controller.

Then she was bundled into the small cargo hold behind the passenger cabin, the plump man pushed a couple of large suitcases in after her and slammed the hatch shut. Almost immediately the plane's engines increased to a deafening roar as they taxied onto the runway and presently she felt the unmistakable sensation of flight as the rumbling wheels left the ground.

After about ten minutes, the plane reached its cruising altitude of just over nineteen thousand feet and Cassie soon began to shiver and shake, as the temperature in the unheated hold plummeted to several degrees below freezing point. She began to feel the first signs of panic, as her breathing became difficult in the rarefied atmosphere and her fingers and toes became numb with the cold.

Perhaps Don Alvarez had forgotten to switch on the ventilation and heating for her she thought desperately, but then she doubted whether anyone would bother putting heating in the hold of an aircraft. After all, only luggage was meant to be carried in the hold.

Cassie had heard of people stowing away in the cargo holds of big jets and being found frozen solid at the destination airport. Surely, as an experienced pilot Don Alvarez knew that she would freeze in the hold. Cassie just couldn't believe he would let that happen, after all, hadn't he just paid fifty five thousand dollars for her But what if it was all a terrible mistake and for some reason he didn't know she was freezing to death!

In a rapidly burgeoning panic, Cassie began to kick out at the suitcases behind her with both feet, but she could barely make any noise above the deafening roar of the engines thundering away only a few feet away. Her anxiety quickly rose to the point where she began to sob and cry out despite the terrible pain in her mouth. Her head began to swim as the combination of panic, oxygen starvation and physical exhaustion overwhelmed her and once again she felt herself begin to slip into merciful oblivion.

Within the air-conditioned comfort of the flight cabin, Don Alvarez' highly attuned pilot's senses immediately recognised the muffled thudding, as Cassie kicked out wildly at the luggage surrounding her. He glanced briefly at the hold temperature gauge and satisfied himself that it was not reading low enough to do her any lasting harm in the short term.

Seated beside him his trusted major-domo, Alphonso, sat gazing out at the endless rainforest rolling away beneath the plane. If he had sensed the girl's distress he gave no outward sign.

As they flew onward Cassie's protests soon became less and less audible, as she eventually slipped into unconsciousness.

As soon as the commotion in the hold ceased, Don Alvarez gently pushed the control yoke forward and allowed the plane to gradually descend to ten thousand feet, before radioing ahead to inform his ground staff that he would be landing at the Fazenda in a few minutes.

The plane's wheels thudded into the grass landing strip, jolting Cassie suddenly back to full consciousness and the welcome realisation that she was still alive and back on the ground.

Despite having flown at low altitude for the past ten minutes, her extremities were still numbed by the cold and she could only groan in agony as Alphonso dragged her out of the cargo hold and deposited her into the back of an electric golf buggy. She lay groaning on the buggy seat, as the blood slowly began to force its painful way back into her fingers and toes. The bloodied saliva which had frozen in her mouth during the flight now began to thaw in the hot sunshine and trailed out of her distorted lips to run in a desultory stream down her chin.

Whilst the major-domo busied himself directing the estate workers in unloading the rest of the luggage from the plane, Cassie was able to crane her neck to get a first look around at her new home.

The plane had come to rest in front of a small hanger erected at the side of a closely mown grass strip. Beyond, she could make out the sprawling white shape of what she took to be the estate mansion through a stand of trees and toward which, Don Alvarez was already disappearing in another buggy with Sandrine.

Even in her wretched state, Cassie was struck by the neatness and order of the place. All of the equipment looked new and the land surrounding the closely mown runway looked well kept. Even the native estate workers were clean and tidy looking, each one wearing a stylised "AZ" badge on his coveralls that signified Don Alvarez' ownership as did the cow label riveted to Cassie's tongue.

When all of the luggage and packing cases were safely loaded on to the buggy's back deck, Alphonso climbed aboard and they set off after Don Alvarez.

Once they had cleared the trees, Alphonso turned off at a fork and steered the buggy away from the mansion down a tree lined track, trundling along for several hundred yards until they came to a large compound surrounded by a high whitewashed stucco wall. Once inside the gates, Cassie could see various warehouses and workshops, as well as a separate area that looked set aside for the estate workers and their families.

Alphonso stopped at what appeared to be a carpentry shop, and instructed the apprentice to unload a packing case from the buggy for the old carpenter who came to stand with Alphonso.

"Did you have a good flight old friend " the carpenter asked Alphonso, smiling slyly. It was well known at the Fazenda that Alphonso hated flying and dreaded the regular trips Don Alvarez made in his light aircraft.

"If I never see another plane …" Alphonso replied grimacing, leaving the sentiment unfinished.

The carpenter offered Alphonso a cheroot and lit it for him. Then he nodded toward Cassie, at the same time bending close to glimpse her face through the dark mass of tangled hair. "Another one of His Excellency's whores " he asked.

"A very special mare, this one," replied Alphonso grinning at his friend, "Don Alvarez prizes her very highly, very highly indeed."

"She looks like a bag of shit and smells twice as bad from where I'm standing," opined the old carpenter, straightening his spine and shaking his head dubiously.

"She's been through a lot," agreed Alphonso, blowing out a thin stream of tobacco smoke, "but she'll scrub up nicely, they always do. The

Don has excellent taste."

"Well he certainly doesn't stint himself of that I'm sure," the old carpenter grunted. "What have you brought her down here for "

"She's going into the mill. His Excellency wants to trot her for a spell to get some of the wanderlust out of her." Both men burst out laughing at this apparently humorous idea.

Listening to them discuss her fate in such a detached and callous fashion, Cassie felt the familiar dread hand of fear slowly gather up her squirming innards.

"Well," said Alphonso flicking the half smoked butt into the sand, "I'll have to be getting back to the big house and I've this bitch to sort out first." With a wave to his friend, he clambered back into the buggy and they set off again this time stopping beside one of the largest buildings from which there emanated a cacophony of mechanical noises and pungent smells.

Cassie had arrived at the mill.

Alphonso helped her up from the buggy none too gently and dragged her inside, leading her through a maze of clattering machinery and whirring conveyor belts until they arrived in what appeared to be a stable of sorts with stalls to one side populated by a handful of mules standing around munching hay.

An ancient muleteer came out of one of the stalls to greet Alphonso with a somewhat vacant, toothless grin.

"His Excellency wants this bitch to push the wheel around for a while, Rufio," Alphonso informed the old man, "and you'd better bring her a belt, we don't want any field hands paying her any evening visits whilst she's here, do we "

Without bothering to answer, the old man ambled off to the tack room for the belt as ordered. Alphonso began to undo the straps of the restraint jacket and pulled the stiff canvas shroud over Cassie's head before standing back to admire the body his employer had paid so much for.

Cassie was aware of his close scrutiny of her nakedness, but she was feeling so utterly exhausted and wretched that she simply stood in the centre of the stable, head bowed, hands hanging limply at her sides and staring hopelessly at her still chained, filthy feet.

Rufio returned with the belt, which was a contraption of thick, double stitched leather and metal, shaped like a pair of pants and secured by an iron bound belt and padlock.

Cassie groaned helplessly as the old muleteer fitted the medieval looking contraption between her legs, slapping her buttocks sharply in order to get her to part her thighs so that he could position the shaped metal gusset pieces precisely over her vulva and anus, thus preventing any unauthorised penetration.

The thick leather pants were duly padlocked closed and the key handed to Alphonso.

"Okay, let's get her fixed up and then I can be about my duties."

They led the girl into an adjacent room dominated by an enormous capstan like structure to which, were harnessed two mules walking perpetually round a straw covered track. Rufio called out a guttural command, "Hoah!" and the two mules slowed to a stop. Cassie was pushed into a vacant slot and Rufio quickly harnessed her wrists to a horizontal bar at chest height.

Once Rufio was satisfied that she was properly secured Alphonso bent to check the snugness of the chastity belt and the strength of the lock.

"Apparently you like to run, missy," laughed Alphonso, "well, you can run all day long in here and you won't even get out of the room."

Cassie groaned again and shook her head. Was everyone in this country completely absolutely crazy she asked herself desperately Now they expected her to work like a fucking horse in some sort of bloody flour-mill!

"What's with the cattle card," asked Rufio, staring at the girl's spiked tongue curiously.

"The silly bitch did a runner on the journey up here and was daft enough to surrender herself to the Feds in La Corunda. She spent all day yesterday with Commandante Estoban and his men. You know what Estoban is like," said Alphonso, "the guy has the weirdest sense of humour."

Rufio shouted, "Yaaha!" and the two mules immediately set off at a pace that had Cassie stumbling along at a fast trot, the chains around her ankles snagging and pulling mercilessly until she was able to get into a rhythm of quick, short steps. It made her totter like some sort of demented geisha girl, she thought, feeling herself suddenly wanting to laugh hysterically at the ludicrousness of the situation.

But after a short while her legs began to tire and a slow burning began to build in her calves and thighs, making her legs feel increasingly leaden, as revolution followed revolution. The floor beneath her feet was thick with manure, where the two mules had simply relieved themselves as they walked, and soon she was covered almost to her knees in animal filth.

For his part, Rufio seemed to take it personally that she was not pushing as hard as his beloved mules and each time she passed his position seated on a high stool by the stable door, he cracked her across the naked shoulders with a long switch, shouting at her to pick up her fat arse and do her fair share of the work.

Round and round she went, pushing at the bar until her legs were two solid lumps of cramp and her breath came in tortured gasps that hacked at her lungs until she thought she would faint. Unable to swallow properly, the blood flecked saliva ran in a constant stream out of her gaping lips and dribbled from her chin into her ample cleavage, where it mixed with the rivers of sweat running out of her every pore.

Eventually, after what seemed like an age, Rufio called "Hoah!" and the mules came to a stop with Cassie collapsed over the bar in a state of near total exhaustion.

The muleteer then unhitched the two mules and led them off to the stables, returning after a few minutes with a single mule, which he harnessed in the trap opposite her. Then he shouted "Yaaha!" and the mule and Cassie began to walk around the track again whilst Rufio disappeared into the stables for his afternoon siesta.

Throughout the rest of the afternoon Cassie trudged around and around the track with only the mule for company. The long minutes merged into hours until she was almost walking in her sleep. At the end of the day Rufio took the mule away to its stall and simply left the girl to sag down into the filthy straw, her legs and body completely exhausted.

The rattling mill machinery slowly ran down around her, as the workers left for home and presently the only sound that could be heard was the occasional whinny of one of the mules in the adjacent stables.

Cassie came awake with a start as Don Alvarez lifted her head gently with a hand under her chin.

It was dark outside and the only light came from the softly hissing hurricane lantern he had brought with him.

"Gently, Cassandra." His voice was soft and mellow. "Be still." He squatted down beside her, smoothing her matted hair away from her face. Cassie shifted nervously, trying to bring her arms together over her breasts, somehow not wanting to appear lewd in front of this man of all men, but the leathers securing her wrists to the push bar prevented all but the smallest of movements.

"I need to take the pin out of your tongue, Cassandra, before the hole becomes permanent, or infected." He peered deeply into her eyes, recognising the fear and desperation he saw there. "I need to cut the pin with these," he held up a pair of wire cutters, the sight of which made her recoil in panic.

Alvarez took hold of her face between his palms his eyes holding hers with the intensity of his gaze.

"Cassandra, I want you to be brave and trust me, I know it hurts so badly, but once the pin is out your tongue will heal within a few days."

Slowly, Cassie nodded her understanding. Closing her eyes tightly, she extended her aching tongue as far as she could, stretching her jaws as wide as possible, trying desperately not to panic as she felt him insert the wire cutters into her mouth and then the sudden sharp pain as the steel jaws closed on the spike and snipped off the top grommet, allowing the hated cow label to fall away.

Cassie whimpered in relief as she was able to relax her mouth and close her lips for the first time in nearly twenty-four hours.

Don Alvarez waited patiently for her to open her eyes.

"The rest of the pin is still embedded in your tongue, you can't feel it because of the swelling," he said and then more firmly, "I have to pull it out."

Once again Cassie closed her eyes and extended her tongue, balling her fists against the pain as he took hold of the base of the pin with the cutters. At the same time, he wrapped his arm around her bare shoulders to prevent her from jumping away and drew the spike swiftly out of the swollen flesh.

Cassie barely made a sound as the steel came out, hanging on to his arm with her shaking hands as the pain washed over her in waves.

As he looked down at her tightly closed eyes and quivering mouth, Alvarez felt a sudden excitement stir in his groin at the way she handled her pain and something more, an unaccustomed pride that she had refused to cry out as he had drawn out the wicked sliver.

The willingness she had shown to place herself into his hands at this early stage gratified him more than he could say. Cassie tried to move her tongue, but it was so swollen and fat that she could hardly form the words of thanks she wanted so much to utter.

"Thaaankuu," she whispered, as two tears squeezed through her eyelids and rolled down her face leaving two crooked trails in the grime covering her cheeks.

Alvarez pushed an antiseptic lozenge between her lips. "Suck this," he murmured, stroking the thick tangle of her hair, "it will dull the pain and help to prevent infection."

He sat with her for a long time until her breathing settled and she drifted back off into an exhausted sleep. Once she was sleeping soundly, he unhitched her wrists from the push bar and settled her down into the filthy straw and fetched a mule blanket from the stable, which he laid over her.

Before he left, The Don sought out Rufio and gave him strict instructions as to Cassie's treatment and care, as well as leaving a blister pack of lozenges for her mouth.

The next morning, Cassie awoke as the mill workers came into the building and started cranking up the thumping mill engines. Rufio brought her a cup of water, some thin porridge and finally the lozenge for her tongue as ordered.

Then, the old muleteer hitched her up with the mules and started the carousel turning, as usual barking at her to keep up with the animals.

But after having watched from the darkness as Don Alvarez tended her during the night, the old man decided against beating her again with the switch.

There was more than a little something of the devil in his mercurial employer, something which Rufio had absolutely no intention of provoking.

Some years ago he had watched The Don whip a field hand almost to the point of death after the ignorant idiot had attempted to force himself on one of the native housemaids. The Don had been terrifying in his coolness as he had stalked around the man, cutting him to ribbons with the long bull-whip piece by piece, as the grovelling wretch had rolled and sobbed in the dirt begging for mercy.

As Cassie tramped around the filthy track pushing the heavy bar before her, she replayed the hazy events of yesterday night over and over in her head, recalling with warmth the tenderness that Don Alvarez had shown her, yet also remembering that he was the one who had, at the very least, indirectly caused her kidnapping, putting her into the hands of Bormann, Abdullah, the Twins and the Commandant and now he had incarcerated her in this mill.

Failing to make any sense out of what was happening to her, Cassie tried to blank out everything from her thoughts as she tramped despondently around the track, her mind once again becoming numb, as the exhausting hours of unending toil piled slowly one on top of another.

At the end of the sixth working day, Rufio unhitched Cassie from the wheel and led her stumbling and pain-wracked form outside. Waiting in the golf buggy, Alphonso looked momentarily askance at the frightful apparition standing hunched and blinking in the evening sunlight. Cassie's once long and lustrous mane hung like a filthy mop over her face and shoulders, the individual strands of hair knotted together in a tangled mass of rats' tails.

Here and there, bits of straw poked out of the dark thatch giving her the look of a witch-cum-scarecrow. The girl's pale skin, ingrained with the sweat and dirt of a week's hard labour looked blotched, grey and sallow, and her legs were caked from toes to buttocks in a thick paste, comprised of the mules' and her own excrement, which the constant trotting had kicked up from the track.

"Do you want her in the buggy with you " asked the ancient muleteer doubtfully.

"Oh no," replied the Major-domo shaking his head, "decent folk have to ride in this thing."

Handing Rufio the key to her chastity belt, he curtly ordered the old man to remove the device, tie a rope around her waist and make the other end of the rope fast to a grab rail at the rear of the buggy.

Cassie was in a state of almost complete mental and physical exhaustion as a result of six twelve-hour days spent pushing the mill wheel round with the mules. So that in her confused state she was barely aware of the half-mile trek back to the mansion, her legs again working with an automatic will of their own, as she plodded doggedly after Alphonso in the electric buggy.

The girl's mental fatigue was so deep seated that she neither heard the insults nor felt the stones flung at her by the laughing and cavorting worker's children, as they made their way out of the compound and on to the long road back to the mansion.

The buggy drew up in a small courtyard at the rear of the house where a tall blonde woman in her late twenties and dressed in a short white tennis dress waited. Her striking blue eyes and finely formed features showed no visible reaction as she swept her gaze over the pathetic zombie-like creature now standing swaying dazedly in the middle of the courtyard.

Alighting, Alphonso untied the rope from the buggy and tugging sharply several times to get her attention, led the hapless Cassie over to the waiting woman.

"Six days in the mill, something of a record, eh Marla " said the Major-domo, handing the woman the ropes end. "The poor bitch doesn't even know what day it is."

As he spoke, he allowed his eyes to glide casually over the blonde woman's superb athletic figure, lingering here and there on the firm swells of her breasts, her trim waist and finally, her long, firmly toned legs.

Not for the first time Alphonso wondered what it would be like to have Marla to himself for just one night. But this cool beauty was far beyond his scope, being reserved only for the personal use of His Excellency and, very occasionally, his houseguests. It was a similar story for all of the foreign girls that Don Alvarez had brought here from time-to-time. And that exclusivity of use was a rule which his employer enforced with absolute and complete inflexibility.

Marla allowed a small, sardonic smile to touch her lips, as she noticed the plump man's hungry eyes rove over her body. As His Excellency's major-domo, Alphonso held a significant position of authority within the household, but as the longest serving body slave and de facto head of His Excellency's harem, Marla held a somewhat different but equally important position of authority. And whilst the two had never seen fit to discuss the differing nuances of their respective roles, each ensured at all times that they did not encroach upon the other's particular areas of authority.

Marla took the leash from Alphonso's sweating fingers and moved coolly away, conveying Cassie to the privacy of the slave wing via a series of back passageways and a service elevator that kept away from the more public areas of the mansion.

Once there, she quickly summoned two body slaves from their rooms and gave a series of quick and precise instructions that saw Cassie led away to a large and opulent bathroom. Here she was gently ushered into a shower cubicle where she finally sagged against the cool marble wall as the two girls gently scrubbed the thick layer of the filth and grime from her body.

By the time they brought her from the shower, Marla had finished drawing a foaming hot bath and Cassie allowed herself to be lowered by gentle hands into the perfumed and welcoming water. A long, low groan of relief broke from her lips as the soothing liquid closed over her aching and shattered body.

For the next hour the two girls worked under Marla's expert supervision, carefully treating Cassie's abused hair and body with a range of soaps and emollients.

Finally, the fussing women wrapped their exhausted charge in a cavernous bath sheet and guided her to a bedroom. Once there, Cassie gratefully collapsed down on to the soft mattress, her mind immediately surrendering to sleep even as the silk counterpane was being drawn over her.

The next day around noon, with the sunlight pouring in through the large second floor windows, Cassie's consciousness began to return by slow degrees, as if her shocked mind was reluctant to leave its protective cocoon of darkness.

Warily, the sleep tousled brunette sat up, slowly uncoiling her leaden limbs and gathering the counterpane up to her chin as she looked around the confusingly pleasant room.

The memories of yesterday evening gradually came back to her one-by-one the major-domo collecting her from the mill, roping her to the buggy and the long trek back to the mansion, the beautiful blonde woman and the two girls who had bathed and soothed her. She looked around carefully. She saw that the room was comfortably furnished with such things as a dressing table, chest of draws, sofa and easy chairs, there was even a hi-fi, but no telephone.

The curtains and décor, whilst tasteful, were nonetheless frankly opulent, and her feet, for so long now used to the harsh rigours of walking outdoors barefoot, sank into the soft, deep pile of the carpet, as she moved hesitantly about the room touching and examining.

The various drawers were all empty and she could find no clothing in any of the cupboards. By contrast however, the en-suite bathroom was more than adequately stocked with all manner of personal toiletries and beauty products of the finest quality.

To Cassie's surprise, the bedroom door was unlocked, but when she looked out into the hall she could detect no signs of activity in the otherwise silent house. As she had no clothing, Cassie decided against venturing out, and in truth she was still physically exhausted and knew that she was in no condition to go exploring.

The young English girl's attention was drawn back into the room by sounds coming from the window and looking outside she was able to see down into the lush gardens surrounding the house and there was the source of the sounds she had heard.

The tall blonde woman was exercising alone on the tennis court, receiving service from a machine. Cassie stood for a while watching the beautiful and powerful woman dodge this way and that, her body moving with easy grace, swinging her racket in alternate forehands and backswings, as the balls flashed toward her over the net.

Despite her physical tiredness, Cassie's mind was far too active to allow her to return to bed and so she began to run herself a bath, deciding to make full use of the facilities before they were withdrawn, and to repair some of the ravages of the past few weeks.

Whilst the water was filling the bath, Cassie tied up her thick mane of hair and took stock of herself in the full-length bathroom mirror. This was the first opportunity she had had to take a close look at herself for almost four weeks and she was shocked to see the changes in her face and body that had taken place over that time.

Her skin, which had rarely been out in the sunlight since her kidnap, was almost translucent in its whiteness, and the thin tracery of blue veins in the taut flesh of her full breasts was clearly visible. The unusual whiteness of her skin also served to accentuate the dark umber cones of her nipples, which now felt permanently thickened and elongated after her treatment at the hands of the Commandant.

The hair in her armpits had grown thickly and in her groin the soft dark pelt had spread out to her inner thighs and up on to the lower slope of her gently curving belly, making her crinkle her nose in distaste.

The weight she had put on at the trading post had long since been lost in the mill, but the cumulative effect of the prolonged stretching and strenuous physical exercise that she had been forcibly subjected to recently, had succeeded in bringing out a pleasing muscular definition in her body that had never been there before.

Having completed her self-critique, Cassie settled herself down into the water and allowed her still protesting muscles to relax as the welcome heat seeped into her body.

Marla called in on Cassie at the end of the afternoon and immediately expressed smiling approval at the improvement in her appearance.

"I see you've made good use of your time, you look much recovered. Another few days of rest and you should be good as new," she smiled.

Marla had changed out of her sport dress and was now naked save for a short diaphanous wrap that she had tied around her waist and which went some way toward disguising her flaxen haired pudendum and flaring buttocks. On her feet she wore a pair of fine golden sandals.

"The master will be home in three days and by then he will expect you to be fully recovered and ready to begin your training," she went on in a matter in fact tone, at the same time handing Cassie a wrap and sandals similar to the ones she wore. "Come along, I'll show you around the slave quarters and introduce you to the other girls."

Cassie hurriedly tied the translucent material around her hips and followed the other woman out of the room.

His Excellency Don Ramon Jesus y' Alvarado leant back in his chair and considered his good friend and business associate, Theo Mandrakos, over the rim of his china coffee cup.

The pair were sitting in Don Alvarez' sumptuous first floor study enjoying a late breakfast and naturally enough, their conversation had quickly turned to the pleasures of women's flesh.

Theo had just asked The Don to describe the differences between an experienced slave and a beginner, or noviciate, as The Don preferred to term them.

One of the main reasons for this, Theo's latest trip to South America, was to become familiar with Don Alvarez' slave training methods so that he could emulate them in his native Greece and hopefully join the incredibly secretive and exclusive world wide fraternity of wealthy slave owners of which Don Alvarez was a leading light and Theo's potential sponsor.

Mandrakos had first become acquainted with the pleasures of slave ownership on a previous business trip, when, as a special thank you for helping one of Don Alvarez' companies to win a lucrative export contract with the Greek Government, he had been invited to the Fazenda and had spent an amazing and extremely pleasurable weekend sampling the delights of his host's special harem.

"In simple terms," began The Don somewhat didactically, "an experienced slave will know instinctively what is expected of her at any given moment, or will have the capacity to adapt instantly to her master's needs. She should have the ability to follow the master's lead in any number of given bondage, sexual, or social situations. Further, she will be able to demonstrate a large number of sexual techniques designed to enhance her master's and," The Don nodded reasonably, "her own sexual pleasure."

Seeing his friend's eyebrows rise in surprise at this last comment The Don went on to explain further.

"Whilst one side of the primary role of the slave's purpose is undoubtedly to be physically exercised and chastised by her master, an experienced slave should enter into the relationship with a high degree of acceptance and it is to encourage this willingness that the slave must be regularly rewarded with sexual pleasure and comfort. Hence, you will see here at the Fazenda that I keep each slave in opulent accommodations and provide generously all manner of trinkets, cosmetics, fancy attire and so forth. As far as a slave's health is concerned, a good diet and physical exercise is essential. All of my slaves are required to use the extensive gymnasium facilities on a daily basis and also exercise their other feminine talents, such as personal grooming, cooking, needlework and cleaning to the full."

The Don paused to drink from his coffee cup whilst Theo digested the first part of the lesson.

"At the outset," he continued, "slaves must be pre-selected for such essentials as physical beauty, intelligence, health, athleticism, and of course innate sensuality and sexuality."

The Don paused to refill his cup from an antique silver pot, before resuming.

"One of the benefits of having slaves brought up river by an experienced handler such as Gunter Bormann is that this affords the opportunity of testing the subject over a period of many days in situations of the utmost rigour. In this fashion weak specimens can be weeded out at an early stage, thereby markedly reducing the likelihood of rejection once a slave has been taken into final ownership."

Mandrakos nodded his growing understanding, his mind already imagining how he would use his family's great wealth and influence to begin selecting and training his own bevy of slave girls.

Sensing the direction his friend's thoughts were taking, Don Alvarez delivered his final opinion.

"Lack of respect or gratitude or refusal to co-operate must be dealt extremely harshly and to this end I maintain certain facilities close at hand, which one might describe as being the absolute opposite of those situated here on the first floor."

Alvarez paused as Mandrakos' eyes took on an interested and frankly hungry look.

"Have patience my friend," The Don laughed reassuringly, "we have two new slaves to begin training today and so perhaps we will have need of severe corrections in due course."

"That," said Mandrakos with a wolfish smile, "is a promise I hope to hold you to, my friend."

Don Alvarez set down his cup decisively, "perhaps an actual demonstration of some of the things I have told you is in order."

He pulled on a bell cord to summon Alphonso and once the major-domo appeared he gave the retainer instructions to send Marla and Cassandra to the study at once.

Cassie had just finished a punishing routine on the computerised step machine and was now relaxing, towelling off her sweat dampened hair, when Marla came into the gymnasium and pointed to the wrap and sandals, which the brunette had changed out of before beginning her exercise programme.

"Quickly now, get out of that sport bra and those shorts, put a brush through your hair and put your wrap back on," said Marla urgently. "His Excellency wants us both in his study immediately."

Sensing the excitement in Marla's voice, Cassie ventured a question, "what does he want us for "

Marla looked at Cassie with a quirky expression, "he wants us there for his pleasure, why else "

As Marla led Cassie quickly down the wide staircase and around the first floor mezzanine toward the study, their sandals clicking rapidly across the highly polished floor, she hissed a stream of advice: "Remember what I taught you. Always refer to His Excellency by his title and his guest as "master", do exactly as you are bidden, say nothing unless you are directly addressed and on no account say "NO."

Cassie had no time to respond as they were now at the study door and Marla was knocking, her small knuckles making almost no sound against the ancient teak. From within came the muted sound of male laughter and then the door was opening and for the first time since he had visited her in the mill Cassie saw The Don.

She had a fleeting impression of perfect white teeth as he smiled, and then the faint smell of citrus cologne came to her nostrils, as he ushered the two women inside.

At the far end of the room, still seated in one of the large bay windows, a darkly handsome thick-set man lounged, his expression relaxed, but his eyes intent as they swept frankly over the almost nude women now stepping into the centre of the room.

Cassie started involuntarily, but managed to remain silent when in an easy gesture The Don pulled the diaphanous wrap from her hips as he walked around her, examining the results of four days pampering and healthy exercise.

"My, my, Cassandra," he said approvingly, "your condition has improved since I tended to you in the mill."

Cassie blushed with furious embarrassment. Partly at her nakedness and partly as she remembered the incredibly filthy state she had been in when he had seen her last. Flustered and unsure how to respond, she simply mumbled "thank you," remembering at the last moment to say, "your Excellency." But The Don was already turning away and seemed not to have noticed her stumble over the honorific.

"We'll start with experience first, I think," The Don said to his guest, as he took a two-inch wide leather tawse from the drawer of an ornate ebony cabinet. Testing the implement's well-oiled flexibility between his hands, he nodded to Marla and gestured with the eighteen-inch length of leather to the expanse of his massive ebony desk.

"I've promised my good friend Mr Mandrakos here that he will see how a true body slave takes her punishment, Marla," he said matter-of-factly. "I know you won't disappoint me."

Without a second's hesitation, Marla discarded her wrap, kicked off her sandals and crossed to the end of the desk where she stood perfectly erect, legs together for a moment, gathering herself and then she bent forward at the waist, bringing her arms over in two perfect butterfly circles to place her steepled fingers between the piles of papers and books - careful to disturb nothing.

As The Don moved to stand on the opposite side of her so that Mandrakos would have an uninterrupted view, Cassie was amazed to see Marla raise her bowed head until she was looking directly forward and then arch her long back so that her belly sank almost onto the dark wood and her beautifully shaped buttocks were upraised.

Marla's facial expression was one of complete calm, although Cassie couldn't help but notice that her coral pink nipples were already crinkled and stiff with fear - or was it anticipation

Deep within her own body, Cassie felt the now familiar serpent of lust uncoiling and outwardly her own dark nipples began to tighten in response to she knew not what, as she stared fixedly at the incredible tableaux before her.

Slowly, like a professional golfer winding up his back swing, The

Don raised his arm and then with blinding speed he brought the tawse down across the blonde's buttocks with a crack that ricocheted around the room like a rifle shot.

Despite herself Cassie flinched and yelped, but incredibly Marla showed no sign that she had felt anything at all. Again, The Don brought the tawse down across her buttocks, this time a couple of inches above the first strike and then his arm was moving with metronome like precision, marching up the smooth expanse of the blonde's tanned back, leaving a scarlet band wherever the insidious leather strap touched the soft skin.

Cassie stared fixedly at Marla's face, but could detect only the merest flicker of her eyelids as the dreadful sounding blows landed one upon another.

By the time The Don had reached her shoulders with the twenty fourth stroke, Marla's mouth was slightly parted as she quietly panted between gritted teeth and her face and taught neck were flushed and sweating. After the sound of the last stroke had faded, he bent forward to examine with fastidious interest the precise reticulated pattern of wheals now blossoming all across Marla's back and buttocks.

Cassie marvelled at the way the woman was able to maintain her posture despite what must be a totally agonising level of pain.

The Don extended his long tongue on to the woman's right buttock and slowly licked the entire length of her back up into the hollow between her shoulder blades and on into the sweat soaked hairline at the nape of her neck. Finally, he whispered into her ear, a few private words that brought a tremulous smile of gratitude to Marla's otherwise quivering mouth.

As The Don straightened up, Marla too slowly raised herself from the desk and, turning, lifted herself so that her scarlet banded rump was now perched on the heavily carved bevel of the desk.

Slowly, she spread her knees and placed her bare feet upon the heads of the carved jungle panthers that pounced snarling from the corners of the ancient desk. And then, spreading her arms behind her, she gripped the sides of the desk so that she was bent backwards in a bow and now her breasts and belly were exposed to The Don's mercy.

Cassie looked on in fascination as The Don once again raised the awful tawse and brought it down across the blonde woman's body. The sharp leather drew a broad stripe of pain across the pale flesh of her lower belly just a fraction of an inch above her carefully trimmed, tawny haired pudendum. Once again Marla showed no outward sign of distress or emotion, simply holding herself immobile, head flung proudly back, as the tawse once again began its slow march up the length of her torso, striping her belly and breasts a further dozen searing times.

Cassie found herself relishing the sight of the handsome Don lashing the beautiful blonde without even a shadow of mercy. So much so that she gasped with disappointment when the last blow had fallen and The Don put the tawse to one side.

Once again, he stooped to examine the marks his arm had raised upon the peerless flesh and once again he used his tongue to sooth the vermilion wheals until Marla's arms quivered and her pale, pink nipples stood out like bullets. Finally, he looked up at Mandrakos, his eyes on fire with excitement.

"Isn't she marvellous, Theo Thirty-six full strokes of the tawse and not so much as a murmur," he said triumphantly, "not a single sound out of her, by God!"

"Absolutely incredible, Ramon," agreed Mandrakos, his voice thickened with lust and his senses so excited that he could hardly frame the English to express himself.

The Don turned his attention back to Marla and he was enchanted to see the evidence of her need trickling on to the oiled black wood of the great desk from her gaping vulva in long silver tendrils. He stepped between the woman's quivering thighs, pulled open his pants and drew out his iron hard erection, immediately sinking himself into the wide-open sex before him.

And for the first time since entering the study, Marla uttered a sound a long groan, issued from deep within her belly to echo around the room.

The electrified Don then began to plunge his hips back and forth between the American girl's wide-spread thighs, bringing her madly excited flesh to an immediate and excruciating orgasm that rolled through her loins and belly like a train wreck played out in slow motion, pounding her senses until she could no longer hold herself up and he had to gather her in his arms and draw her to him, so that she could wrap her shaking arms about his neck and shoulders, clinging on to him, their wide open mouths jammed together in an unending series of deep sucking kisses, their tongues writhing serpent-like, as his own orgasm vented his copious fluids into her gratefully suckling vagina.

Cassie was almost beside herself with a strange mixture of excitement and fear, as she surveyed the aftermath of the encounter between the handsome Don and the athletic Marla. The blonde now lay slackly across the broad desktop, her splayed thighs still visibly twitching and her heated body coated in a thick sheen of perspiration.

The Don stood over her, avidly drinking in the sight of her dishevelled and plundered beauty revelling in the strength of his whip arm as he slowly tucked his still thickened phallus back into his trousers. And then he ran both hands through his hair, hair which Marla had ruffled with her fingers at the height of her massive orgasm.

But it was with a feeling of dread mixed with strange anticipation that Cassie regarded The Don as he turned his attention to her and Mandrakos.

"And now Theo," he smiled widely, "for the second part of the demonstration - I give you the inexperienced and untested Cassandra."

Cassie stood ignorant and bemused as The Don brought an aluminium spreader bar from the ebony cabinet and bent to fix it between her ankles. As if in a dream, the English girl automatically moved her feet apart the required distance without being instructed.

It was with a detached part of her mind that Cassie considered the change in her behaviour over the past three weeks her lack of shame in standing nude before these men, the acceptance of imprisonment and bondage as a normal part of her day-to-day life, her voyeuristic pleasure at watching others being whipped and fornicating, and, inescapably, her own heightened appetite for sex and the dark pleasure of the whip.

By now, Marla had managed to rouse herself from the desk and crossed somewhat unsteadily to the window where she reached behind the silk drapes to operate an unseen switch. Slowly the huge wooden chandelier set into the centre of the high ceiling began to lower.

Once again The Don was speaking to Mandrakos. "My great, great, great grandfather, Don Archilla, had this chandelier fashioned by the estate's craftsmen from the wheel of a Paraguayan army field gun his cavalry unit captured during the war of 1864," he said proudly. "I had it remounted with a different purpose in mind - its twin adorns my bedchamber"

As Marla lowered the great wheel, a number of iron rings with an obvious application became visible. Marla stopped the wheel a bare twelve inches above Cassie's head so that Don Alvarez could attach a set of chains to opposite sides of the wheel which terminated in a set of padded wrist cuffs. As soon as the cuffs were snapped shut, Marla began to raise the wheel until Cassie was drawn up into a widely spread X, to stand balancing precariously on the balls of her wide spread feet.

Behind Cassie's back The Don handed the tawse to Mandrakos together with a few discrete words of advice.

"The leather should be applied with vigorous but consistent force," he advised. "You might like to start at the base of the buttocks and move up to the top of the shoulders. When using a heavy implement care should always be taken whilst moving over the area of the kidneys so as not to cause permanent damage, which, for any whip-master worthy of the title would be an unforgivable lapse."

Mandrakos impatiently nodded his agreement. He clenched his hand tightly around the dark wooden haft of the tawse, as his eyes raked over the superb expanse of Cassie's naked flesh spread invitingly before him. Flesh that he was desperate to test his untried arm upon. The sight of his friend and sponsor scourging and then fucking the fabulous Marla had excited him to fever pitch and his need to sate his sexual tension through the whip and his rigid, aching cock was palpable.

For her part, the trussed and spread-eagled Cassie was almost completely paralysed with fear, as she strained her ears to catch the whispered conversation going on behind her. In front of her, Marla, unable to speak aloud whilst Don Alvarez was conversing, fixed the wretched girl with an intent stare and shook her head from side-to-side almost imperceptivity to signify that she should make no sound and then Marla drew her lips back from her clenched teeth to show Cassie that she should clench hers against the pain to come.

Even as he was speaking with Mandrakos, Alvarez noted the subtle interplay between the two women, but for once he chose to ignore the sisterly concern shown by Marla, who he was immensely pleased with after her magnificent performance under the tawse. In any event, the new and untried Cassandra would be completely alone with her pain in due course. He moved off to one side, as Mandrakos stepped in and described a few practice swings. The sound of the leather cutting through the air forced a strangled whine through Cassie's tightly clamped lips.

Impervious to her terror, Mandrakos gathered himself and then brought the tawse down upon Cassie's ample rump, pausing only to stare at the livid stripe of crimson that burst across the girl's beautiful white buttock flesh. Instantly, fire exploded through Cassie's backside like a blowtorch, but somehow she managed to contain the pain and grit her teeth as she tried to focus upon Marla's impassive face where the blonde woman stood motionless against the wall. Again and again the leather bit into Cassie's soft flesh, as the powerful Greek rained a succession on blows down upon her arching body, climbing up her back to her shoulders in two-dozen flaming steps.

By the time he had finished with her back Mandrakos was almost delirious with lust and he marched around to her front to recommence the beating without allowing the helpless Cassie a moment's respite. Marla looked imploringly at Don Alvarez, but the tall Brazilian simply lounged against his desk with one leg idly swinging back and forth as Mandrakos resumed his work, beating a harsh tattoo across Cassie's rounded belly and up over her full hard nippled breasts, wringing a long series of agonised cries from the helpless brunette, as she shuddered and bucked against her chains.

Finishing the flagellation, the stocky Mandrakos threw aside the tawse and ripped open his pants, bringing forth his dark and steeply up-curving cock in an incredibly hard state of erection. The Greek stepped over the spreader so that he was in between Cassie's widely spaced thighs, barking over his shoulder at Marla to lower the Chandelier. The blonde quickly complied, dropping Cassie so that she sank down on to Mandrakos' immense hardness. A hardness, which he immediately began to pump in and out of her, battering her soaking sex in a series of savage lunges, as he held her steady, pulling her sweated thighs around him with his huge hands.

Cassie groaned long and hard as the powerful Greek's cock slid deep into her sex, almost instantly converting the agonising all-over burning of the flogging into a deep seated sexual heat. A heat that exploded outward from the depths of her belly to send gouts of love juice cascading into her cunt to intermingle with the thick stream of semen that Mandrakos' sudden orgasm sent flooding into her now intensely spasming belly.

Don Alvarez instantly realised that his friend Mandrakos, probably through pure excitement and novelty, had peaked too early and would deny Cassie her much needed orgasm. Signalling to Marla to assist him he quickly took hold of the brunette by a thick hank of hair and dragging her head backward fastened his lips over hers, sucking her tongue deep into his mouth, as at the same time Marla took hold of one of Cassie's swollen breasts and drew the turgid flesh into her mouth, swirling her tongue around the solid nipple, sucking the sensitive teat into an even harder state.

Groaning helplessly, Mandrakos pumped the last of his scalding seed into the bucking girl's churning womb, as Don Alvarez thrust his index finger deep into her sweat soaked anus and at long last Cassie grunted her shattering orgasm deep into Don Alvarez' mouth, their tongues writhing together, as he moved his finger against her perineum, massaging the hypersensitive tissue against the iron hardness of the cock still embedded deep within her sex.

Slowly, the three detached themselves from Cassie, who slumped to hang limp in her chains. The Don watched transfixed as her thigh and belly muscles continued to twitch and ripple spasmodically beneath the damp skin, whilst the slowly ebbing tide of her orgasm ran its course and finally petered out.

After Cassie and Marla had departed for the second floor slave quarters the two men resumed their discussion.

"So now you have seen for yourself the difference between an experienced slave and a novice," The Don said. "On the one hand, Marla, unhesitating, obedient and able to remain still and silent under a severe scourging."

The Greek nodded. "Yes, she was magnificent, such control, the way she displayed herself for you, like an athlete, no, more like a gymnast."

"And then there was Cassandra, equally passionate perhaps, but as yet untrained and unsure of herself and in no way able to emulate the control displayed by Marla."

"But, My God, Ramon," said the Greek, his voice quaking with residual passion, "never have I felt a woman grip with such force in her cunt, and her thighs around my waist - I could hardly breathe - she just sucked it out of me, like, like, a machine," he finished finally, bursting out laughing.

Don Alvarez nodded agreeably, sharing in his friend's delight. "The reports I received from the handler, Bormann who brought her up river and the Commandant at La Corunda who recovered her, lead me to believe that Cassandra has great innate sexuality, which she is only just beginning to realise and understand. Her responses to chastisement have shown that her sexual appetite is greatly amplified by the application of pain and discomfort far more so than the average female, perhaps even more so than Marla."

The Don's Greek guest again laughed uproariously, slapping his leg, "I think you will have much pleasure finding out if you are correct, my friend."

After they left Don Alvarez' study, Marla took Cassie to her room where she drew them both a warm bath, adding a selection of fragrant oils to the foaming water.

Both girls then sank gratefully but gingerly into the soothing liquid, each groaning softly, as the water scratched over their glowing, sensitised flesh, until they lay submerged with only their heads above the foam, each maintaining a reflective silence for many minutes.

"You handled that well enough, for a beginner," Marla eventually remarked with a wan smile, "I was afraid you would start howling and leaping about after Ramon laid it on me and you saw what was in store for you."

"You should have seen me ten days ago," Cassie snorted, "some police sadist types really made me howl and leap about."

"Yes, I heard Ramon telling the Greek all about it," said Marla. Then she added mischievously, "he said you fucked those three cops to a standstill."

Cassie's already heated complexion plunged to an even deeper hue, "I couldn't help it," she spluttered guiltily, "the situation was weird, this whole damn thing is. One minute I'm having a great time, you know single girl, good job, great friends, lots of parties and then whoosh! All this happens and suddenly I don't know where I am, or what's going on, or even who I really am anymore."

Marla nodded her understanding, "it's like that for all the girls, you either learn to accept it, or..."

"Or, what "

"Or, you get traded out."

"Out where "

"Some place a hell of a lot worse."

The pair lay in silence for a long while, allowing the warmth of the water to gradually sooth their many aches.

"Is it the same for you " Cassie eventually asked, awkwardly.

"The same "

"The sex I mean, when they whip you, does it make you want to screw their brains out too "

"Every Goddamned time," laughed the pretty blonde wryly, "oh, I was like you in the beginning. I couldn't work what was wrong with me, harangued myself constantly for being a slut and a whore, fought against it every waking minute. Then it just hit me one day when I was standing outside his study door ready to go in. I couldn't wait, I just couldn't bloody wait. I really wanted it and not just the sex. I mean I wanted it his way, the discipline, the pain and then the sex when he had me so wound up I thought my ass would catch on fire."

"What did he say to you when you were bent over his desk After he had leathered you and he licked the sweat from your back, he whispered something in your ear that made you smile, what was it "

Marla's face softened, as she climbed gingerly out of the tub and wrapped herself in a soft, pink bath sheet.

"He said I tasted like honey."

Marla led Cassie into the bedroom and carefully took the towel from around the English girl's damp body. The pair climbed into the centre of the large bed and Marla examined Cassie's brutalised skin minutely before taking a pot from her dresser and gently spreading a sweet smelling cooling balm over the many angry wheals.

Mandrakos was an inexperienced whip hand and he had crossed and re-crossed his strokes at several points on Cassie's belly and breasts, as his fever had increased and his arm had tired.

When Marla had finished, Cassie performed the same task for her. In Marla's case The Don had struck with an almost robotic precision so that the thirty-six stripes gracing the blonde's body were all quite separate and distinct and long experience had taught her they would fade within a few days.

When Cassie had finished working the balm into the swells of Marla's breasts she found herself lingering over the coral nipples, her fingers suddenly reluctant to leave the buds, which had quickly become erect under her touch.

Marla responded by placing her cupped palm over Cassie's damp, pouting sex lips and when Cassie issued a soft sigh of pleasure at the delicate touch she allowed her middle finger to slide up into the heat of Cassie's vagina. With a simultaneous moan of pleasure both woman brought their mouths together in a soft, but deep kiss, their tongues slipping past like tiny serpents to plumb the other's sweet mouth as they fell on to the soft eiderdown, their hands gently stimulating one another's bruised bodies.

Adeptly, Marla reversed her position so that they could lie with their mouths over one another's heated sexes, each lapping gently at the other's tender loins until they came softly and repeatedly their exhausted bodies finally succumbing to much needed slumber.

Several days later Cassie was again summoned to Don Alvarez's study, this time alone and it was with a tremendous feeling of trepidation, tempered with not a little excitement, that she made her way quickly downstairs to stand trembling before the heavily carved door.

Her knock was answered almost immediately by a flushed and bare chested Mandrakos, who waved her cheerfully into the room with a hand towel he had been using to wipe perspiration from his powerful upper body.

Cassie paused abruptly after barely two steps into the room, when she caught sight of the wretched female lying supine in the centre of the rich Chinese rug before The Don's great desk. Cassie moved reluctantly as Mandrakos' firm hand in the small of her back propelled her forward.

"Do not be shy little one," the Greek laughed cruelly, delighting in the sudden nervousness the beautiful English girl displayed in his presence. The hirsute Greek gestured with a nod to the figure on the floor, "this ungrateful wretch has just spent the last hour learning the meaning of the word obedience."

The wretch in question, Tanya, was the daughter of a Russian merchant banker who had been taken up by slavers six months ago, whilst enjoying a family holiday in Mexico.

The pretty, mousy haired, small breasted Russian girl had come to the notice of her kidnappers because of her incredibly large scarlet nipples, which she had delighted in showing off to all and sundry in her daily topless promenades at the beach. Taken quite simply as a speciality item', her handler had been delighted to discover that her unusual nipples were complimented by her similarly outsized labia, which hung like a pair of pink, fleshy curtains almost two inches beneath her vulva.

Tanya was lying on her back with her ankles shackled together and folded beneath her buttocks. Her thighs were spread at an almost impossible one hundred and sixty degrees by a long spreader fastened between her knees and her elbows and lower arms were enclosed in a heavily laced leather sheath, which, forced her elbows tightly together, causing her shoulder and neck bones to project sharply through her flesh. Her wrists were secured to her ankles and a foot thick diameter bolster had been thrust into the space between her legs and the small of her back, forcing her body into a pronounced arch.

Finally, the helpless girl was prevented from voicing her obvious discomfort by the presence of an oversized red rubber ball gag crammed into her wide stretched mouth and secured by straps buckled behind her head.

Cassie fought to suppress her outrage as she gazed at the poor creature so tightly trussed up before her. From just above her knees to a point just below her throat, Tanya's tortured flesh was covered in mesh of closely spaced wheals where she had been systematically flogged by Mandrakos. Her hugely erect nipples had obviously been a special target for his whip arm. Her belly gave a sudden and unwelcome heave, as she saw the thick stream of semen running from Tanya's wide-open sex. The massively pouting labial lips glistening redly in silent witness to her recent ravishment.

The girl must have been fucked by Mandrakos only moments before Cassie had been summoned to the study and she flushed hotly at the sudden realisation that she would have much preferred to have been called earlier, so that she could have watched the sex take place between Mandrakos and Tanya.

The bitter irony was not lost on her. Only a few short weeks ago she would have considered what had just happened in this room to have been aggravated rape. A serious crime demanding harsh punishment for the two men involved, but now she simply termed it rough sex and wanted to watch.

Mandrakos' voice broke into Cassie's confused thoughts. "If you will excuse me, my friend, I promised Marla and Sandrine that I would join them for a game of croquet and a picnic lunch on the lawn." Sensing that the Greek was not speaking to her, Cassie looked around to find Don Alvarez regarding her quizzically from behind his imposing desk.

"Enjoy!" The Don remarked simply without taking his eyes from hers, as the other man gathered up his shirt and strode quickly from the room.

Presently, he got up and came around the desk to stand beside her looking down at Tanya. "Do you know why she is being punished in this fashion " he asked unexpectedly.

Cassie shook her head, murmuring uncertainly, "no, Your Excellency". In truth, Cassie could think of several ways Tanya could have gotten herself into trouble with her Masters. The Russian girl was not the most popular member of Don Alvarez' harem, being a lazy and fractious personality who shirked her fair share of the many domestic tasks that took place on the upper two floors of the mansion.

All of the girls in the harem took turns to cook and clean when they were not exercising or grooming themselves, and Tanya's tardiness had been the cause of more than one bad tempered catfight.

No domestic servants, other than the major-domo, Alphonso and the elderly female housekeeper, Hortense, were allowed on the first or second floors, where the responsibility for maintaining the slave quarters, and more particularly, Don Alvarez' sumptuous personal comfort, was the exclusive responsibility of the harem - and one which Marla took very seriously indeed.

"It has been reported to me that Tanya refuses to attend to her duties in the proper fashion and that she perhaps resents her position here."

Cassie noted that the tone of The Don's voice was tinged with more than a little disappointment.

"And this," he continued with subtle menace, "after I have already had cause to chastise her for these very same infractions on two previous occasions. Very well, now that our guest has warmed her up for us, I think we can proceed with the rest of the lesson."

On the floor, Tanya craned her neck and shook her head wildly from side to side, her eyes wide and staring, as she sought desperately to signal her renewed compliance to the tall Brazilian. The Don seemed to consider his options for several moments, apparently oblivious to the helpless girl's desperate protestations.

"We'll use the chandelier," he said finally, signalling to Cassie to attend the electrical switchgear behind the drapes. The brunette crossed to the window in a daze, her legs moving woodenly, the sudden elevation to slave master's assistant only serving to add to the compote of confusion she had been experiencing since entering the study.

Whilst she lowered the huge cannon wheel from the ceiling, Cassie was fighting a desperate mental battle. Telling herself that she should be protesting against what was happening, not helping this patently cruel and arrogant man to further brutalise the helpless creature further. But even as she battled with these thoughts, Cassie knew that she would not refuse to obey. She told herself simply that if she refused, she herself would be punished, and another girl would be summoned to take her place.

Whilst the huge wheel descended, The Don brought two shackles from the large side cabinet and, rolling the helpless girl over, removed the wide spreader from between her knees and discarded the bolster cushion. Next he fastened a short length of chain to her wrist cuffs, which he attached to one side of the wheel rim where Cassie had stopped it four feet from the floor. He then affixed another chain to Tanya's ankle cuffs and thence to the opposite side of the wheel. When he had finally satisfied himself with the arrangement he signalled Cassie to raise it all up.

Cassie flicked the switch, catching her breath as the silent electric winch in the attic above began to draw the huge cannon wheel slowly upward. The groaning victim found herself dangling between the two chains, her wrists and ankles pulled agonisingly taught behind her, as her body was slowly swayed up from the rug to hang suspended in a deep bow at head height in the centre of the room.

The Don took hold of Tanya's hair and yanked her head up so that he could look directly into her agonised face.

"Now my dear, you will hang here all afternoon, whilst you reflect upon the disappointment you have again caused me," he said through lips pinched with annoyance. And then turning to Cassie he snapped, "bring me the ivory inlaid case, the large one - there, on top of the cabinet."

Quickly, her excitement rising, Cassie scampered across the room to fetch the case as ordered. She brought it over to The Don, cradled in her arms, surreptitiously crushing the solid weight against her suddenly sensitive breasts.

Alvarez opened the lavishly inlaid lid to reveal a multiplicity of curious articles, each so beautifully crafted from gold and silver metals as to be truly worthy of the term Art. He selected a pair of golden nipple rings, which he fitted through holes already present in the middle of Tanya's thick stalks. This was the first time Cassie had been able to study Tanya's amazing teats close to and she was intrigued to see that the bright crimson peaks were every bit of two inches long and as thick as her thumb, each surrounded by a broad aureole covering fully half of the small, pert breast.

Having affixed the rings, he next took two heavy elaborately enamelled balls the size of lemons and hung them by twelve inch silken cords from the nipple rings. The considerable weight immediately stretched the nipple and breast tissue into long tear drops and extracted a strangled gurgle of pain from the helpless girl.

Next, The Don pulled Tanya's thighs apart and examined her sex, which he found to be still febrile and thick with Mandrakos' ejaculate.

He took the heavy case from Cassie and set it down upon his desk, then again parted the girl's legs and jerked his head, indicating that she should get between the moaning Russian's thighs.

"Her cunt is thick with come, clean her with your mouth so that I can find the piercings in her flaps," he instructed tersely.

Once again, Don Alvarez's tone brooked little room for any squeamish considerations on Cassie's part, who in any case was beginning to relish her part in the treatment being meted out to the lazy and sluttish Tanya.

Cassie pushed her head between the other girl's thighs, extended her tongue into the gaping vulva and lapped the thick mixture of spunk and love juice from the heated flesh. She took care to suck the prodigious labial folds into her mouth, rolling the thick flaps with her avid tongue, removing the glutinous, savoury coating as instructed.

As she licked, Cassie could feel the other girl's vulva begin to tighten and flutter and when she extended the tip of her tongue to the front of the sex, she was amazed to feel Tanya's massive clitoris standing painfully tumescent. For a moment Cassie was unsure how to proceed, she badly wanted to continue what she was doing, but was uncertain of the mercurial Don's response if she began to do her own thing.

Behind her, Alvarez' critical attention immediately noted the change in both girls' body language and after a mere second's consideration he decided to allow them to continue, pushing Tanya's straining thighs further apart to allow Cassie easier access. Sensing her master's tacit approval, Cassie redoubled her efforts, concentrating upon rolling the erect clitoris with the tip of her tongue, flogging the sensitive flesh until Tanya began to moan and slaver around the fat ball-gag wedged uncomfortably between her teeth.

Alvarez allowed Cassie to slurp away until Tanya was literally squeaking with need and then, at the last moment he grabbed a thick hank of Cassie's hair and pulled her face out of Tanya's quivering sex, leaving the unfortunate Russian to toss her head and wail disconsolately, as the prospect of her much needed orgasm was suddenly withdrawn.

For her part, Cassie could only stand licking her lips stupidly, as Tanya teetered helplessly on the rapidly receding verge of satisfaction.

Alvarez crossed to his desk and chose a handful of items from the case and returned to fit four rings, two to each of Tanya's hugely distended inner labial petals, careful not to let his deft fingers trigger the orgasm she so desperately craved.

Again, he suspended a heavy enamelled ball from each piercing, stretching the sensitive membranes half as long again so that the late morning sunlight flooding the room shone clearly through the bat-like wings, illuminating the delicate tracery of blood vessels within the succulent flesh.

Finally, he took a small clamp from the box and fastened this to Tanya's massively thrusting clitoris, crushing the hot, pink flesh between the small flanges as he screwed the jaws shut with a small wing nut, wringing a fresh cry of anguish from the miserable girl.

Cassie stood back, aghast at the sight of Tanya hanging in chains with the six heavy weights dragging at her most intimate and tender parts. Yet she thrilled to the sensual feelings surging through her body, as the suspended girl hung sobbing at the cruelties visited upon her breasts and sex, or perhaps more accurately, she thought, because of The Don's refusal to allow her the orgasm she had so clearly craved.

Cassie's own body was now in a state of deep arousal and she ran her hands down over her hips, casting off the gossamer wrap, wishing she were alone in her room, so that she might plunge her fingers into her hot pussy and relieve the sudden need burning there.

Turning his attention away from the snivelling girl, Alvarez took Cassie by the elbow and guided her across to one of the tall bay windows, which was filled by a large object covered with a heavy damask sheet.

"Do you like to ride Cassandra " he asked innocently, his hand taking hold of the covering.

Cassie fought to drag her attention away from the wretched Russian.

"Why, y-yes, I like to ride very much," she replied, taken aback by the obliqueness of his question and somewhat wistfully thinking back half a life-time to the day her parents had bought her a pony for her eleventh birthday.

"Good, then you may like this."

With a flourish, the Brazilian pulled the cloth away to reveal a three quarter life size wooden rocking horse, most accurately carved from solid ebony.

"This was made for my grandmother, shortly after the First World War," he told her. "I found it stored away in the attic, where it must have been for many years I had it brought down and refurbished."

Cassie ran her fingers over the dark, freshly oiled wood. The horse was carved in exquisite detail, with every feature lovingly recreated by the unknown artisan, even down to the teeth fashioned in ivory, yellowed with age and the hooves shod with real iron shoes.

"Well, what do you think, do you like it "

"Y-yes, it's absolutely wonderful," said Cassie, uncertain as to what was coming next.

"Did you have a pony when you were a child " he asked.

"Erm, yes, I did, my father bought me one for my eleventh birthday." The girl's face softened as she recalled the day. "I asked Daddy for a white

Lipizzaner and was terribly disappointed when Little Spot arrived." Cassie stopped suddenly, afraid that she had presumed to say too much, but The Don was listening to her intently.

"Up you get," he said, placing his hand upon her rump. It was the first time he had touched her since she had come into the room and his palm on the flesh of her bottom sent an immediate wave of excitement coursing through her belly.

Smiling self consciously, Cassie kicked off her sandals, placed her foot in the padded stirrup and lifted herself into the saddle. Alvarez brought two broad sheep skin cuffs from the cabinet and buckled them on to her wrists. Cassie felt an immediate flutter of unease at the use of the restraints, but allowed herself to be somewhat reassured by the feel of the soft wool against her skin. She placed her hands on the carved bar-holds sprouting from the horses neck, eliciting a nod of approval from The Don, as he fastened the cuffs to rings at the bar ends. Alvarez stepped on a switch set into the marble plinth and Cassie gasped with surprise and delight as the horse began to walk on', the gentle hum of an electric motor powering the smooth undulations.

Alvarez stood back smiling, savouring the delightful imagery he had created the magnificent ebony stallion carrying away the exquisite, pale beauty.

In the garden below, Herve, the head gardener, choked back an oath, as he gazed up at the unexpected sight of one of the master's beautiful foreign whores riding the wooden horse. By the time the afternoon drew to a close, all six-estate gardeners would find compelling reasons to attend to the roses beneath the large study window.

After a few moments, the sensation of her pudendum rubbing on the hard leather saddle began to inflame Cassie so much that she was forced to stand up in the stirrups to ease her situation.

Smiling to himself, Alvarez crossed to the cabinet and took out a twelve-inch rubber dildo, which he brought over to Cassie and reaching between her spread thighs slid half of its thick, cunningly ridged length easily into her moist sex, wringing a fretful groan from her lips as the broad girth stretched her delicate vaginal tissues. Then he clipped the base of the dildo to a pivot ring set into centre of the saddle and stepped on the throttle again, bringing the horse up to a gentle canter.

Cassie immediately let out a, deep, long, tremulous "Ohhhh," as the increased undulations alternatively drew out, and then thrust in, the cock-like dildo anchored beneath her rapidly juicing sex.

After allowing her a few minutes to find her balance, Alvarez again stepped on the throttle, bringing the horse on another gear.

Realising that Don Alvarez was not going to let her get off after a quick canter around the room, Cassie raised herself up into a more orthodox riding stance, leaning forward over the plunging neck and lifting her superb flanks high, as the stallion's powerful undulations began to send shock wave after shock wave through her vulva and up into her roiling belly.

Judging her ready, The Don again stepped on the throttle, making Cassie groan long and loud as the stallion bolted into a fast gallop, ramming the dildo rapidly in and out of her soaking sex, sending furnace blasts of heat throughout her body, as her heavy breasts began to flog heavily back and forth.

Behind her, Don Alvarez swung his riding crop in a tight arc, landing the braid across the brunette's rippling buttock meat, extracting a sharp squeal of pain from her, as the supple leather bit lengthwise across the furiously bobbing orbs.

Cassie bared her teeth against the wicked pain, but was helpless to prevent herself from pushing her buttocks up into an even higher steeple of invitation. The fire-like sensations flashed instantaneously into her vagina, causing the muscles there to spasm around the invading dildo.

With studied precision, The Don applied the crop, starting at the base of her rump, just above her spread thighs and moving up incrementally an inch at a time. Each carefully measured blow landed as Cassie's buttocks arrived at the very top of their arc, the pain exploding in the heated flesh in perfect time to be absorbed and converted by her madly sucking vagina, as her hips plunged down on to the thick cock beneath her. By the time he had finished laying on the desired baker's dozen, Cassie's anguished face was flushed and sweating. Her green eyes bulged above her gritted teeth, as she fought desperately to endure the white-hot incendiary her arse had suddenly become without screaming out loud.

Once again, Alvarez stood back for a few moments to savour the spectacle of the fabulous young woman galloping along at top speed.

Although saying nothing, he was privately delighted at the way in which Cassie had accepted the crop without the usual sobbing and shrieking and, most significantly, by the way in which she had actively presented her buttocks to him during the scourging. It proved beyond doubt his belief that the English girl was now truly beginning to discover the latent masochism he had so fervently hoped she possessed.

Turning his attention reluctantly back to Tanya, hanging patiently from the chandelier, the tall Brazilian took hold of her scalp and jerked her head up roughly so that he could look into her face.

The Russian girl's normally flawless complexion was blotched and mottled with strain and her icy blue eyes were puffy and red-rimmed. The delicate tip-tilted nose ran with mucus from her constant snivelling, and strands of saliva hung from her lips and chin where the ball gag prevented her from closing her mouth.

Alvarez sneered with disgust and pushed her away with a heave of his shoulder, setting her body swaying violently back and forth, setting all of the balls hanging from her sex parts madly orbiting their tortured piercings, once again wringing a long, gurgling wail of horrified pain from the woebegone female.

"You will hang all evening and then Alphonso will take you to the Mill and you can prance with Rufio's donkeys until you learn the meaning of obedience and gratitude," the handsome aristocrat told the Russian, turning away as the hapless girl whined miserably from behind her gag.

Don Alvarez relaxed back into the chair behind his great desk and put his feet up on the finely polished surface, carelessly kicking off his hand-lasted Italian loafers as he did so. He crossed his hands contentedly behind his head and settled down to watch, as Cassie worked up a considerable lather, her magnificent body bathed in the warm afternoon sunlight pouring in through the large bay window.

Presently, a knock at the study door announced Alphonso with his master's afternoon coffee. If the Major-domo was surprised to see two obviously distressed nudes one hanging from the ceiling and the other riding a rocking horse at top speed, he showed none of it. Having been in the remarkable Alvarez family's service since boyhood, he had long ago learned to find the bizarre and unusual quite commonplace.

After allowing Cassie to strain mightily at full tilt for several more minutes, The Don pressed a button on a control pad on his desk and the horse slowed to a walk, allowing Cassie a desperately needed respite. She had been galloping for over twenty minutes and was now in real danger of fainting from sheer physical exhaustion, not to mention the deep sexual arousal that had been gnawing at her insides ever since Alvarez had thrust the huge rubber dildo into her.

Don Alvarez finished his second cup of coffee and then decided that it was time to broaden Cassie's repertoire now that she had begun to show definite promise. He crossed to the large cabinet where he selected a small, flanged rubber butt plug and liberally coated the end with a thick lubricant gel. Next he took out an aerosol of Burneeze' and approaching her from behind sprayed the cooling unguent liberally across her inflamed buttocks, making her groan appreciatively as the topical anaesthetic began to take effect.

Still rocking gently back and forth, Cassie closed her eyes and began to drift, putting up no resistance as he began to gently stroke her buttocks, his soft palm working in the cooling balm, relaxing the hitherto tense haunches. Even when he parted her buttocks and sprayed more coolant across the pink bud of her exposed anus, Cassie remained relaxed, her only movement the now almost automatic upturning of her hips, allowing The Don to insert the first flange of the plug before she even knew it was there.

With a yelp of alarm Cassie attempted to turn, but the wrist cuffs kept her firmly in place.

"What are you doing " she gasped. "P-please no! not that, anything but that," she pleaded, as he slowly rotated the plug, screwing it in over the second flange.

"Hold still and relax your muscles again," was all he replied, slipping his hand under her and gently massaging the tension from her belly. "It will be uncomfortable for a while, but that will pass as the muscles learn to relax." He again rotated the plug and forced it slowly in until the third flange disappeared beyond the greedily sucking anal sphincter.

"That's enough for now," he said, going back to his desk.

Cassie squirmed her hips and clenched her buttocks, as she tried to sense exactly what had been done to her. Now that the initial shock of the unexpected invasion was wearing off, she had to admit that the strange pressure in her back passage was not completely unwelcome, almost complimenting the much heavier dildo slowly riding in and out of her burning sex.

As he watched her slowly dawning acceptance, Alvarez felt himself once again hugely gratified and smiled broadly at her as he reached for the control pad.

"Time for a little more exercise," he said happily. "This time we'll use a special programme that will simulate a real hack through your charming English countryside – eh, what "

Cassie resolutely took up her posture again, and for the next hour she went through a myriad equestrian evolutions, as the wooden horse undulated its tireless way through the seemingly unending exercise programme.

"I'll take Marla as the lead mare for my team," decided the stocky Greek at last, indicating with a twitch of his whip that the athletic blonde should move over to his side of the courtyard.

The tall Brazilian nodded agreeably to his friend. "A good first choice, Theo. Marla's power will be advantageous in the climbs, but to counter that advantage I will choose Cassandra, as my main engine." He motioned the brunette to stand by his side.

The Greek beetled his dark eyebrows and pursed his lips in a mock show of disappointment. He had intended to match Marla and Cassandra together for his team, but was unsurprised at The Don's counter-balancing choice of the statuesque English girl.

"Very well my friend, then I will have Sandrine as my second, not as powerful as Marla, or Cassandra perhaps, but from what I have seen in the gymnasium, she is fast and should have plenty of stamina for the later stages."

Don Alvarez pointed at Tanya. It was almost a week since the Russian girl had returned from the mill and she seemed to have found a new delight in The Don's service. What she lacked in physical strength, he calculated, she would more than make up for in spirit. She skipped nimbly over to stand beside her teammate, Cassie.

All four girls were dressed similarly, in knee length laced up leather boots with pointed toes, ridged soles and high Cuban style stack heels. Each wore a simple but stoutly made leather harness comprising of a wide waist belt and neck collar connected by a pair of straps, which tightly encircled their bare breasts, passed over their shoulders and down through slots in the belt to delve deeply between their buttock cheeks, running back up through their vulval clefts, to be secured once again at the waist. The gladiator-like outfits were finished off by polished Roman style helmets, each adorned with a tall ostrich plume Cassie and Tanya now sported green and yellow for the House of Alvarez and Marla and Sandrine donned blue and white for the House of Mandrakos.

When they were ready, Alvarez and Mandrakos hitched their respective teams up to the super light titanium framed chariots standing nearby. Each pair of slaves took up their side-by-side positions against the crosstrees, whilst their Masters hooked up the traces to metal rings on their harnesses. Finally fitting leather covered bits between their teeth buckled to the cheek pieces of their helmets, lightweight reins were then lead back from the bit ends to allow easy steering from the narrow, half enclosed platforms, which the two charioteers now mounted.

"Walk on," barked The Don, slapping the reigns against his team's shoulders. Cassie and Tanya instantly bent forward, pushing against the bar, striding purposely out of the courtyard and on to the road leading off toward the airstrip.

On the platform behind, Alvarez sighed with pleasure, as he watched the pronounced muscular interplay of the girls' superb arses and upper thighs as they took up the strain. Once out of the courtyard he flicked the reigns again and the girls increased their speed to a fast trot.

Looking behind him The Don was treated to the equally splendid sight of the matched blondes Marla and Sandrine bouncing along closely behind, their heads thrown back and their tightly encircled breasts out thrust as they sought to match his speed.

Alvarez grinned hugely, savouring the exhilaration of being borne along in the sunshine by a brace of beautiful Amazons in his latest toy.

When he had first invited Theo to stay at the estate, he knew that he had to celebrate his good friend's visit with a special treat and the idea of a chariot race had come to him, whilst watching the epic movie Ben Hur one evening. It had been simplicity itself to have the state-of-the-art chariots made up to his own design by the light aircraft division of one of his fabrication companies on the outskirts of Sao Paulo. At the same time he had subtly altered the exercise regime in the harem to take account of his requirements so that each slave girl developed increased running speed and endurance.

They were running alongside the airstrip now and as they passed the airplane hangar several workers paused to stare open mouthed as the two silver chariots rolled quickly past, drawn by the semi-naked women, their brightly coloured helmet plumes waving coquettishly as they swept by.

Satisfied that both teams were warmed up and the chariots performing as intended, The Don plucked the long coach whip out of its scabbard and cracked the tasselled end between Cassie's and Tanya's heads. Immediately he felt the chariot surge forward as the two startled girls opened their stride and began to power away.

Behind, Alvarez could hear the insistent crack of Mandrakos' whip as he spurred on Marla and Sandrine to keep pace.

Cassie opened her mouth wide around the thin leather covered bit as she struggled to suck in more air to supply her rapidly pumping muscles.

They had left the airstrip far behind now, commencing the long shallow climb up one of the many service tracks that led into the rolling foothills to the west of the mansion.

It was incredibly hot as the tropical sun advanced toward its zenith and the perspiration had long since begun to spring in torrents from every pore of her straining body. The teaming sweat began to mix with the sunscreen Cassie had liberally protected herself with at the start. The mixture quickly covered her skin in an oily slick that ran down her back and belly and into her silky pubes and buttock crease.

Whether or not it was a deliberate part of Don Alvarez' design, the thick leather harness rubbed against her delicate flesh at every step, mashing her clitoris and working the base of the butt plug, which he had insisted she wear ever since her first session on the rocking horse.

Cassie began to grunt helplessly as the building sensations in her belly began to presage a long series of low-level orgasms. Beside her, Tanya's ragged panting betrayed that the slim Russian was beginning to suffer similar tortures, and Cassie winced in sympathy as she recalled the other girl's extraordinarily large clitoris and labia, all of which must be being rubbed raw by the coarse harness.

As they rattled past the tall neatly laid out rubber trees that Don Alvarez cultivated on this part of the plantation, Cassie thanked God that she had put her heart and soul into her gym work in the time she had been at the plantation, otherwise she knew she would have been on her knees by now.

Beside her, she could hear Tanya panting deeply, as the smaller girl strove to keep up the effort of hauling the chariot. When they had first started off, Cassie had been surprised by the contraption's apparent lightness, but as the run went on the chariot seemed to increase its dragging resistance minute-by-minute, necessitating ever more frequent cracks of Don Alvarez' whip behind their ears. As their ability to respond began to fade, the implacable Don began to play the stinging tip across their naked shoulders and buttock cheeks with increasing regularity, wringing ever more effort from their burning muscles.

After what seemed like an age of pounding along the service tracks, Don Alvarez steered them off into a small clearing where Alphonso awaited them. The redoubtable major-domo had come ahead in a Land Rover and had already set up a picnic table, complete with a large parasol for the two masters.

Alvarez brought his chariot to a shuddering halt allowing Cassie and Tanya to immediately sink to their knees in a state of near exhaustion, their heads bowed to the ground as they gasped desperately for breath in the hot and humid air. Drawing up beside them Marla and Sandrine collapsed in a similar state, as the oblivious Don and his friend stepped down from their chariots laughing with delight at the exhilarating ride up to the picnic site.

"That was absolutely fantastic," enthused the brawny Greek, repeatedly clapping the beaming Alvarez on the shoulder with his bear-like paw. "My friend, I swear, you have a flair for the dramatic that is quite unparalleled, never have I had so much fun, never!"

Alvarez nodded ecstatically, as he flopped into one of the recliners Alphonso had set up and gratefully accepted a flute of chilled Dom Perignon '66 from the major domo.

"The ride up here certainly exceeded all of my expectations," agreed The Don, quaffing his champagne as he swept his eyes across the crumpled, steaming figures of the panting slave girls. "My God! these four bitches certainly looked delicious harnessed up like that, hauling their fancy asses for all they were worth."

Indicating the women with his empty champagne flute, The Don instructed Alphonso to release their mouth bits and give each a half a pint of water and an energy bar. "Just enough to fuel them for the run home," he explained to his companion, "no sense in giving them colic."

For the next thirty minutes the two friends feasted on smoked salmon and a crisp salad, followed by some ultra light honeyed crepes cooked on a portable burner by the multi-talented butler. After they had finished their lunch, Alphonso cleared up the dishes and departed in the Land Rover, leaving the Masters and their slave girls in privacy.

Don Alvarez smiled at his friend as if an idea had just occurred to him. "How would you like to take part in a little competition " he asked.

Mandrakos sat up in his chair, instantly galvanised by the tall Brazilian, who had proved his uncanny ability on numerous occasions over the past two weeks to bring all manner of fun out of the simplest situations.

"What do you have in mind, Ramon "

Clapping his hands to gain the now dozing girls' attention, he crooked his index finger. "Come here my pretties, quickly now, form up here, front and centre." The two slavers roved their lascivious gaze over the four superb creatures as they climbed wearily to their feet and pulled the empty chariots over the grass to stand to attention before their masters.

"A simple competition in two parts," Alvarez announced. "We are about three miles from home and it's pretty much all downhill from here - the first team home wins."

"And the finishing line is where " asked Mandrakos.

The Don grinned, "Alphonso already has instructions to stretch out a tape between the water tower and the wind sock mast at the far end of the airstrip, that's where we will finish."

"You said a competition in two parts," reminded Mandrakos.

The Don nodded, smiling broadly. "Before either team can set off, all team members must achieve a full sexual climax, driver as well as mares."

Mandrakos grinned lasciviously at the prospect. "Ramon, you are inspired. But perhaps we should build in a little incentive to make sure that the mares give it their all, eh "

"What did you have in mind "

Mandrakos considered for a moment. "The winning mares dine at table with us in high style this evening and are excused all domestic drudgery for three days," he said expansively, and then injecting a harder tone into his voice, "however, the loosing mares go to the Mill for three days."

"And what shall be our incentive " inquired The Don.

"A cash wager," suggested Mandrakos, "say fifty thousand dollars to the winner."

Alvarez watched the four women's faces intently after Mandrakos had finished speaking. Each girl glanced nervously at the others, feet shifting fretfully, their faces betraying the tangle of emotions the wager had suddenly aroused in them.

None of the four wanted to be the cause of any of the others going to the dreaded mill, but each instantly realised that to give the slightest quarter, the slightest diminution of effort, might well mean going to the great wheel herself.

As the tall Brazilian got up from his chair, four pairs of bright, apprehensive eyes watched his every move.

"I'll take the wager, but at a quarter of a million dollars," he responded, enjoying the momentary flicker of doubt that flashed across his friend's upturned face. Mandrakos quickly swept his eyes over Marla and Sandrine, his businessman's mind calculating the many variables involved in bringing each women to orgasm, not to mention himself, and then the long dash home - three miles.

Suddenly, he burst out into a smile, once again his intriguing host had raised the stakes to an almost narcotic level of excitement. "A quarter of a million dollars it is. How do we proceed " he asked, jumping up, instantly hungry to start on the two suddenly skittish blondes.

Alvarez pointed to a low, spreading tree a short distance away. "You take your team over yonder, start as soon as you get there. I'll wait here until you are ready before I begin."

Alvarez waited patiently whilst Mandrakos led his team over to the tree before turning to consider Cassie and Tanya. He knew that both girls would be terrified at the prospect of returning to the mill, each having recently been a guest of that old bugger Rufio and his miserable mules. He decided to put aside any thoughts of coercion, instead choosing to rely upon the women's individual sense of self-preservation.

"Listen carefully," he said, pulling them gently down by the bridle to sit on their heels. His voice adopted a deep, soft tone, as his fingers quickly began to unfasten the crotch straps running between the thighs, which each girl now quickly spread for his convenience.

"Master Theo will most probably attempt to rush Marla and Sandrine into orgasm, but that will only make them tense and delay their ability to achieve their climaxes. We will proceed more sedately and, as the tale of the hare and the tortoise, arrive at our destination more quickly."

He slipped his fingers into Tanya's sex first, banking on the Russian girl's inveterate love of masturbation and hugely sensitive clitoris to provide them with their first orgasm. Her sex was already soaking wet from the run up to the picnic site and the heady mixture of fear and The Don's fingers stretching and rubbing her stalk soon had her at full erection and the juice streaming hotly into his palm.

After only a few minutes, Tanya began to groan and thrust her crotch out in time to his swirling fingers. She lifted one of her pert breasts and pointed the two inch long crimson teat at The Don's mouth.

"Bite on it Master," she hissed desperately, as a fresh spasm rippled through her vagina, the tight chasm sucking hungrily at the four fingers he had crammed into her heat, whilst he worked the pad of his thumb rhythmically over her stone hard clitoris.

Alvarez dipped his head and swallowed the hot flesh deep into his mouth, drawing on the long stalk with all of the suction he could muster, pulling the whole breast out into a taught cone before closing his sharp teeth on to the succulent flesh as she had begged. Instantly, Tanya threw her head back and wailed out loud, her climax surging through her cunt like a dam bursting, the relief at delivering her orgasm making her sob. Alvarez continued only long enough to be sure that she had passed the point of no return and then withdrew his hand from her sopping vulva, ignoring her automatic cry of disappointment as he did so.

Quickly, he unhooked Tanya from the traces and removed her bridle, pulling her under the crossbar and opening his fly so that the still spasming Russian could take his iron hard cock into her eager mouth. Then he slipped his tongue into Cassie's mouth, mashing her lips and sucking on her tongue, drinking in her sweet saliva - plundering her full lips, as he knew she loved him to do.

At the same time he sought out her much more delicate stamen with his fingers. He quickly found the proud bud, which had risen to erection whilst she had watched Tanya give herself up so brazenly. Alvarez deftly masturbated Cassie for several minutes, succeeding in getting the tall brunette to writhe and pump her haunches in time to his ministrations, but such was her level of nervousness that she could not attain the final release. In desperation he reached around her hip and slipped his finger through the soft rubber ring at the base of her butt-plug, gently, but firmly he pumped the plug in and out over the second and third flanges, making her toss her head back and grunt loudly, as the invasive sensations consumed her flaming bowels.

Finally, his own climax exploded up his pulsating shaft, as Tanya clenched her tiny fingers around his balls and milked the scalding jets of semen from him. The Russian holding his massively swollen glans between her tightly pursed lips, flogging the sensitive underside with the tip of her sharp tongue and finally gulping down the thick jism as it jetted into the back of her throat.

The Don felt himself swooning as the tiny Russian's avid mouth sucked the last drops of seed from him, her head bobbing back and forth panting harshly through her nose, still rolling his balls together in her palm, determined to leave not a drop of the precious fluid behind.

At the last moment, Cassie gave up her orgasm, shouting harshly out loud, her face contorted in agony, the white hot sensations, more pain than pleasure, wracked through the length of her vagina, twisting her belly into a tight knot, as the hard won detonations rolled through her in a ragged broadside.

Don Alvarez allowed Cassie to fall twitching to the ground and staggered unsteadily to his feet, disengaging the persistent Tanya from his drained, flaccid shaft as he did so, hurriedly pushing her back into the traces and refastening her bridle.

He cursed under his breath as he tried vainly to pull Cassie to her feet, but the brunette's pleasure wracked body still vibrated with the orgasm that he had forced from her.

Glancing across to the other team Alvarez grinned, as he saw that Mandrakos had resorted to flogging the French girl's buttocks, as Marla simultaneously buried her face in Sandrine's crotch. Apparently, Theo was having the same problem that he had had with Cassie, but the Greek had adopted a radically different resolution.

Eventually, Cassie was able to stagger drunkenly to her feet and Alvarez struggled desperately to refit her bridle. The Brazilian looked across again at the other team and saw that Theo had lifted Sandrine by the hips and was now plunging his huge, curved cock into her like a man possessed, as the blonde gripped her legs about his waist with Marla now suckling determinedly at the French girl's coral buds.

As The Don clambered somewhat shakily into the chariot he heard Sandrine begin to shriek out her orgasm and glancing across at the other team as he slewed his team around, he spied Theo, his darkly bearded face contorted into an animalistic mask as he pumped his seed into the svelte blonde, both of them clinging together hips bucking madly as their orgasms clashed with simultaneous violence.

Alvarez laughed triumphantly at the sight of Marla vainly trying to separate the two dazed copulants. The tall American girl literally jumping up and down gesticulating urgently at The Don's rapidly disappearing chariot as he headed out of the clearing.

Alvarez was more than a hundred and fifty yards down the track when he next looked back to see the other chariot come thundering out of the clearing. Marla and Sandrine had their heads and shoulders bent steeply forward into the crossbar their legs cycling madly and kicking up dust, as the harried pair strove to catch up.

The excitable Greek's long black whip cracked insistently about the blonde pair's unfortunate shoulders and buttocks, spurring them madly onward.

Alvarez snapped his whip in the air above Cassie and Tanya, calling for them to lengthen their stride as they commenced the long run downhill. With three miles to go Alvarez was loath to lay the whip directly on to their flesh at this early stage, knowing that the livening effect of the leather would quickly fade if it were used too soon and over too great a distance. Better to allow the inexperienced Theo to flog his team into exhaustion in the early stages and then when the time was right, Alvarez would simply use the power of his whip arm to force the fresher Cassie and Tanya through in the final half mile.

For her part, Cassie was simply thankful that Don Alvarez was apparently content to simply crack the whip in the air above them and call out instructions as they galloped downhill.

On the final part of the ascent to the picnic site he had played the thin stinging tip of the whip across their shoulders and buttocks with a mastery that had had both girls high stepping long after exhaustion had set in, each female finding hidden reserves of stamina that only the insidious pain of the whip could discover.

As they ran, Cassie and Tanya once again began to suffer' from the movement of the thick body harness straps sawing back and forth in their crotches. Once again, rivulets of perspiration sprang from their steaming hides and gravitated into their nether clefts to mix with the left over sexual juices, forming a foaming effluvium that lubricated the coarse leather as it scoured mercilessly over their turgescent clitorises and dripped from them in thick white clots as they pumped their powerful thighs up and down.

After a mile, or so, Alvarez twitched the reins to the left, guiding Cassie and Tanya over slightly so that Theo could bring his team through on the outside, deliberately surrendering the lead so that the Greek could carry on setting an impossible pace.

As Marla and Sandrine drew level, Alvarez noted the strain etched on their faces. Their eyeballs protruded and their mouths gaped as they sucked in great lung-fulls of air, their sweat soaked skins bearing a myriad scarlet wheals where the whip had bitten into their hard driven flesh.

With a triumphant shout and a wave of goodbye, Theo rumbled past, the thin alloy wheels of his chariot throwing up a dusty haze in the mid afternoon sunshine. Alvarez allowed him to stretch his lead to a bare ten yards before he cracked his whip and picked up the pace, pressurising his friend so that he could not rest his already tiring team even for an instant.

Mandrakos had been forced to drive his team hard from the start to make up for the lead Alvarez had stolen out of the clearing, whereas The Don's team had been able to reserve more of their energy for the final run downhill past the airstrip to the finishing tape.

As the airstrip came in sight at the bottom of the hill, Alvarez cracked his whip insistently several times high in the air, ostensibly to spur Cassie and Tanya on, but in reality to panic Theo into making his dash for the line now less than a mile distant.

As Alvarez had expected, as soon as his Greek friend heard the crack of his whip he immediately began to lay into Marla and Sandrine, calling for them to stride out for the line. Squealing desperately around the leather covered bits, the two blonde girls burst forward, breasts flogging madly as they vainly tried to outrun the flickering tongue of the whip scorching across their shoulders and buttocks.

But their final effort was doomed to be short lived. As their by now non-existent energy reserves petered out completely, their strides became foreshortened and disjointed and no amount of flogging from Mandrakos' huge arm could rekindle their flagging efforts.

Sensing that the time was right to make his move, Alvarez brought the tip of his whip down in a flurry of stinging strikes across both girls' haunches. The sudden pain catapulted them forward to draw level as both chariots began to race along the edge of the airstrip heading for the finish.

As the two teams whirred past the aircraft hangar all of the maintenance staff came out to applaud and yell their approval, as Don Alvarez' team easily passed the frustrated Greek's exhausted blondes and powered into the lead to cross the tape several chariot lengths in front.

As soon as Alvarez brought them to a halt, Cassie and Tanya crumpled to their knees, heads hanging down between their arms as they gasped for breath in the humid air. Behind them, the utterly exhausted Marla and Sandrine staggered drunkenly over the line and collapsed heavily on top of one another in a tangle of shaking limbs. Both girls simultaneously retched and sobbed with both the pains of exhaustion and the merciless whipping Mandrakos had subjected them to over the final half mile.

Don Alvarez jumped down and ran immediately to the hunched, steaming figure of Cassie and reached underneath her heaving belly to slip loose her crotch straps before unzipping his trousers and thrusting his hugely erect cock deep into the depths of her incandescent vagina. The molten fluids she had been producing since the start of the run dripped freely from her puffed and distended labia, running over the tight knot of his balls as he pumped himself vigorously in and out of the gasping girl.

Not to be out done yet again, the bear like Mandrakos turned away from his own shattered team his lips twisted in disgust at their failure, and falling in behind Tanya he began to batter her equally heated sex with his fierce erection, driving the exhausted Russian's body into the rich, dark sod with the force of his frustration.

The next morning Cassie was curtly informed by a somewhat sour faced and pensive looking Alphonso that she would be taking a flight with His Excellency down to the state capitol.

And so it was with not a little excitement that she hurried to her room to collect a few essential items, which she popped into a small Italian handbag. Then she donned a short white sport dress and went to sit in one of the two huge carved chairs that flanked His Excellency's study door as she had been instructed.

Cassie's mind felt numb as she considered the import of the major-domo's message. She was being taken back to the city, back to civilisation. This was something she could not have anticipated even in her wildest dreams. Naturally enough, her thoughts quickly turned to the opportunity for escape, something that she had, over recent weeks, put out of her mind. Not only because of the dreadful punishment she had suffered after her last bid for freedom, but also because of the manifest impossibility of trekking hundreds of miles through the unknown depths of the rainforest back to the coast.

Strangely, Cassie found herself unable to even begin to frame any ideas for effecting an escape. Each time she tried to imagine how she might slip away, the mental image of Don Alvarez' face flooded into her mind and she felt a frisson of disquiet as she considered breaking her strange bond with the devilishly handsome Brazilian.

Presently, Don Alvarez opened the heavy teak door and beckoned her inside. As she entered, her eyes involuntarily settled upon the huge ebony rocking horse now standing silent and immobile in the large bay. The sight of the strange machine made her stomach flip as she recalled the long and not entirely unpleasant hours she had spent riding it over recent days. Following her glance Alvarez let out a short bark of laughter.

"I'm afraid there will be no horse riding this morning Cassandra," he said. "In a short while we will be going over to the airstrip to fly Master Theo down to the city airport in readiness for his transfer to a commercial flight to Europe."

As he spoke, he took her by the hand and led her to a small, well-stuffed sofa. "But first," he said, parting her thighs with his hands as she sat, "I want you to wear this." He held out his palm to show her a smooth silver tube about four inches long and an inch in diameter, a thin wire issued from one end and was connected to a small plastic box the size of a cigarette carton.

"What is it " Cassie asked nervously, remembering at the last moment to add: "Your Excellency."

"It's a simple and safe device that will allow me to stimulate you during our journey." As he spoke his fingers deftly affixed the slim plastic box midway up her inner thigh with a broad Velcro strap and then he began to stroke the smooth end of the tube against her moist labia, slowly working the tube into her vagina as her now sexualised flesh relaxed after only the briefest contact with his fingers.

As the tube disappeared from sight, Cassie strained her legs apart so that The Don could thrust his index and middle fingers deeply into her tunnel, pushing the device up to rest against the sensitive cervix. Satisfied that he had the location correct, Don Alvarez handed Cassie a pair of white cotton panties and bade her put them on, which she did with a little difficulty, as they were far too small. The leg seams cut into the tops of her thighs and the narrow gusset immediately sank deeply into the heated gash of her pubis.

"That should stop any slippage as you become succulent," he opined with a boyish grin that made Cassie's heart miss a beat.

Cassie stood up gingerly, her hands quivering as she smoothed down the tight material of the dress over her flaring hips. She now had two objects lodged inside her: The omnipresent rubber butt plug, as well as the vibrator. Their combined weight made her bowels feel heavy and yet strangely pleasant, as she flexed her various internal muscles in a vain attempt to settle the unfamiliar sensations suddenly beginning to thresh like a nest of serpents deep within her belly.

The Don reached into the pocket of his slacks and pulled out a slim plastic box. Recognising it as the control unit for the vibrator, Cassie held her breath in dreadful anticipation. Her mind travelled back in time to the similar but far more brutal treatment meted out by the dreadful commandant of police, as The Don's thumb pressed down on the first button.

Instantly, Cassie felt the silver tube begin to energise, though minutely at first, as the tiny vibrations sprang into existence almost on the other side of her senses and then became steadily more insistent.

The Don adjusted the control, ramping up the power until Cassie was forced to clamp her knees together against the keening vibrations suddenly threatening to turn her insides to mush and making her feel as if she was about to urinate where she stood.

Cassie stared at the Brazilian with something akin to panic showing in her wide, green eyes. Her white teeth bit down on her bottom lip as she fought to control the internal seething threatening to overwhelm her momentarily.

Once more, Don Alvarez increased the gain, this time adding an electrical pulse into the routine. In actual fact the voltages concerned were very small, but within the ultra sensitive folds of Cassie's liquefied vagina the shocks felt intense.

The Don stood immobile, his dark eyes glittering and the muscle in his cheek twitching as Cassie slowly bent over double, one hand clutching the sofa arm for support and the other pressed hard into her fluttering pudendum. The English girl's mouth fell open as she expelled a voluble series of groans at the incredible riot of sensations knotting up her belly.

Satisfied that the device was fitted and working as intended, Don Alvarez reduced the power to a tick-over' setting, which allowed Cassie to slowly unbend as the tension gradually leeched out of her aching stomach muscles. Trying her utmost to recover her composure in front of the suave Don, she was once again shocked to feel raw sexual heat coursing through her body. Already, the gusset of the knickers she wore had become sodden with juice where it cut in between her engorged labia.

As always, Don Alvarez' smile was knowing as he took hold of one of Cassie's massively tumescent nipples through the bodice of her dress, pinching the hard stalk until, helpless to hide her sudden concupiscence, Cassie arched her spine forcing the hard globe onto his hand. The Brazilian's smile hardened, as he suddenly walloped his hand back and forth across her bloated breasts half a dozen times, wringing gasps of pleasure from her as she swayed with the force of the blows.

Not for the first time Alvarez had to force himself to disengage from this captivating and irresistible woman. It seemed that whatever new variance he introduced her to, the gorgeous brunette rose to the challenge and never failed to derive some measure sexual pleasure from the episode.

Stone faced, so as to hide his immense satisfaction and ignoring her gasp of disappointment, The Don turned on his heel and strode from the room, barking a sharp command for her to follow.

Cassie sat in the rear of the twin engined Cessna alongside the lachrymose Alphonso, whilst Don Alvarez and Mandrakos flew the plane toward the distant coast.

Within her sex, the insidious vibrations and electrical impulses rose and fell as the whimsical Don periodically adjusted the remote on his lap, varying the intensity and frequency, forcing the girl to cross and uncross her legs and squirm in her seat hour after hour until the soft hide beneath her rump was sodden with the slick juices that had long since soaked through the seat of her dress.

By the time the plane touched down four hours later, the heavy bumping of the undercarriage on the tarmac was all that was required to bring a sweat stained woman to a very intense and very public orgasm. Cassie groaned helplessly out loud, her teeth buried into the back of her hand, the long climax rolling over her in gut wrenching waves that made her sob at the intensity of the release.

As she continued to shake and yelp, the implacable Don still found the time to ratchet up the power of the vibrator as he guided the plane along the taxiway, determined to wring every last ounce of sensation from her well-stoked core.

Once the engines had stopped the two grinning pilots clambered out on to the tarmac followed by Alphonso. The latter gave Cassie a long and shamelessly hungry look as he disembarked.

Having been acutely aware of what she had had to endure through-out the long flight and conscious of her fecund thigh squirming against his in the confined space in the rear of the cockpit, the major-domo had had his own work cut out not to allow his intense proximity to the over-heated bitch to tempt him to transgress his Master's inflexible rule about frater-nising with the house girls.

Outside the plane, Alphonso busied himself transferring Master Theo's many suitcases on to a luggage cart, thankful for the cooling ef-fect of the late afternoon breeze and that the Master's attention was else-where than on the dark stain in the front of his trousers where, ten thousand feet above the rain forest he had silently ejaculated into his pants, his hand inside his trouser pocket lining milking his turgid glans be-tween forefinger and thumb as the fabulous English whore had inces-santly twitched and whimpered in torment beside him.

Once the luggage was unloaded, Don Alvarez opened the door be-side Cassie and helped her to the ground, where she, like the butler a few minutes earlier, blessed the cool breeze as it played over her body, quickly evaporating the sheen of sweat that lay on her neck and breasts and coated her shapely legs.

His farewells said, Mandrakos shook hands finally with Don Alvarez and startled Cassie by taking hold of her arms and pushing her back over the Cessna's wing root, covered her mouth with his in a deeply invasive French kiss.

Cassie was still in a state of lingering arousal and her mouth fell open the moment his lips touched hers, allowing his insistent tongue to plumb her mouth. At the same time, his bear like paw swept up beneath the short hem of her dress and cupped her mound his three longest fingers dragging out the saturated panty gusset before stabbing easily into her moist cunt and quickly triggering another powerful orgasm as he worked his fingers rapidly to and fro.

Despite their relatively public situation on the light aircraft apron, Cassie was powerless to stop herself spreading and raising her legs up on to the wing as the climax wracked her body. Pulling his fingers out of the clutching well of her sex Mandrakos held his fingers up to her face and the still gasping brunette obediently licked her own glutinous fluids from his fingers, taking care to suck each thick digit deeply into her mouth as she did so.

Satisfied finally, Mandrakos nodded to the Negroid baggage handler who had stood by goggle-eyed and speechless throughout, whilst this obviously wealthy and important personage had ravished the gorgeous white whore. What a story he would have to tell his mates when he got back to the loading ramp. But even as he thought about it he knew that they would never believe a word of it.

Nodding obsequiously to Mandrakos, the handler waited until the Greek was safely seated and then stepped on to the driving platform. The baggage handler set off toward the international terminal, looking backward more than once at the tall beauty who now stood beside the handsome aristocrat, busily running a brush through the rich, dark hair that fell all the way to the middle of her back.

By the time Cassie had finished making herself presentable, Alphonso was drawing up beside the plane behind the wheel of the black Cadillac Seville The Don kept in the hangar, whilst he was up country and where the Cessna would now be taken for service and valeting. Cassie cringed with embarrassment as she wondered what the valeting staff would make of the soaking wet patch she had left on the aircraft seat.

Don Alvarez waited patiently in the breeze, his hand absentmindedly caressing Cassie's buttocks through the thin dress whilst the major-domo loaded the suitcases. Eventually, the servant stood stiffly to attention and held open the door for his employer and attendant slave girl.

Once inside and with the chauffeur's partition sealed, Cassie was again alone with the mercurial Brazilian. Secure within the sound proofed and armour plated cocoon of the opulent limousine, as its V8 engine swept them rapidly past the sprawling clutter of airport buildings and out on to the highway.

Cassie suddenly realised with something akin to shock that she cherished these moments alone with Ramon', as she privately liked to call him. There was definitely something special about the way he treated her. It was strange she thought, as she struggled to overlay some sort of sense onto the whirling maelstrom of her feelings. Yes, there was an insouciant cruelness about him. An almost clinical, semi-detached attitude, but no matter what he did to her, she always knew that he was in control of himself and therefore of her and this gave her a inexplicable sense of security, even when she was straining in the most excruciating bondage and he was lacing into her with the whip.

And always the moments of equally excruciating tenderness at the end, when she had worked so hard to please him and he rewarded her with his mouth and his hands and, she thought flushing hotly, his cock.

God! how she wanted it now, here in the car. Cassie glanced sidelong at him. The Don was reading a newspaper, heaven knows where Alphonso had found it the super efficient butler probably had one delivered to the car every day on the off chance The Don might fly in.

Cassie settled back into the deep cushions and allowed her eyes to close against the late afternoon sunshine burning dimly through the heavy tints. She had been strung out' and agitated by the gyrations of the vibrator throughout the long flight and tiredness was now settling heavily upon her, even as the silver gadget still hummed happily away inside her on its minimum setting keeping her need gently simmering and the crotch of her panties soaked with warm sexual flux.

Cassie awoke with a start. Fighting off the fog of sleep she realised that Ramon was speaking to her. Quickly, she uncoiled her legs and sat upright. She had fallen asleep against his shoulder and from the mushy feel of her cheek he had allowed her to remain there while she slumbered.

"I'm sorry, I was asleep, what did you say, Master " Cassie asked, instantly wondering why she had used that term. She usually called him Your Excellency' somehow it had always sounded less servile to her western ears. She saw that Alphonso had stopped the car and was getting out to open the rear door next to her.

Don Alvarez held out a fifty-dollar bill.

"I said, would you be kind enough to buy me a copy of Time' " he repeated, his voice caught in his throat slightly, as his eyes feasted upon her heart stopping beauty her softly vulnerable expression was a heady mixture of just having awoken and confusion as she tried to gather her slumbering thoughts.

Cassie looked out beyond the door held open for her by the major-domo come chauffer. They had entered the city whilst she slept and were now in a densely populated and somewhat seedy area of the down town district. Don Alvarez indicated a newspaper stand some twenty, or thirty yards distant along the pavement as he pressed the crisp, unused bill into her hand.

"As you wish, Master." Again she used the term of total subservience rather than his title without quite knowing why, except that when she thought about it later, she would realise that it simply felt more comfortable and somehow right.

Cassie got out of the car and walked toward the newsstand, conscious of the many male eyes turned toward her, following her, as she slotted through the early evening crowd. Within her superheated sex, the vibrator increased its delicious background purring to the point where she could only just maintain her bearing without any outward affectation.

As she arrived at the counter, several male customers moved aside for her, each cloaking her with frank stares of approval. Cassie tossed a quick look over her shoulder through the bustling crowd to the car, where Alphonso stood waiting patiently by the still open door, his attention fixed upon two teenage whores arguing with their pimp on the opposite side of the street. Cassie thought she saw a slight movement within the car's darkened interior where The Don waited. She turned back to the counter her eyes roaming over the neatly laid out titles.

The fat old man behind the counter spoke whilst staring fixedly and with brutal frankness at the rounds of her tightly constrained breasts with their visibly erect nipples.

"Yes, Signora, what would you like "

Cassie's mouth went suddenly dry. She felt herself pressed to the counter by the men who had made way for her, but who now had moved in close. She could feel their eyes roving over her body and was suddenly shamefully aware that the seat of her dress was clinging wetly to her rump.

In something akin to panic she looked around her. She had fifty U.S. dollars in her hand. If she ran away now she would soon be lost amongst the crowds. She could hail a taxi and be almost anywhere within a few short minutes her apartment, the BRAZCO offices, the British Embassy perhaps. Her capture and torment would finally be over and swift and terrible retribution brought down upon all those who had conspired in her kidnapping.

Cassie was shocked out of this thought pattern by a hand sliding up the back of her thigh and coming to rest on her buttock, the hard fingers kneading her flesh through the thin, wet material of her panties.

Galvanised by the unseen stranger's lewd touch, she swiftly snatched up a copy of Time' and dropped the fifty-dollar bill on to the counter. In the same movement, she turned and swatted a second hand from her breast with the magazine before plunging back into the crowd, ignoring the obscene comments of the men behind her as she strode quickly back to the car, all thoughts of flight gone from her mind as she desperately sought the air conditioned sanctuary of Don Alvarez' limousine.

As she approached the open door, the vibrator lodged deep within her cunt began to keen with increasing urgency, its pitch increasing at every step. The complementary electrical shocks suddenly flashed through the delicate inner folds of her sex, making her crush the glossy magazine to her aching breasts with her crossed arms as she staggered gasping the last few paces and virtually fell into the cool, welcoming interior of the car.

She was barely aware of the solid clunk of the door closing and the sudden surge of power as the mighty V8 swept the heavy vehicle back out into the stream of evening rush hour traffic.

As soon as the car was in motion Don Alvarez ramped the vibrator up to full power, twisting Cassie up into a tight ball as if she had been punched in the solar plexus. Her hands clawed talon-like at her spasming crotch and her breath rasped sharply through her clenched teeth.

The Don took hold of Cassie's wrists and forced her arms behind her behind her, buckling them together with a pair of broad leather cuffs just above the elbows so that her shoulders were forced backward and her breasts out-thrust. Then he pushed her back into the corner of the seat and dragged her legs apart, jamming her left thigh wide open with his right knee and tucking her right thigh behind his left hip so that he sat between her legs with her crotch wide open to him.

Unable to either touch her sex, or clamp her legs together against the fierce internal sensations, Cassie could only wail out loud her head thrown back, as the towering vibrations smashed through her loins, the searing electrical impulses flashing through her nerve endings to bring her clitoris and nipples to a mind shattering state of hardness.

The Don kept her like that for long minutes, his fingers kneading and pulling at her rock hard teats, savouring the play of desperate emotions sweeping over her sweating face, as she fought to deal with the intense pain/pleasure/pain/pleasure sensations he doled out to her.

Only when it was clear to him that Cassie could bear no more and was on the verge of fainting, did he cut the insidious flow of power to the vibrator. But allowing her no time for respite, he stretched her across the seat and tore her now totally sodden panties down, wrenching the narrow gusset from deep between her swollen labia with a roughness that brought a grunt of gratitude from her slack mouth.

He dragged her along the wide seat, positioned her shaking legs over his shoulders and supported her lavish buttocks in his palms so that he could study her gaping vulva. The outer and inner labia were massively tumescent and her rapidly flooding juices were flowing thickly out before his eyes to further soak the already saturated dark brown pubic pelt before running down into her anal cleft.

With a groan of heartfelt appreciation Don Alvarez plunged his mouth into the glutinous goblet of her soaking maw, his lips and tongue avidly gathering up the copious pool of nectar from her hypersensitive tissues. His strong hands slipped round to hold her hips steady, as she bucked and writhed against the intolerable stimulation as his tongue flogged at her proud standing clitoris. Sending the brunette into her third orgasm of the hour, her long, ululating scream of release piercing his ears for long seconds as her body was racked from stem to stern' within the dim, sound-proofed interior of the speeding car.

Don Alvarez held her like that for many moments, as she slowly subsided into a deep, post climactic torpidity. His tongue was languorous as it laved gently at the hot, distended folds of her crushed sex, exploring every nook and hollow, drinking in the final spurts of her love juices, as they continued to issue from her exhausted vulva. Only when he was sure that Cassie had nothing left for him did he close his perfect white incisors down onto the protruding wire of the vibrator, tugging the tiny torpedo from her still erratically spasming vagina, the clutching muscles reluctantly surrendering their prize with a warm, viscid slurp.

Closing his eyes, the enraptured Brazilian fastidiously licked the hot, clotted effluvium from the tiny, silver tube, slowly savouring the thickest and most delicious secretions from her deepest recess.

Finally, he unbuckled her elbow cuffs and allowed the exhausted creature to subside back into the plush leather and that was where she remained, drifting in a warm, limpid sea of complete sexual satisfaction.

The shattered girl stirring from her pleasure induced slumber only when the limousine eventually pulled into the courtyard of Don Alvarez' palatial town house.

Cassie followed Don Alvarez into a truly imposing Italian interior, complete with huge expanses of marble flooring and vaulting pillars, which soared up through three suspended landings to support a complex series of roof lights.

Following them inside, Alphonso quickly disappeared into a nineteenth century type elevator with The Don's luggage. Cassie stood patiently looking around at the opulent fittings and various art works whilst The Don sorted through a small stack of mail on a hall table.

Cassie was suddenly surprised by the appearance of a young man coming down the stairs toward her. He was in his early twenties and extremely good looking in a languid, slender sort of way. His blonde hair hung in a ponytail and he moved, she thought, with a fluid, almost feminine grace. He was dressed in a pair of the closest fitting white, spandex pants she had ever seen outside of the Royal Ballet the style and cut clearly designed to accentuate his hugely bulging genitals, which were clearly discernable in full detail through the skin tight fabric.

The young man returned Cassie's scrutiny with equal frankness. His bright, blue eyes wandered over every inch of her by now somewhat dishevelled appearance, pausing pointedly to linger upon her heavy breasts, as she somewhat self-consciously smoothed her soiled dress down over her wide hips. The newcomer's lips twitched in what she took to be amusement at her obvious discomfort.

However, the smile was immediately wiped from his face as Don Alvarez finished sorting through his mail to be replaced by a look of respectful attention.

"Good evening, Pierre," said The Don with his customary punctiliousness. "Where is my sister "

"Madame is resting before dinner, but asked if you would go up as soon as you arrived, Excellency," replied Pierre. His softly accented English reminding Cassie of the wonderful season she had spent working in Paris five summers ago at the start of her university gap-year.

"Very well," said The Don mounting the stairs, "kindly show Cassandra to one of the guest rooms on your floor and then bring some champagne to Madame's rooms."

"Immediately, Excellency," replied Pierre, who then waited deferentially for Don Alvarez to attain the first floor landing before motioning Cassie to follow him upstairs, his expression once more becoming one of interested amusement.

Cassie followed Pierre along several passageways to what seemed to be the rear of the house, although the outrageous opulence of the place hardly varied in what she presumed to be the servant's quarters, for that was obviously what Pierre was, if not a sex-slave like herself, judging from his provocative dress.

"This is the room where I sleep," said Pierre gesturing lazily to a door as they past "and this will be yours," he told her, opening the next door they came to, politely standing aside for her to pass by.

When she entered Cassie was not surprised to see that the room was extremely spacious and at least as well appointed as her room at the Fazenda. She turned suddenly and with not a little alarm when Pierre also entered and closed the door behind him. Once again his eyes roved over her body in a frank appraisal, the bulge in his pants visibly thickening as his manhood began to react to her obvious fecundity.

"He fucked you in the Limo' didn't he " he said with a lascivious, although not altogether unattractive leer.

"That's none of your business," replied Cassie hotly, putting more outrage into her tone than she really felt. She was becoming inured to embarrassment in sexual matters, so much so that things that would have incensed her only weeks ago now seemed almost banal.

Pierre held up his hands palms outward in a mock gesture of surrender, his smile broadening, "no need to get frosty. Besides," he shrugged, "it's obvious what you've been up to, you stink like a Breton trawler - I could smell you from the top of the stairs."

Cassie groaned somewhat theatrically, "you would stink too, if you had been through what I have today," pushing her fingers through her dishevelled hair.

Pierre pointed to a door. "The bathroom is through there, I'm sure you'll find everything you need, and in here," he said, throwing open the closet, "is what you should wear tonight for dinner."

"How do you know " she asked, pulling out the skimpy garments and examining the impressive succession of designer labels.

"I know because he had them delivered for you this afternoon," replied Pierre simply.

"What time do we sit down to eat " asked Cassie looking longingly toward the bathroom door. "I need a long, hot shower."

"We don't sit down at all," laughed Pierre shortly, "WE aren't having dinner, we ARE dinner, or at least," he allowed, "the final course," and then changing the subject, "would you like me to scrub your back "

"You had better take them their Champagne, or it will be him scrubbing your back and not with a sponge," Cassie returned tartly, enjoying Pierre's sudden look of panic as he belatedly remembered The Don's order.

"Eight o'clock sharp in the dining room, don't be late," Pierre quipped over his shoulder as the door clicked shut behind him.

Cassie entered the dining room at eight precisely. She felt greatly refreshed after her shower and having hurriedly tried on each of the three outfits Don Alvarez had ordered in for her.

Cassie plumped for the least revealing a strapless, body hugging sheath of fine silver cloth that clung like a second skin to her voluptuous curves, clearly outlining the heavy rounds of her breasts with their prominent nipples as well as her gently curving belly.

Twin slashes soared up from the knee length hem at both front and rear to crotch level. There had been no underwear in the closet and so, of course, she supposed he had intended that she wear none. The result being to display her dark pubic curls at each slight movement of the delicate fabric. The dress was complemented by a pair of improbably high silver stiletto sandals, which caused her to totter precariously as she made her careful way downstairs.

If Cassie had expected any kind of reaction to her entrance she was to be disappointed. Don Alvarez was seated with his back to her at the one end of the long table around which sat five other people, none of whom she had ever seen before.

Four of them were obviously couples. A heavily built man tending toward fat and his equally plump wife sat opposite one another nearest The Don. Next, there was a smooth haired, darkly handsome man opposite a very pretty if brittle looking wife and it was she who was the only one to look up from the conversation as Cassie entered. The quick blue-chip eyes made a detailed inspection before returning her attention to the striking black haired woman who sat at the far end of the table from the facial resemblance Cassie adjudged that this must be Don Alvarez' sister.

Cassie hesitated in the doorway for a moment, uncertain of what to do until she saw that Pierre was discretely motioning her to join him by a side table. Then her eyes widened in surprise as she took in Pierre's equally revealing attire. The French youth wore a brief, skintight leather bolero jacket fastened across his tightly muscled chest by three thin thongs. His slim legs were sheathed in a matching pair of chaps cut so that both his buttocks and crotch were left totally exposed.

But it was his penis that really grabbed Cassie's attention. As she had guessed at their first meeting, Pierre was quite simply hugely endowed. His abnormally heavy shaft jutted out fully twelve inches in a thick, semi-erect twist of flesh. The heavily veined length supported within a tight golden metal helix that wound from his bulging scrotal sack two thirds of the way up the awesome length of dark skinned meat.

As she approached him, her stilettos cracking like castanets on the polished brown marble tiles, the scant dress flapped open and shut performing a sort of pornographic semaphore across her dark mound at every step.

Pierre's reaction was as instant as it was obvious, his cock quickly tumescing to stand at full attention, the thick flesh confined inside the tight metal helix bulging out from between the constraining coils, the trapped gristle darkening as it became fully engorged, a tell-tale bead of seminal fluid weeping from the painfully bulbous purple head.

Tearing his eyes reluctantly away from Cassie's crotch, Pierre swallowed, his voice thickened as he addressed her quietly.

"The first course will arrive momentarily via the dumb waiter' behind us," he explained. "Our job is simply to keep the food and drink coming like good servants." He paused for a moment, once more raking his eyes across her breasts before asking somewhat fretfully, "you do know how to wait table, don't you "

"Yes, we all take turns in serving His Excellency's meals at the Fazenda," Cassie replied, her own eyes dropping to further examine the huge erection quivering only inches away from her silver clad belly. She shifted her feet slightly as her own traitorous juices began to slowly trickle into her vagina.

"Bon," whispered Pierre, apparently relieved, "it would not do to ruin Donna Esperanza's dinner through your ignorance."

Even as he finished speaking the first course announced its arrival behind them with a soft thump. Pierre slid back the hatch in the wall and lifted a silver tureen out on to a waiting trolley. Cassie then accompanied him around the dining table, lifting the fine China dishes up for him to ladle in the soup.

Donna Esperanza was the first to be served and as Cassie set down her plate she spoke to the other guests, her tone that of a harbinger of important news.

"This is Ramon's new interest' - Cassandra," she announced smiling - and then to her brother, "she really is quite ravishing Ramon, wherever did you find her "

"A special purchase," The Don replied. "I almost lost her at one point, but happily I wasn't without her for long." His eyes fastened upon Cassie's as he spoke, sending a small shiver down her spine as she thought to divine a hidden message in what he had said.

"She's English," Esperanza informed the blonde woman beside her, "Ramon tells me he bought her for her speaking voice, he says he finds it enchanting, don't you Ramon "

"Pah! Ramon bought her for her looks and her body I'd say," snorted the smooth haired man derisively, at the same time treating Cassie to a minute top-to-toe inspection.

The blonde woman gave her husband a sour glance before replying to her hostess, "I find the English to be such a cold breed, like their climate, dank, miserable and more than a little wet."

"Is she cold and miserable Ramon, like Anna says " asked Esperanza giggling.

"Far from it," The Don replied. "I find her to be both passionate and ardent."

As Cassie turned away from serving the fat man he stopped her with a hand on her buttock, at the same time slipping his other hand through the slit in the front of her dress to cup her pudendum in his large palm. Instinctively, Cassie parted her legs so used was she by now to being manhandled.

Mistaking her movement for skittishness the fat man said sharply, "be still girl, I am a doctor." Cassie glanced uneasily at his wife, but the plump woman's attention was fixed firmly on Pierre's phallus, which still strained at more-or-less full erection.

The fat doctor seemed most interested in the delicate folds of Cassie's labia, running his thick fingers over her damp inner lips, pinching them and drawing them out to their full length and then he released her as suddenly as he had started, dipping his soiled digits into a finger bowl and drying them on his napkin.

"You must forgive Dr Suzman, my dear," laughed Donna Esperanza gaily, "as a gynaecologist he thinks all women should spread their legs for him, don't you Herman "

The doctor shrugged smiling, "not many of my patients have a fox hole as neat as Cassandra's."

"There you are my dear, high praise indeed," giggled the doctor's wife. Herman must have had most of the quality pussy in the Capitol on his examination couch at one time or another."

The meal progressed with Cassie and Pierre endlessly moving back and forth, alternatively setting down then removing plates and refilling wine glasses from a succession of expensive vintages.

Occasionally, The Don would call Cassie to him and feed her morsels of the exquisite food from his fingers, something that she was extremely grateful for, as she had not eaten since breakfast.

Following The Don's example, the doctor's plump wife did the same for Pierre, until by the time coffee came she had progressed to openly fondling his heavy balls with her free hand, rolling the massive testicles against one another, crushing the fully charged weights together until Pierre gasped, jutting his slim hips forward in obedient anticipation.

"When was the last time you milked him " the doctor's wife asked Esperanza.

"Last night, my dear Mercedes," laughed Esperanza delightedly, "can't you tell by the weight The rascal's full to bursting."

The plump Mercedes hefted Pierre's scrotum in a thoroughly theatrical gesture.

"It feels like he hasn't come in days." she grinned, licking her lips lubriciously.

Esperanza turned to the sharp-featured Anna.

"Ordinarily Pierre requires relieving morning, noon and night," she confided, "otherwise he becomes surly and perspires incessantly, not to mention becoming a menace to the housemaids. Isn't that right Pierre "

"Yes Mistress," replied Pierre immediately, gritting his teeth as Mercedes dug her long red nails deep into his scrotal sack.

"I purposefully denied him his breakfast and lunch-time relief in preparation for tonight's little gathering."

Esperanza looked up at Cassie where she stood next to her brother's chair.

"How much did Ramon pay for you " she snapped suddenly.

Cassie hesitated for a moment, taken aback by the obliqueness of the question.

"Fifty-five thousand dollars, Mistress," supplied Cassie miserably, hating to be reminded of her slave status in front of the three obviously wealthy and free' women.

"Fifty-five thousand dollars for an untrained and untested slave," said Esperanza archly, "you must have wanted her very much, Ramon."

"As I said," smiled The Don, "she has an excellent speaking voice."

"I paid one hundred and twenty five thousand dollars for Pierre at the market in Lisbon earlier this year," Esperanza announced, smiling at Anna's gasp of amazement. "Cocks as large as Pierre's are very rare indeed," she explained, "especially when coupled with such a strong and subservient libido as his."

Pierre stood proudly as the women ogled his stupendous genitals, the plump Mercedes eventually dipping her head and taking the bulging glans into her brightly lipsticked mouth, sucking deeply on his turgescent flesh until the muscles in his thighs began to shiver.

"Be careful Mercedes," Esperanza giggled after a few moments, "if you make him come he may choke you."

Standing beside Don Alvarez, his fingers gently stroking her inner thigh, Cassie shivered involuntarily as she imagined the overwhelming sensations of such a large quantity of semen flooding into her own wanton mouth. Pierre was almost as large as that pig Abdullah, and if the French youth produced only half as much semen as the giant Afghan, then Cassie knew from experience that Mercedes might well choke herself.

Mercedes reluctantly, or so it seemed, allowed Pierre's quivering phallus to slip from between her lips and dabbed delicately at the corners of her mouth with her napkin as she permitted the slave to step away.

"Perhaps we should let Ramon have his surprise now," suggested Esperanza, her dark eyes bright and avid with anticipation.

Doctor Suzman nodded to Pierre who hastened to open a door set into the wall and which, was indiscernible until opened, as it seemed to form part of the intricately painted fresco covering the walls.

Pierre reappeared after a moment and Cassie gasped in voyeuristic surprise, as the young Frenchman led a blindfolded female into the room. The olive skinned girl was entirely nude save for a soft, black, velvet cloak that hung from her shoulders to the floor her glossy black hair had been piled high in an intricate column of waves and curls.

But it was her hugely distended breasts pushing aside the thick halves of the cloak that commanded the attention of every person in the room. The football sized globes stood out like two torpedoes. The painfully stretched skin was covered with a dense tracery of deep blue green veins, which formed a livid pattern clearly visible from across the room.

Pierre led the girl slowly by the hand over to the table and helped her to sit in the carved wooden seat the doctor had brought up for her.

"Meet your coming home present, my dear Ramon," smiled the doctor expansively. To Cassie's surprise the physician switched to speak in heavily accented English. "Her name is Pilar Sancho Ybanez and she was recently admitted to the clinic to be delivered of twin boys."

The doctor slipped the cloak from Pilar's shoulders so that her entire body could be properly viewed. Deftly, the medical man fastened the girl's wrists and forearms to the arms of the chair with heavy leather straps, so preventing her from moving her arms or rising.

"I delivered Pilar of twin boys over four weeks ago," he continued casually, as if lecturing to a group of medical students, "and she has been breast feeding ever since."

Cassie saw by his rapt expression that The Don was indeed enthralled and titillated by the novel nature of his surprise'.

"When Esperanza told me that you were coming home for a few days I thought you might appreciate Pilar's particular attributes," the doctor explained.

The unfortunate girl groaned and bit her lower lip, as the physician slipped his hand under her left breast and hefted one of the phenomenal weights.

"She has been lactating prodigiously with the demands of her own two infants to satisfy," said the doctor, "nonetheless, I increased her daily yield by having her wet-nurse an additional two babies whose mother's are dry."

As he spoke the doctor peeled off the two thick cotton nipple pads that served to soak up the perpetually leaking fluids and immediately two arcs of milk spurted powerfully forth on to the damask tablecloth.

"I stopped her breast feeding all four infants this morning, hence the massive amount of congestion in the breast tissue."

The Don moved around to sit on the edge of the table slightly to the side of the miserable, whimpering girl.

"Bring something to catch her milk in," he ordered Pierre, who quickly fetched two crystal bowls from the sideboard and placed them directly in front of the girl's huge mammaries, both of which continued to leak copious amounts of milk from the remarkably thickened and extended teats.

From across the table Anna asked somewhat breathlessly in halting English, "If she is a patient of yours, how on Earth did you get her to agree to come along tonight, Herman "

"One of her infants was born with a fairly minor birth defect, which can easily be rectified by simple surgery, but she is from one of the townships and has no money for the operation." The doctor shrugged casually, "it was a simple matter to persuade her to pay for my highly expensive private medical services with the use of her body for an evening."

"How harsh can we be with her, Herman " breathed Esperanza heavily, her eyes darkened demonically, the coal black orbs sparkling with a tiny hail of kaleidoscopic reflections from the candelabra in front of her.

The physician nodded reassuringly to his exquisitely beautiful, ebony haired hostess.

"I have promised Pilar that she will suffer no permanent injury, but she understands that she will be roughly handled and subjected to various sexual practices."

Cassie now realised why everyone was speaking in English. The girl was from one of the poverty stricken shanties outside the city and as such would hardly be likely to speak a foreign tongue. The blindfold ensured that she would not see where she was brought to, nor whom she was meeting with, although given her lowly peasant status and the Alvarez family's lofty social position it was hardly likely that anything would come of a complaint from the likes of her.

"She looks to be in great pain Herman," Maria said, noting the sweat standing out on the girl's brow and upper lip. The blonde woman's tone was openly approving and not at all sympathetic to the poor girl's plight.

"Yes," confirmed the doctor smiling grimly, "if the breasts are left un-milked for even a short period, the pressure can build up to truly excruciating levels of discomfort - that is precisely why I stopped her breast feeding this morning."

"The poor creature must be desperate for relief," opined Don Alvarez, his voice deceptively neutral as he considered the best way to enjoy this novel opportunity.

Reaching over Pilar's hunched shoulders, The Don took hold of her left breast in both hands and ignoring her agonised gasps slowly began to apply pressure with his palms, forcing a powerful stream of milky fluid to hiss from the long, puce coloured nipple into one of the crystal bowls. The Don worked diligently, enjoying the hitherto unknown pleasure of milking the groaning female, quickly perfecting his technique until he could cause the milk to issue forth in a sizzling stream with each compression of the colossal globe. The aristocrat stopped only when Pilar had yielded up about half a pint into the left hand bowl.

Dragging her eyes away from the weird scene, Cassie looked surreptitiously around the table. Each of the women was looking on with an expression akin to fascinated disgust. The blonde Anna stared fixedly at Don Alvarez as he pumped his hands around the hugely distended mammary. The plump Mercedes had once again dipped her head to nurse on the hugely swollen tip of Pierre's cock, craning her heck so that she could simultaneously watch The Don's enjoyment of the helpless peon.

Pilar was a somewhat plump girl and the skin of her belly was still slack and dimpled after her pregnancy. She had the olive skin and glossy, jet-black hair of an octoroon and despite the blindfold Cassie could see that atop her long neck she had a fine caste to her cheekbones and was obviously a very pretty girl.

"How much milk can she give " asked The Don, moving to Pilar's other shoulder to begin milking her other breast.

"A female with such large mammaries as this can easily produce about a full pint from each side at a single sitting," replied the doctor matter of factly.

"It seems a shame to waste such a rare delicacy," laughed the smooth haired man cruelly, his eyes narrowed and fervent as he watched The Don at work.

"Never fear Luca," The Don assured his guest and smiling broadly, "we will have cook prepare us something with Pilar's precious milk. Some chocolate crepes perhaps, what do you say to that my friend "

The vulpine-faced Luca smacked his thin lips loudly in approval.

Having perfected his technique on the left breast, Don Alvarez went to work on Pilar's second milk filled globe with a will, adeptly forcing the lacteal fluid from the bloated breast in a series of powerful, sizzling streams, quickly filling the second bowl with the now sobbing girl's hot, creamy milk.

When he had expressed an identical amount into the second bowl he released the still rock hard mammary, which like its twin continued to stand almost straight out from her chest despite the phenomenal weight the internal fluid pressure serving to maintain a steady drip, drip, drip of milk from both nipples.

The Don pulled Pilar's chair away from the table and dragged his own chair up to face hers, at the same time motioning the dark haired Luca join him.

"A competition eh, Luca," he suggested grinning and gesturing toward Pilar's out-thrust torpedoes, "the first to finish suckling the remaining half pint from his breast wins."

Luca peeled his thin, cruel lips back from his teeth in a carnivorous smile of acceptance and moved with undisguised alacrity to reposition his chair beside The Don in front of Pilar's right breast.

"Esperanza, you can be referee," said The Don.

The doctor lent over her shoulder to whisper a few words of calm into Pilar's ear, reminding her of her baby awaiting surgery in his clinic. Pilar ceased her sniffling and straightened her back in the chair, mumbling a few halting words of gratitude to the unseen Cassie as the English girl wiped the tears and perspiration from her flushed face with a soft napkin.

Each man took hold of one of the wretched female's mammoth

breasts in both palms, each weeping globe still painfully distended and obviously bursting with milk despite the partial draining.

"One, two, three go!" shouted Esperanza at the same time rapping her palm down on the tabletop.

Simultaneously, the two men's heads darted forward, their mouths opening wide to seize upon Pilar's hugely thickened nipples. As soon as their tightly pursed lips closed on the darkly pigmented stalks the girl flung her head back in the chair her teeth gritted against the sudden agony as the two men, heedless of her pain, began to suckle at her breasts with all of the force they could bring to bear, their cheeks hollowing as they sought to gulp down the pulses of hot, sweet fluid, their cruel hands pumping rhythmically at the red hot flesh clenched between their iron hard fingers.

Behind the chair, the doctor took hold of Pilar's shoulders and held her back firmly against the heavily carved wood so that her chest was presented to the maximum advantage of the two avid competitors.

Standing off to the side Cassie's expression was aghast as she stared fixedly at The Don guzzling like a starving man at Pilar's stupendous gourd. The brunette shifted her feet slightly, seeking to ease the lurid itching of her sex as she took in the weird scene before her. She parted her full lips in a silent hiss of amazement as a sudden flood of heat ignited deep within her body, as if a furnace door had been flung open, her belly beginning to roil with its now familiar hunger, her breasts becoming volcanoes and the nipples erupting into searing hardness like two smoking fumaroles and making her wish fervently that it was she who had the privilege of feeding The Don such an erotic meal.

Across the table, Pierre was battling to avoid ejaculating prematurely into Mercedes' rapacious mouth as the plump forty-year-old blonde sucked avidly at his saliva-slicked rod, her greedy fingers clutching cruelly at his naked buttocks and scrotum as she toiled. The Frenchman's spine began to twist backward, his slim arms outspread to steady himself against the high backs of the adjacent dining chairs his eyes slits of concentration as he stared back at Cassie his lithe body rocking gently back and forth with the force of Mercedes' assault.

From her position at the head of the table Donna Esperanza surveyed the concupiscent tableaux with unashamed delight. The present' the doctor had arranged for her brother was as fascinating as it was unusual and the gusto with which Ramon was enjoying the wretched girl's monstrously distended jugs was plain for all to see.

Esperanza chuckled delightedly at her friend Mercedes who was desperately trying to force Pierre to shoot into her mouth, but the well trained Frenchman new better than to ejaculate before his mistress had given him permission and besides, they both knew it was far too early in the evening for that.

Since bringing Pierre home from Lisbon, Esperanza had spent many long hours training her personal slave to orgasm almost to order. Training given with long, repeated applications of her clever, voracious mouth and stinging leather crop.

Amazingly, Pilar's agony was slowly turning to pleasure as the two men's greedy mouths gradually reduced the painful pressure in her breasts and stimulated her over sensitive nipples with their feverish suckling. Slowly, the girl from the shanty began to arch her back, helplessly thrusting her ribcage nearer to the two men as her lips parted and she began to pant raggedly, her upper body rocked back and forth by the hands and lips assaulting her breasts. Between her olive skinned thighs her recently over-stretched vulva gaped slackly as the pleasure she was beginning to feel in her breasts sank deep into her abdomen, heating her flesh and making her juices begin to churn.

The two contestants finished in a dead heat, dropping Pilar's parched breasts down onto her slack belly, leaving the girl to groan loudly with sudden disappointment, the ravaged, spout-like nipples now hanging almost to the level of her navel.

"A draw," laughed Anna, clapping her hands with delight, her thin face flushed with excitement as she handed the grinning contestants a brace of napkins to wipe their mouths.

"Perhaps," said Esperanza approaching Pilar's slumped form with quick purposeful strides, "then again, perhaps not."

The Doctor dragged the girl upright in the chair once again, as Esperanza took hold of each slack globe in her heavily bejewelled fingers, her long and perfectly lacquered blood red nails stood out starkly against the sallow veined flesh for a moment before she crushed the already bruised roundels together with all of her strength.

Once again, the hapless Pilar threw back her head her mouth gaping fish-like as she issued another harsh cry of agony. The cruel hostess stared intently at the thumb-like nipples. Slowly, as the crowd watched, a single bead of milk issued from the breast The Don had sucked upon, whilst the other remained stubbornly dry, allowing the victorious Luca to raise his fists high in victory.

The Don spread his hands in a gesture of acceptance.

"I accept my defeat like a man," he laughed, "Luca is tonight's breast suckling champion."

Esperanza reached down to cruelly tweak one of Pilar's raw looking nipples, bringing a grunt of pain from the perspiring female.

"I think the slut enjoyed being milked," she laughed shortly, bending from the waist to thrust her hand between Pilar's fulsome thighs, she jammed all five digits into the unsuspecting maw, forcing yet another yelp of complaint from the girl.

Withdrawing her fingers, Esperanza slapped her hand rapidly back and forth across Pilar's face, snapping, "silence slave!" Contemptuously she wiped the glutinous evidence of the wretched girl's obvious need across her desiccated breasts.

"Perhaps we should give her something to show our appreciation," Esperanza continued and turning to Pierre snapped out a quick order.

"Get over here and fuck this ignorant harlot before she slides off the chair in her own juice."

Esperanza had purposely spoken in Portuguese so that Pilar would hear and understand what was about to happen to her. The girl struggled as Luca and the doctor unfastened her restraints and forced her on to the table top, rolling her on to her back and pinning her there as Pierre came around the table his huge cock swaying ponderously from side-to-side as he walked.

Esperanza reached out and ripped away Pilar's blindfold so that the helpless female could see the massive weapon that was about to be used on her. Pilar blinked against the lights of the grand chandelier above her for a moment before finally fastening her eyes on the approaching cock, instantly clamping her legs together in panic and shaking her head wildly from side-to-side.

"Please no, it's too big," she gasped, once again beginning to sob. Once more the doctor lent over to whisper in her ear and after a long moment of tortured indecision Pilar acquiesced, allowing Pierre to drag her thighs apart as he positioned himself before the gaping entrance to her sex.

Esperanza took hold of Pierre's huge phallus in her small, alabaster fist pumping the already iron hard column until she was satisfied that he was ready before guiding the bulging head, smeared with Mercedes' scarlet lipstick, into the glutinous entrance.

As soon as Esperanza released her hand the Frenchman rammed his hips forward and bottomed himself in Pilar's viscous trench, immediately propelling his narrow hips into a rapid lunging motion, raping the helpless female in the only way he knew his exacting mistress would accept.

Despite her initial protestations, Pilar groaned mightily almost as soon as the huge cock began to pummel at her cervix. She rolled her head from side-to-side, as if in disbelief at the force of the sensations building up inside of her flaccid belly, biting her lip against the strangely addictive pain of her brutalised udders as they flogged up and down on her chest in time to Pierre's massive lunges.

Cassie tore her eyes away and made her way around the clustered voyeurs to where The Don was once again sitting in his place at the head of the table calmly observing Pilar's enravishment.

As Cassie approached, Don Alvarez took immediate note of the high colour in her pale cheeks and the scintillating brilliance of her emerald eyes and not for the first time since he had first laid eyes upon her at the trading post his mouth felt dry and his chest became suddenly constrained as he beheld her loveliness.

The Don reached out and pulled her down on to his lap, his cock responding immediately to the heavy warmth of her glorious silver sheathed rump as she settled comfortably into his crotch.

In silence the pair turned to watch as The Don's sister increased the power and tempo of Pierre's thrusting by the simple expedient of laying her thin whippy crop across his naked arse.

For a full minute the ebony haired beauty thrashed at her slave's pumping buttocks, laying down a perfectly blocked pattern of densely reticulated wheals across the rock hard musculature, driving Pierre on until the recipient of his thrusting reared up from the table top, her face contorted into a twisted mask of agonised pleasure as she bellowed out a seemingly endless orgasm, her mouth falling open to hang slack and gaping as she crashed back down on to the table top, her sweat covered breasts and belly heaving in the aftermath of the brutal experience.

Seeing that Pierre was nearing the end of his self-control, Esperanza slipped her hand between his thighs and grasped at the tightly bunched scrotum and abruptly wrenched him out of the cloying chasm that still clutched at his iron hard shaft.

Pierre allowed himself to be spun around arching his back and jutting out his hips in a haze of lust as Esperanza flogged the length of his penis with the crop she had used on his buttocks only moments before. The slave fought desperately to suppress his urge to orgasm as his erection grew to even greater rigidity standing vertically against his belly as the smarting blows blazed up and down the underside of the darkly veined meat.

Beside herself with excitement, the plump Mercedes threw herself to her knees in front of Pierre and, grasping his cock in both hands, plunged her greedy mouth down over the damson coloured glans, hollowing her cheeks as she sucked and bobbed her immaculately coiffured blonde head.

Once again, Mercedes clenched her long fingers around the massive scrotum, massaging the brimming testes together in an effort to force the Frenchman to vent his precious fluid.

The anguished slave clamped his jaws together so tightly that the muscles began to twitch below his slitted blue eyes, eyes that remained riveted upon his mistress, silently imploring her to grant him permission to climax.

Esperanza withheld her consent for a long time, enjoying both the agony of her slave, whom she privately thought had done well to withstand the flogging as he had pounded the shanty slut's cunt and the desperation of her friend who was almost sobbing with her need for the Frenchman's thick jism.

Finally, and with the smallest of nods Esperanza consented, her attention rapt as Pierre released the pent up pressure in his stupendous gonads, thrusting his penis into the very back of Mercedes' throat to discharge himself in a chain of massive pulses. The heavy fluid sludging into her wanton mouth to be swallowed down the throbbing throat with a desperation that was matched only by the woman's palpable greed.

Mercedes' voracious mouth continued to suck at the exhausted flesh long after the final gout of semen had been consumed, surrendering the fading cock only when her husband intervened to push her across tabletop. A signal for her to hastily gather up the hem of her dress and lie legs splayed alongside the still exhausted Pilar, as the doctor produced his own iron hard cock and plunged himself into his moaning wife, battering into the well prepared moisture of her hirsute crotch as it became Mercedes' turn to grunt out her orgasm.

Don Alvarez turned away from the licentious scene to gaze deeply into the iridescent mists of Cassie's huge eyes floating only inches from his own and for a strange, brief moment he considered sparing her the rigours he had brought her here to experience.

Incredibly, he felt a sudden urge to be away from the house in the city, to return to the peace and solitude of the hinterland where he could have this marvellous English girl all to himself in whatever way, shape, or form he desired.

He knew, as he looked into her eyes that she was rapidly becoming besotted with him. To his immeasurable delight, Cassie had come so very far in such a very short time and her apparent willingness to place herself at his meagre mercy only served to amplify the strength of his feelings for her. Wonderingly, he asked himself if it was not he who was besotted and in danger of becoming her slave.

Alvarez had spent all of his adult life developing his tastes for domination and the concomitant use of pain as the master key to unlock the incredibly sweet sexual appetites hidden deep within a seemingly endless succession of fabulous women. The bizarre notion that he might suddenly be minded to veer off at some banal emotional tangent was a singularly unusual and shocking experience for him and one that caused him to harden his heart lest he loose himself forever in the Venus fly trap that the English girl represented.

He must not, could not, show her the slightest mercy nor favour in what was to come. Steeling his resolve, The Don finally began to speak to her in hushed tones, his mouth pushing through the luxuriant curtain of her hair to nuzzle at her ear, sending shivers down her spine as she listened to the sibilant words.

"Do you trust me Cassandra "

"Ever since you took the spike out of my tongue in the mill, Master," the girl replied without hesitation, her voice barely more than a whisper against his cheek.

Alvarez paused, thinking back to the moment she had mentioned, replaying the incident in his mind, and once again drawing satisfaction from the memory.

"Well, I need you to trust me like that again," he said.

"Will it hurt very much, Master " Cassie asked after a short hesitation, her voice faltering only slightly over the words.

"Yes," he replied shortly.

Cassie closed her eyes and nodded slowly, "I trust you, Master."

Taking Cassie by the hand, Don Alvarez led the way through yet another concealed door, similar to the one through which, Pilar had made her memorable entrance a short while earlier.

Once inside, Cassie looked around to see a large room set out with a variety of deeply upholstered chairs, and couches many of strange design. A thick post of solid rosewood stood totem-like in a deep, floodlit alcove and all about the assorted paraphernalia required for slave training the walls covered in a mesmerising display of torture implements, both current and antique, some of the more abstruse articles dating back to the days of the Inquisition.

Above her head, the elaborate plaster moulded ceiling was dominated by an imposing stainless steel carousel fully fifteen feet in diameter. Hanging a equidistant points around the shinning circumference of the great wheel were four electric winches and it was to stand beneath one of these that Don Alvarez led the submissive brunette.

Pierre and Pilar were placed in opposing quadrants, each slave being shackled to a ring in the floor before the four dominants silently repaired to an anteroom.

Cassie stood stock still with her arms at her sides, closing her eyes rather than look at the various torture implements scattered about the room. She fought desperately to quell the fear gradually building inside her chest and threatening at any moment to breakout and overwhelm her.

As she stood there light headed and swaying with the now familiar deluge of cold sweat beginning to trickle from her armpits, Cassie could hardly begin fathom precisely what these mercurial people might have in store for her, but from the look of Donna Esperanza and her vampire-like friends, not to mention the treatment already meted out to the wretched Pilar by Don Alvarez and his two male cohorts, she could be certain of one thing only and that was that whatever was about to happen to her it was going to hurt.

Cassie thought back over the many strange and harrowing things that had happened to her since she had been taken up by Gunter Bormann at Allessandro's tiny garage flat so many weeks ago. She told herself that if she could cope with the beatings and the indignities she had suffered thus far, then she could surely survive what was about to come.

Yet even in this the moment of her greatest fear, Cassie could feel the solid weight of her lust hanging heavy in her belly, as she awaited her Master's dark pleasure. Whatever happened she was certain of one thing, Don Alvarez would expect that she bear herself with dignity and courage before his sister and their guests and to behave that way for him was, she knew, quite simply the single most important thing anyone had ever asked of her.

Cassie stiffened to attention as the grim looking sextet began to file slowly out of the anteroom led by the diminutive Donna Esperanza, who along with the others had shed her sumptuous designer evening wear to be replaced by startling individual confections of metal, leather and cloth.

Esperanza wore a corset fashioned from heavy black brocade edged with silver bullion and laced so tightly that the doll like woman's waist was swaged like an hourglass. Her tiny beasts thrust upward, the sharp coal black nipples peeping through solid silver circlets stitched into the constraining bodice. Below the corset her sex was naked, the delicate, creamy skinned mons smoothly shaven and the delicate labia glistening where she had oiled the waiting flesh. About her shoulders she had draped a soft black leather cape complete with high Mandarin collar gathered at the neck with an ornate silver clasp fashioned in the shape of a spider, its multiple eyes picked out with individual rubies. Her finely muscled legs were encased in towering thigh high platform boots, again fashioned from the softest skins and complimented by a huge pair of silver spurs, the wickedly spiked wheels jingling at her heels as she walked.

Next came Anna, her body encased in a gleaming black cuirass, the highly polished hide moulded into an erotic caricature of the female form with sharply jutting breasts, distended belly and deeply sculpted navel. Her forearms and shins were sheathed in matching greaves the ornate leather tooling picked out in gold leaf. Fastened to the shoulder plates by

159

golden clasps shaped like claws she wore a flowing cloak of rich, white samite that fell to the tops of her gleaming stack heeled ankle boots. Below the cuirass Anna's sex was also nude, but unlike Esperanza's shaven mound, hers was covered in a luxurious golden thatch through which the pouting pink labia could be readily discerned.

Behind Anna, the plump Mercedes tottered on six inch stilettos, her heavy body encased from throat to ankle in a black spandex cat suit, a wide belt fashioned from heavy gold links was cinched tightly about her midriff, which together with the elasticised material conspired to mould her body into a series of curves each more voluptuous than the last. As with the others, the shiny cloth was cut away generously at the crotch and buttocks to allow access to the darkly haired vulva that glistened wetly where she had been serviced by her physician husband only fifteen short minutes before.

All three women had slicked back their hair with mousse and re-applied their make-up in heavy Gothic style so as to hollow their cheekbones and darken their lips and eyelids and, as a result, looked for all the World like the vampires Cassie had previously thought them to be.

The doctor wore heavy sandals that slapped noisily against the cool stone as he approached. His brawny, bear like frame was encased in a well oiled leather harness made up of broad, studded straps encircling and criss-crossing his hirsute body, the ponderous cock he had so recently used on his wife poked through a black iron ring that divided the heavy crotch strap at the groin where it split in two before encircling his heavy scrotum and sinking into the dark cleft of his tough hog-like buttocks.

Behind the physician the saturnine Luca emerged from the anteroom and marched resolutely across the floor toward the visibly shaking Pilar. The slender, fit man wore his costume with obvious panache, glancing at himself in the many full-length mirrors as he passed. The black kirtle he wore an exact replica of that worn by a Roman legionary officer of Caligula's time, correct even down to the razor sharp pugio sheathed across his chest and the multi thonged scourge dangling from his leather cuffed wrist. The only compromise to the original design of his costume, a deep slit cut into the front of the kirtle to allow his long, up curving prick - of which he was equally proud - unfettered egress.

"How long before she's ready to produce milk again " he called to the doctor, as he stood over the cowering girl.

The doctor considered for a moment before answering, "she should be full to bursting again in about four hours, a little too long for our purposes I'm afraid," the physician laughed softy.

"A pity," responded Luca, bitter disappointment evident in his tone, "I really wanted to flog it out of her."

"Then you will just have to whip her tits dry, darling," sniggered Anna over her shoulder, as she helped Esperanza and Mercedes strip off Pierre's brief leather clothing and manacle his wrists to the large hook dangling from the winch above his head.

At the opposite side of the circle, Luca fastened the quietly whimpering Pilar's wrists to a short spreader bar and hooked her up to the waiting winch.

Don Alvarez was the last to emerge from the changing room his tall, athletic body naked save for the soft leather kilt that fell to his mid thighs. His slim waist was encircled by a broad, intricately stitched belt from which hung a two-foot long, ivory handled tawse.

He strode up to Cassie and abruptly divested her of her gown tearing the gossamer thin material away from her body with one swift wrench of his arm.

Taking a simple harness from the attendant doctor, he slipped the broad, flat loops of leather around the circumference of each of the brunette's breasts, taking care to ensure that the well oiled bands were cinched tightly about each breast root and hard up against her ribs so that the ample meat was forced out into two slowly darkening cones. Next he wrapped a strap about each of her upper arms, which he drew behind her back and fastened together, forcing her elbows together increasing the incredible thrust of her massively ripening breasts. Finally, he clipped two chains to the tops of the breast loops and fastened these to the hook above.

At a sign from The Don, the doctor walked over to the winch control plate mounted on the wall and raised each of the trepidants slowly from the floor. Firstly, Pierre and then Pilar were suspended by their arms, the doctor continuing to hoist until their feet were well clear of the floor and their gently swaying bodies positioned at exactly the correct height to receive their chastisement.

But for Cassie there was to be no such mundane suspension, and to her mounting horror her not inconsiderable body weight was lifted from her feet and inexorably transferred to the twin bands gripping her breasts the agonised flesh rapidly becoming deeply mottled and puce tinted as the blood flow was constricted by the ever tightening straps encircling each bulging mammary.

Once her toes were clear of the floor the doctor stopped the winch and all eyes in the room including those of the other two slaves were fastened upon the statuesque brunette, as her body hung limply in a gentle arc, her head flung back and her breasts pointing skyward like two artillery shells. Her only bodily movement was the slow pumping of her diaphragm as she panted against the searing pain.

Don Alvarez carefully examined the position and bite of the chest harness before taking one of the girl's hugely congested nipples into his mouth and sucking on the engorged flesh. The wet sound of his greedy suckling was incredibly loud in the otherwise silent room. As he satisfied himself Cassie swayed to and fro, her jaws clamped together against the horrendous pain, each breath ragged and anguished as it hissed from between her clenched teeth.

The tall Brazilian reluctantly allowed the delicious saliva soaked teat to slip from his lips as the doctor put the carousel in motion. At equal distances all around the circle the dominants positioned themselves in readiness, their assorted scourges whistling through the air as they described a few limbering practice swings.

Perhaps predictably, Esperanza was the first to strike, laying her thin black crop across the centre of Pilar's plump buttocks, wringing an immediate squeal of anguish from the girl as a thin red wheal sprang up in a vivid diagonal across the quivering flesh.

Across the circle from his sister The Don laid his ivory handled tawse across Pierre's solar plexus driving the air out of the youth's lungs with the force of the blow. Don Alvarez did not derive any sexual pleasure from flagellating males, but as a means of punishment it ranked highly.

"Perhaps you will remember not to keep me waiting for my Champagne in future, Pierre," The Don suggested, as the gasping slave swung away.

Cassie screwed her eyes tightly shut as she came abreast of the doctor. The hirsute physician stood casually, a broad wooden paddle held loosely in his hand as the exquisite brunette rotated into position. With snake like speed the doctor brought the hard paddle up in a solid forehand stroke thudding into Cassie's bulging right breast and then a complimentary backhand catching the underside of her left breast as she passed bye, her mouth failing open in a silent scream as the already tortured breast meat was further agonised by the cruel impacts.

The room was suddenly full of the sound of leather and wood on flesh, as the dinner guests began to lay into the three helpless slaves as the carousel slowly revolved, bringing each twitching piece of body-meat into range for a few precious strokes of their favoured implement.

Each dominant had their preferred target area: For Mercedes it was Pierre's stupendous cock that drew her fire, the short tailed cat o' nine tails she preferred, blazing into the handsome Frenchman's crotch at every pass forcing the thick length of meat she had so recently feasted upon to rise up swaying once more against his tightly muscled belly. Anna reserved her harshest efforts for Cassie whom she despised simply because Don Alvarez favoured her. She laid her varnished rattan cane across the brunette's rich, dark pudendum as she approached and across the backs of her silky thighs as she swung away.

The doctor treated each slave clinically, striking at that part of the anatomy which would illicit the greatest pain, but cause the least physical damage for Cassie and Pilar it was their breasts, albeit for different reasons and for Pierre his overlarge testicles.

Luca had little interest in Pierre whom he used only for full power practice swings, whilst he waited for the two women to come around. He delighted in the small splashes of milk his Roman scourge forced from Pilar's hopelessly vulnerable gourds as she trundled slowly past.

Esperanza flogged each slave in equal measure, her dark eyes glittering as her tiny arm rose and fell, always seeking out the most tender parts to excoriate with her insidious, whippy crop. The pocket sized Latin beauty's sharp white teeth bared with glee as she sought to elicit the sharpest, most anguished cry from her hapless target.

But for his part, Don Alvarez only had eyes for Cassie, watching intently as she ran the merciless gauntlet of his companions, his naked chest swelling with indescribable satisfaction as the brunette refused to emulate Pilar's dreadfully tedious shrieking, instead, bearing her ordeal in almost total silence, only giving way to the occasional anguished gasp when a singularly painful blow found its way past her proud defences.

By the time the English girl had completed a half dozen revolutions her body was covered from shoulders to her knees in a plethora of wheals, stripes, blotches and bruises where the disparate array of instruments wielded by The Don's sadistic companions had savaged her alabaster flesh.

The pain of the continuous flogging, together with the unspeakable agony of her over-stretched breast tissues had long since past over the threshold of what her mind could deal with as a normal sensation and as she moved on from dominant to dominant, the initial stirrings of dark sexual pleasure began to manifest itself as the first of a series of shattering orgasms began to gather in the pit of her heaving belly.

Each of the experienced dominants immediately recognised the point at which Cassie began to cross over from the realms of pain to pleasure and each redoubled their efforts at wringing a series of increasingly ardent cries of ecstasy from the pliable brunette as she passed them by.

As the carousel brought her around to Don Alvarez for the thirteenth time, Cassie's agonised expression changed to one of burgeoning pleasure, her slack mouth cracking into a tremulous smile of acceptance as her Master brought the biting length of his tawse down upon the raw peaks of her nipples, leaving yet another scarlet streak across the already annihilated flesh and drawing a sharp exclamation of joy from the delirious girl.

His excitement surging, The Don brought the tawse down again, this time across the girl's desperately out-thrust groin, sending a lazy spatter of vulval juice high into the air and then as she was passing away he flayed at her tremulous buttocks, which were already covered in a mass of purple and crimson furrows until the room was filled with the sound of her orgasm bursting forth in a long ululating wail.

Seeing that the moment he longed for had finally arrived, The Don walked after the screaming brunette, using the two foot tawse to maintain her orgasmic fervour by beating her in alternate strokes across the vulva and the buttocks until the clear, silver sexual flux ran in thick streams down her shaking thighs.

At this unspoken signal, his companions fell upon the other two victims. The three women surrounding Pierre and lashing excitedly at his hardened body, which twitched and flexed in silent torment beneath the winch. His cock stood straight up against his hard belly as Esperanza repeatedly cropped the iron hard column until he spurted forth a sudden, scintillating stream of jism that reached its arc well above his head before falling back to spatter on her upturned face, her expression rapturous as her delicate pink tongue flickered out to catch the pearly droplets.

At the other side of the carousel, the fulsome bodied Pilar was soaking up a torrent of punishment from both Luca and the Doctor, who were taking it in turns to thrash the ample rounds of her breasts, belly and buttocks as she wailed and shook on the spreader, screaming out in disbelief as Luca's Roman scourge unexpectedly ploughed into her richly haired pudendum, mashing her prominent clitoris and thick labial folds and sending thick gobbets of vaginal spume into the air.

Luca shouted to make himself heard above the girl's howling, "she's about ready to burst, but she needs a little help."

Nodding his agreement, the doctor stopped the carousel so that Luca could thrust himself into Pilar's gaping sex, grinding his cock back and forth within her slack maw, his strong hands holding her tightly behind the knees as he thrust repeatedly, whilst the doctor quickly returned to batter her arse cheeks with great swings of his hard paddle.

The girl's mouth opened up into a huge straining circle, as her shrieking abruptly ceased as she held her breath for what seemed like an age, her eyes bulging, the shining face turning blue as she hung impaled on Luca's thick cock. The attentive dominant released his grip on one of her legs and brought his free hand up in a swift series of slaps across the girl's congested cheeks. These few sharp shocks were all Pilar needed to trigger her orgasm and she again began to scream, but this time her cries were those of a female experiencing a hard won orgasm dredged up from the very bottom of her guts.

Luca wrenched the girl's thighs apart and heaved himself forward, impaling her right up to his tightly clumped gonads so that he could feel the rippling of her vaginal muscles as they clutched at the not insignificant diameter of his iron hard rod.

Pilar groaned as Luca continued to ream her soaking wet channel, the fabulous sensations the cock was creating in her cramping belly making her body shiver and pour with sweat. Steeling herself, she looked directly into his eyes, something she had not dared to do all evening.

"M-m-my nipples, please, in you m-mouth Senior," she hissed hoarsely, and then hauling herself up on the spreader she locked her heavy thighs about his slim hips and repeated the plea her voice cracking with desperation, "please, suck on them again, I have milk for you, please I beg you."

Luca grinned wolfishly into the pretty, perspiring face.

"I am going to come to you in the hospital, Pilar Sancho Ybanez," he hissed between gritted teeth, "I am going to come by every day and you are going to suckle me and when you leave the hospital you are going to come and work in my household where I will bend you over the furniture and fuck you up the cunt and the arse whenever I want to and you will learn to call me, Master."

Pilar's staring, doe like eyes slowly darkened, becoming hooded and brooding as she listened to his words. Her belly muscles fluttered wildly as she absorbed his threats to continue this viciously licentious liaison far into the future. She winced as the saturnine Luca punctuated his dreadful words with repeated stabs of his magnificent cock, her protests no longer rooted in pain, but in pleasure, as the dark side of her febrile libido suddenly arose to take control.

"I'll do anything you say, ... Master," the girl from the shanties finally gasped, at the same time leaning back to present her aching, veined udders to him, sobbing gratefully as the sleek head dipped down and the thin, cruel lips drew in the first long, purple teat and began to suck.

Whilst the others continued to be preoccupied with Pierre and Pilar, Don Alvarez lifted Cassie down from the winch and released the ligatures from her breasts, supporting her as he guided her to a curiously high couch.

From a cabinet he brought a jar of cool, scented lotion. Scooping out two large dollops he began to massage her brutalised breast flesh, tweaking her nipples whenever she cried out as he encouraged the circulation back into the mottled tissues.

The girl lay back against the cool leather. Despite her discomfort she was elated by what she knew to have been her very creditable performance under extreme duress. She could tell by the way he carefully massaged the balm into her body that Don Alvarez was pleased with her and when he turned her over on to her belly and pulled her legs down over the rolled edge of the couch she accepted his actions without demur, even when he fastened her ankles to the feet of the couch she remained strangely calm.

He had left the straps securing her arms behind her back in place and now he clipped on a pair of wrist cuffs which he fastened in turn to a chain dangling from the ceiling directly above the couch.

Cassie had not spent weeks aboard Gunter Bormann's slave boat without learning a thing or two, and so she was not in the least surprised when she felt her wrists begin to be hauled up toward the ceiling with the immediate attendant agony blossoming in her shoulder joints as her torso was lifted off the couch.

Cassie hung like that for several minutes whilst The Don helped Luca move in another couch and they secured Pilar in similar fashion.

At the far side of the room, Pierre was lying on his back draped across a low bench, with Donna Esperanza straddling his monstrous cock, which the three women had succeeded in flogging back to erection. Anna was sat on his face, grinding her sex onto his noisily sucking mouth as both she and Esperanza exchanged a languorous succession of French kisses. Mercedes seemed more than content to squat between Pierre's slender thighs slurping her long, pink tongue in endless convolutions over the Frenchman's writhing scrotum, occasionally dipping down to ram her face into his buttocks and ream at the sensitive anal sphincter.

Once Pilar was set up, The Don returned to Cassie and looped his finger into the soft rubber ring at the base of the butt plug she had been wearing for well over a week. Instinctively, Cassie thrust out her haunches as she felt his fingers fondling her, so used was she now to his interest in the that forbidden part of her anatomy.

The Don pulled out the butt plug in one smooth motion, causing Cassie to utter a soft, guttural "Ohhhhhhh," her lower bowel imploding softly as the familiar companion was removed. Cassie knew what was coming next she had never been sodomised before, but had come to enjoy the presence of the ubiquitous butt plug and knew that this was simply another important step in her ever-expanding relationship with her Master.

Alvarez smeared a generous helping of the cream he had used on her breasts over the bell of his fiercely urgent cock before advancing to place the tip against her pouting sphincter. He waited until Cassie felt the first touch and entered as she peaked her buttocks for him.

Cassie grunted as the fat cock forced its way in. The girth was much larger that the training plugs she had been wearing and she was grateful that The Don did not ram himself in, in one huge thrust. Instead, he pushed a little more each time until he was fully home, pausing to savour the incredibly tight grip of her colon around his straining organ, marvelling at he way she took his cock into her glorious arse for the first time, revelling in the way she held herself proudly for him as he began to pump back and forth.

Unfortunately, Pilar was not to be so lucky and despite the training plug the doctor had fitted her with two days earlier she felt the full force of Luca's impatient penetration as he sodomised her with swift athletic lunges, her only defence the plaited leather haft of a crop that Luca had seen fit to slip between her jaws moments before mounting her.

As soon as the two men were into their stride, Esperanza and Anna appeared, leaving Mercedes to enjoy a hard, solo shagging from the redoubtable Pierre.

Esperanza hopped lightly up on to the couch where Pilar was gradually coming to enjoy Luca's pounding of her arse and slid along on her back so that her sex was right in front of Pilar's sweating face. The intent was unmistakable and it only took an insistent thrust from Luca to make her dip her face directly into Esperanza's gluten filled crotch and begin feeding on the succulent flesh.

Cassie was destined to perform the same service for Anna who was simultaneously slipping herself into position under the English girl's nose.

"Lick me Cassandra", she ordered tartly, "I'm full of Pierre's stale spunk and I want to be pristine for Ramon to take me next."

Cassie knew instinctively that Anna disliked her and could guess at the reason why, but once again her need to please The Don far outweighed any personal rivalry she might have with the waspish female. Cassie smiled broadly back at Anna, her breath coming in short, sharp gusts as The Don stepped up his pounding of her fecund arse.

"Mmmm," she breathed hotly, "thank … you … mistress, … I've … been … dying … all … evening … for … a … taste … of … Pierre," and so saying, Cassie dropped her head and went to work with a will on Anna's delicate, steaming portal. First of all licking out all of the seed she could find and then laving the tender pink petals nestling within the soft golden thatch.

Despite her frosty manner Anna really did have a delightful pussy, and in her highly sexualised state Cassie was more than happy to slurp at the heated flower for as long as The Don continued to make her head buzz with the wonderful new sensations his magnificent cock was visiting upon her heretofore-virgin anus.

For his part, The Don saw Cassie's adept put down of the occasionally tiresome Anna as yet another example of his new slave's instinctive surefootedness and he was delighted when his orgasm chose this moment to arrive so that he could reward her with a full load of ejaculate right where he hoped she would appreciate it most.

Abruptly, The Don hauled her hips up and back toward his groin and thrusting his phallus as deep as he could he delivered a squall of boiling spunk into the very heart of her bowels where her sensitive membranes would feel every searing blast.

Cassie raised her face from Anna's dripping sex for a brief moment, her expression ecstatic, as the arrival of her Master's precious offering pummelled at her innards and triggered her own orgasm, which she gasped out in unison with his before sinking down to resume Anna's belated service.

His athletic shoulders slumped in momentary exhaustion The Don withdrew from Cassie's gaping rectum, pausing to carefully de-spumate his spent cock against the sweated flesh of her quivering haunches as he did so.

Luca had also spent himself and now it was the burly doctor's turn to hump his hirsute cock in and out of the gasping Pilar, who was still buried nose deep in Esperanza's crotch, having brought the doll like dominatrix to her third orgasm in as many minutes.

Mercedes was flat out over the low bench where Pierre had fucked her into unconsciousness, or so it seemed and the rapacious youth was now staring fixedly at Cassie's abandoned buttocks, willing The Don to give him permission to couple with her.

Alvarez immediately noticed his interest and decided to allow him to have what he wanted, but only because the aristocrat had an overpowering curiosity to see how Cassie would cope with the abnormally huge Frenchman.

At his signal, Pierre leapt forward, quickly coating his stupendous cock with a liberal amount of lubricant before sliding himself cautiously into the void vacated moments earlier by his Master. Pierre was desperate to violate the superb English girl and had been since he had first laid eyes upon her, but he knew instinctively that she was the subject of the Master's special interest. So much was obvious and as such, Cassie needed to be treated with almost as much respect and care as the Master's own sister.

Cassie felt the invasion begin and glanced back over her shoulder in momentary alarm as Pierre slid his bulging glans past the expanding rim of her sphincter. She gasped at the pain as her delicate passage was stretched beyond reason, but looking around for The Don she took immediate heart from his stoical expression, as he lounged nonchalantly back against a racking table, his hypnotic brown eyes never leaving hers, as Pierre slowly thrust himself in inch by inch until his tautly muscled belly rested against her buttocks.

Slowly she returned her face once again to Anna's crotch and resumed her duties as Pierre began the slow in and out shagging, gradually building up his speed as her anus relaxed to accommodate his fantastic hugeness. Thankfully, Anna finally gasped out a sharp, staccato orgasm and rolled from the table leaving Cassie to concentrate on the devastating sensations Pierre was conjuring up inside her belly. She could not help but be stimulated by the Frenchman's massive dimensions, as he pulled and stretched at her delicate innards, compressing her adjacent vaginal tract and stimulating that which had already been stimulated almost beyond belief.

For Pierre too, the incredible tightness of Cassie's newly breached passage was rapidly overloading his senses and he knew that he was quickly approaching his fourth orgasm of the evening.

All of a sudden, Cassie reared up and began to grunt out her climax in a series of harsh coughing cries and that was enough to trigger off Pierre who slid out of her arse and plunged into her molten, puffed sex, immediately releasing his final fluids in a flurry of desperate lunges, carrying Cassie along with him as she switched her brutalised buttocks from side-to-side and clenched her amazingly strong vaginal muscles around his shaft, trapping him and preventing him from withdrawing for what seemed like an eternity, as the pair remained locked together in an agonising rictus of mutual pleasure.

As the two slaves gasped and groaned together their masters and mistresses fell onto the unoccupied couches and began to copulate with languid ease and familiarity Luca with Mercedes, the doctor with Esperanza and The Don finally with Anna.

Eventually, the dominants finished with one another and returned to the dining room leaving Cassie and Pilar secured to their couches where they were visited by all three men at various times throughout the night to be fucked and sodomised with varying degrees of cruelty.

Pierre remained tied against the heavy post in the alcove and provided service for the three nocturnally voracious women who appeared at regular intervals to thrust themselves onto his seemingly endlessly erect cock.

Two days after Don Alvarez' return from Europe, Alphonso brought a message for Cassie to attend her Master in the stables.

In a rush of girlish excitement, Cassie hurried to her room to slip into her briefest tennis dress and a pair of white outdoor pumps. She paused only for a fleeting moment to check her minimalist makeup in one of the huge French mirrors, as she dashed through the vestibule.

It had been over two weeks since The Don had spent time with her and to her consternation she had pined dreadfully for him every single day. Cassie ran around the side of the large house to the stable block where she found The Don sitting patiently astride his favourite Appaloosa stallion, Vasco.

"I came as soon as I heard Master," Cassie gasped, suddenly feeling incredibly foolish at the way she had sprinted pell-mell around the corner like a moon-struck schoolgirl rushing to meet her first date.

Smiling, Don Alvarez simply nodded toward a snow-white Lipizzana mare being walked out of the stable by two grooms and said, "no harm done, climb aboard."

Cassie accepted the bridle and crop from one of the grooms and mounted the fabulous horse in something of a daze. The Don watched with polite interest as Cassie walked the mare slowly around the stable yard, reacquainting herself with the techniques and skills she had not practiced for many years.

"Master, what is she called " Cassie asked leaning forward to pat the mare's neck.

"I'm not sure," The Don laughed, "it will be on the papers somewhere I expect." He dismissed the grooms with a curt nod and steered Vasco in close.

"I suppose we could always call her Little Spot'," he suggested poker faced, "anyway, it's up to you to name her, she's your horse," and with that he wheeled Vasco around and trotted out of the yard.

The couple rode across the meadow past the airstrip and up into the hills overlooking the mansion, eventually leaving the carefully managed estate behind, they cantered through the increasingly dense forest winding this way and that until Cassie had no idea where they were going, or more importantly what might be in The Don's mercurial mind.

Nevertheless, she found it only too easy to let her own thoughts wander hither and yon, just like their track, as she set out to simply enjoy the pleasure of riding in her Master's company.

Eventually, they came into a small clearing, filled almost entirely by an old ruin, which even after so many years still showed the unmistakable signs of having been destroyed by fire. Most of the walls had long since collapsed and the ever-present forest had moved in to reclaim as much space as it could amongst the toppled stones.

Don Alvarez slipped lithely out of Vasco's saddle and held up his hands to Cassie who swung a shapely leg high over the mare's arched neck and slid down, the sudden feel of his hands on her waist as he caught her sending a visible frisson of pleasure shimmering through the breathless girl.

The Don led her toward what would once have been a rather grand portico and sat down on the lichen-covered steps below.

"What is this place, Master " she asked, looking around at the jumble of old walls with genuine if bemused interest.

"It was the first Alvarez mansion," he told her, his eyes moving from stone to stone, as if visiting with old friends. "Not as large, or as grand as the present house, but I like the tranquillity of the setting very much. It burned down over a century ago, after which catastrophe my great grandfather constructed the present house."

They sat for a while in silence, content to savour the relative quiet of the scene, which was broken only by the soft calling of a distant troop of Howler Monkeys high up in the forest canopy.

"Do you like the horse, Cassandra " he asked, finally breaking the long silence.

"Of course I do, Master, she's absolutely wonderful."

"What have you decided to call her "

Cassie hesitated, unsure of her ground for a moment, "is she really mine, Master " she asked tentatively.

"Yes, I had her shipped by air from Spain especially for you she arrived last night. I recall that you once asked your father for one, but perhaps understandably, thirty thousand dollars was beyond the means of a public school teacher."

Cassie nodded smiling, "yes, I rather fancy Daddy went out on a long limb for Little Spot, Master." The girl looked up, her expression suddenly quizzical, "may I ask how you know my father was a teacher, Master " she asked softly.

Don Alvarez stood slowly, pulling her up by the hand, guiding her around the ruin toward a sheltered place where the garden would once have been.

"I know all about your family, Cassandra and about you," he said turning to face her, slipping his arms around her waist as he spoke, "that's why I went to Europe, to visit England and make certain inquiries and to buy Little Spot on the way back."

Cassie said, "I don't understand Master, why didn't you just ask me, I could have told you all about me, after all, there's little enough to tell."

"I had to find out for myself, to satisfy myself about certain things, family, friends and so on. Bearing in mind how I came to know you, which was, shall we say, in a rather unorthodox manner."

"What is there to know " she asked simply. "My parents are both dead, I have no close relatives and my only real friends are hundreds of miles away and have probably forgotten me by now." And then she added somewhat ruefully, waiving her arm toward the trees, "this is my home now, here with you and the other girls, Master."

The Don closed his eyes for a moment, his arms tightening about her waist as he savoured her simple yet poignant words. When he opened his eyes she was staring up at him with eyes as huge and as green as the forest and he new once and for all that he loved her as he had never loved another woman.

With infinite slowness, he bent his head and kissed the soft redness of her lips, slipping his tongue into her mouth as her ripening mouth fell open and they began to gorge themselves upon one another with ever increasing passion.

Eventually, their lips parted and Cassie fell heavily against him, whispering for the first time, "I love you Master," into his chest in the softest of sibilant whispers, so softly that he almost fancied that she had never spoken.

The tall Brazilian cleared his throat finally and said, "Cassandra, I have for some time been conscious of a void in my life, a lack of something, a lack of something if you will and that something has become more and more apparent to me since your arrival." He put his finger over her lips as she made to question him and carried on with a rush. "I have decided to take a wife and hopefully, have a son and so, to that end, I have made arrangements to do away with the women of the house, to dissolve the harem once and for all. …"

Cassie's eyes widened in horror as he spoke and she blurted out, interrupting him, "no Master, please don't send me a way, I couldn't bear it if I never saw you again, I don't know what I would do without you to serve!"

The Don laughed with sheer delight at the unexpected force of her misplaced passion. "Oh, my lovely, sweet Cassandra, you silly little fool, don't you see, it's you I want, I want to marry you, not send you away."

Cassandra stood for a full minute staring into the handsome aristocratic face whilst her addled mind tried to sort out the roaring crescendo of thoughts whirling around inside her head. And then she was sobbing and laughing at the same time, raining kisses on to his grinning face as her joy overflowed.

Once she had quietened down he spoke again, this time in a more serious tone.

"I love you very much Cassandra, of that I am very sure, but you must know that I am a man of dark, complex and often violent lusts, and these things will never change, and whilst I can assure you that I will always be true to you in terms of my deepest innermost feelings, as both my wife and the mother of my children, I will still avail myself of the flesh of other women and consort with those same like minded friends, as I have done all my adult life. And, I shall expect you to continue to embrace those same pleasures as well. Although, obviously, no longer as a lowly house slave, but as Donna Cassandra Alvarado, public wife, as well as private slave."

Cassie listened to The Don's words in silence and when he had finished she slowly turned away to walk toward the horses where they stood munching grass at the other side of the ruin.

She took down The Don's crop from his saddle horn and made her way back toward him, kicking off her pumps as she came, handing him the crop as she stripped off her dress to stand naked before him, her superb breasts rising and falling with suppressed excitement, her umber nipples unmistakably tumescent.

"Whilst I cannot pretend to fully understand you, Master, I can tell you that I love you and that I will strive every day to be worthy of the faith you have seen fit to place in me. And now, as a token of my love and devotion to you, I beg you to flog me as you have never flogged any woman before. I want you to flog me until I bleed and not stop even though I beg for mercy at the top of my lungs. I love you Master and only live to serve you." And with that the shaking brunette turned away and knelt down on all fours, proudly arching her buttocks and shoulders so that her lover would have unfettered access to beat her as he pleased.

Groaning with the rapidly burgeoning lust her words had kindled, The Don stripped off his own garments to stand naked over Cassie's gorgeous body, pausing for a moment to drink in her heart stopping beauty as she strained the target areas of her body toward him. She moaned out loud as he drew the looped tip of his crop over the pouting lips of her sex, turning the leather in her succulent maw until it glistened thickly with the evidence of her need. And then he brought the crop down across her quivering arse cheeks, as hard as he could, as hard as she had demanded of him.

The pain was intense as it lanced through the dense buttock meat and flashed into her already heating belly like a lightening strike, wringing a long wail of agony from her open mouth.

Alvarez waited breathless, as the peerless white skin that had remained un-whipped for over two weeks erupted into a raised scarlet wheal just above the crease where her buttocks met her thighs. Slowly he raised his arm again and brought the crop down no more than half an inch above the first strike, wringing another tortured scream from the girl as she dug her long fingers into the soft grass to prevent herself rearing up. As the second wave of pain subsided Cassie raised her buttocks another inch as she waited, knowing that her willingness would not escape him. Again the crop came screaming down three, four, five, six times and more as he crammed the livid scarlet wheals into the densest pattern possible, excoriating the abundance of her arse as she had begged, the sweat stood out on his shoulders as he continued the onslaught, turning her whole of her fabulous rump into one solid plateau of pain.

By the time he had completed the hard two dozen, Cassie was grunting like a beast through slack lips, long silver tendrils of love juice leeching from her sex, which gaped open like a tiny mouth, the depths of her vagina glistening and ready for penetration.

The Don once again reamed the entrance to her sex with the tip of his crop, snapping at the taught nub of her clitoris until she gasped and shook her ravaged rear from side-to-side, sending the thick strands of sexual effluxion swinging like bell ropes between her quivering thighs.

Then he resumed the assault. This time he laid down a dozen fiery chevrons across either shoulder blade, smashing her almost flat into the grass with the final blows, before he sank to his knees between her splayed thighs and entered her sex. With one smooth thrust he instantly detonated a whole cluster of orgasms deep within her super-heated core, as her vaginal muscles clamped down on his shaft with the force of a fist and held him secure as Cassie pumped her hips madly, wailing out loud at the top of her lungs. The girl's agonised ululations set off a whole cacophony of howling and screaming from the treetops as the local wildlife reacted to her ecstatic anguish.

Unable to contain himself, The Don wrenched himself out of Cassie's fulminating sex and plunged into the tight pucker of her anus, the thick coating of love juice covering his cock allowing him to plough straight into her in one urgent thrust. Madly, he began to saw back and forth, servicing her, revelling in the appreciative tossing of her head and the warm groans emanating from the depths of her belly.

The Don gasped as his own orgasm exploded out of his solid balls in torrents of hot, cloying spunk, that filled her bowels with a sensational compote of heat and pleasure, sending her into another towering orgasm that left her fainting face down and gasping into in the thick sward.

Cassie lay in the grass only as long as it took her to gather together her stupefied senses and then she was clambering to her feet and staggering unsteadily over to the two still happily grazing horses. She unclipped the two bridles and walked back to where The Don stood, his deep chest heaving as he watched her approach. Cassie handed him the long reins and then walked over to the nearest substantial object - an ancient crooked fruit tree that had once adorned the long gone ornamental garden. She pressed her ruined back and buttocks up against the broad hunched trunk, biting her lips as the excoriated flesh sizzled anew against the weathered bark and stretched her arms behind her for the tall aristocrat to bind tightly with the first strip of leather so that her swollen breasts jutted forward into the cool air.

She waited patiently for him to fetch some thin vines from the fringes of the forest with which to bind her ankles to the base of the tree and then he stood to the side swishing the bridle back and forth as he gauged its properties.

"Whip me, Master," Cassie begged again, "let me show you how much I love... Ahhhhh!" Her words were choked off as The Don flayed the leather across her hopelessly exposed breasts, making the lily-white orbs bounce as the strap landed four-square across both nipples.

Cassie gagged at the intensity of the agony visited upon her over sensitive teats, but she had little time to dwell upon that first strike, as The Don whirled the bridle around his head in a singing blur before landing it once again in the very same spot. And then the lash was falling with dreadful regularity, down over her quickly ravaged breast meat and on to the unsteady plains of her heaving belly.

By the time Alvarez arrived at her crotch the juice trickling from her previously plundered vulva had reached the level of her knees and the first touch of the leather across her pudendum catapulted the shrieking brunette into an orgasm that continued for several long minutes as he worked the biting length of hide over every untouched area of her body.

Finally, Don Alvarez could no longer swing the leather, such was his exhaustion. Never had he scourged a woman so harshly and yet still she looked at him with an expression akin to worship flickering in her red rimmed, tear filled eyes. As he knelt to free her ankles Cassie gasped out to him, her voice agonised and thick with her sobbing.

"Fuck me, Master, take me now, let me serve you with what remains of my strength," and so saying, she dragged her tiger striped thighs apart and balancing on the balls of her arched feet upon the trees knarled roots, she hunched her crotch forward toward his once again fiercely upstanding cock.

Alvarez threw back his head and gave a great bellow of triumph, at the same time spearing the lewdly proffered cunt and then bending to feed upon Cassie's wide, eager mouth with his.

For many long minutes the couple lay against the old fruit tree, their sexes joined, the congested flesh sliding together in a riot of orgasmic pleasure as they rocked against one another. Alvarez' coarse beard had long since blazed the sensitive satin of her face, but still she thrust her mouth at him, sucking in his tongue and lips, devouring him, just as her nether mouth sucked and devoured his smoothly pumping cock.

She crooned to him as he came, the intensity of his orgasm so severe that it seemed to be almost all pain as he seeded his second deluge of precious semen into her waiting belly. The bitter sweet agony of his climax ensuring that he arched his body to the limit, forcing the spitting head of his cock hard against her cervix, impregnating her with his seed as he groaned into her mouth.

Afterward, they lay together for several hours beneath the old tree, naked in the late afternoon sunshine, basking warmly in the lingering afterglow of their incredible orgasms. In blissful silence The Don listened to the balmy melody of her voice as she told him of her parents and her life before she had come to Brazil.

Unexpectedly, she changed the subject as her mind returned to the present day. "What will happen to Marla, Master, where will she go, and Sandy and Tanya and ..."

"Whoa there cowboy, hold your horses a minute." The Don laughed softly. "Arrangements are still being made, but Marla has agreed to accept a splendid offer of a place with Master Theo in Athens, as has Sandrine," he explained. "Ruth has been offered a home with Master Luca and Lulu wishes to go back to her medical career and will therefore be under the care of Doctor Suzman. Tanya has three offers from friends of mine in Paris, Madrid and Tokyo and so is spoilt for choice. All will go with a substantial personal severance paid into a Bahamian, or Swiss bank of their choice, as is my practice when releasing valued slaves."

Eventually the air began to cool and so he helped Cassie into her dress and found her pumps for her. Cassie's well used body was so sore from the merciless scourging that she could not mount her horse and had to have him lift her into the saddle, where she perched uncomfortably with her raw buttocks smarting hotly at every movement of the docile Lipizzana.

As they walked their mounts slowly away from the ruin he said to her, "I think we shall rebuild the old house and make it a private place for only you and I to come, no servants, or visitors of any kind allowed."

Cassie's face was instantly wreathed in smiles as she gushed, "oh, yes please, could we Master, that would be so nice and you could bring me up here whenever you wanted and thrash me soundly against that lovely old fruit tree and then you could ravish me endlessly."

"I'll have the construction company start tomorrow morning!"

"But, won't it be very expensive, Master " Cassie asked innocently, "to rebuild an old ruin this far out into the wilderness "

Once again Alvarez marvelled at her total lack of guile.

"I'm a multi-billionaire."

"Oh quite!" She thought for a moment. "Then I think I shall keep you as my Master!" she said demurely.

URSULA'S REVENGE
Allan Aldiss

Lesbian domination with male assistance:-

This book continues the Emma 'secret world' series which Allan Aldiss wrote as 'Hilary James'.

Emma, a young bi-sexual married woman, cannot escape from the influence of her dominant lover Ursula, an older rich lesbian, despite cruel abuse from Ursula and her big brutish Haitian 'butler' Sabhu, a former animal trainer. Ursula is furious when Emma twice has an abortion when pregnant due to Ursula's highly unusual forced breeding program and decides to auction her into actual slavery with a group of cruel Eastern Potentates.

Our stories of erotic male domination are described overleaf

BARBARY SLAVESHIP, Allan Aldiss

The success of the Barbary pirates, coupled with the brutal repression of a revolt in the Turkish Sultan's Balkan provinces, have caused a glut in the regional slave markets. The Pasha of Marsa orders renegade Rory Fitzgerald, late of Her Majesty's Hussars, to take a shipload of beautiful European women to the Caribbean and open up a market there.

DARK OBSESSION, Argus

Dara, a young deputy sheriff, meets Emery, a mountain of black flesh, his body rippling with muscles, glistening in the hot sun, his face sullen with anger and resentment, just out of prison and full of rage and violence towards her. In an instant she becomes obsessed, her body afire, her mind overpowered by her own uncontrollable lust. What a wicked, wicked thing it would be to have sex with a Black man!

JUSTINE, de Sade retold be Rex Saviour

Simplified and with less philosophy but retaining the power, flavour and cruelty of the novel that spawned sadism.

THE SECRET SADIST, Ted Edwards

Warning – very disturbing. Both Bondage Books and the author wish to make it clear that they do not agree with the views expressed by the late Sir Harry Champion, DSO.

PIRATE'S PRIZE, Mark Slade

Shara falls into the hands of modern Mediterranean pirates, who are quick to realise her value in the white slave trade in Northern Africa. Now she faces a future that promises nothing but humiliation, degradation and abuse.

SLAVERS OF THE AMAZON, Boyd Agate

A steamy tale of kidnap, punishment and dark pleasures with a romantic element.

OUR FAMOUS KLITZMAN SERIES!!!

By PAUL BLADES

KLITZMAN'S ISLE

A young French girl and a street smart small-time hood named Harry Wiggins are 'recruited' by the notorious international criminal known only as Klitzman to serve at his exclusive island resort – one as a potential manager, the other to join the enslaved young women who are offered to those cruel enough and rich enough to visit the 'Resort'. The French girl was just unfortunate, but Harry plays a dangerous game of double-cross among the temptations of unbridled depravity.

KLITZMAN'S EMPIRE

Forced to participate in the subjugation of the girls who have fallen prey to Klitzman's henchmen, Harry struggles to save some remnant of his soul while he is drawn ever more deeply into the dark horrors of Klitzman's Empire.

Klitzman's Empire is 'Pleasure's of Klitzman's Isle' as an e-book

KLITZMAN'S PARADISE

Will Harry surrender to the allure's of Klitzman's Paradise, or will he risk a painful and excruciating death to bring justice to the mad Klitzman and his equally cruel henchmen?

SELF CONTAINED, CAN BE READ IN ANY ORDER

Lightning Source UK Ltd.
Milton Keynes UK
27 October 2010

161968UK00001B/46/P